The Dark Manual

Colin O'Sullivan

Also by Colin O'Sullivan

Killarney Blues (Betimes Books, 2013)
The Starved Lover Sings (Betimes Books, 2017)

The Dark Manual

COLIN O'SULLIVAN

BETIMES BOOKS

First published in the English language in 2018
by Betimes Books

www.betimesbooks.com

ISBN 978-0-9934331-7-7

Cover art © Baptiste Tavernier

Cover design by JT Lindroos

PRAISE FOR COLIN O'SULLIVAN

"A hard, poignant novel of great humanity… remarkably well written…" —*Rolling Stone* (France)

"O'Sullivan's voice—unique, strong, startlingly expressive—both comes from and adds to Ireland's long and lovely literary lineage. Like many of that island's sons and daughters, O'Sullivan sends language out on a gleeful spree, exuberant, defiant, ever-ready for a party. Only a soul of stone could resist joining in." —Niall Griffiths

"His words swagger with purpose, never meandering too long on a scene, always moving the story forward, even when it goes back in time, like a faded photograph coming into view. Lyrical to a point, one word flowing to the next, hardly stopping. I read this novel and saw a movie in my mind – that's how each page appeared to me – and that's a good thing. This story reminded me of a beautiful vase, now shattered to pieces on the floor. But with each piece picked up and glued back into place, a narrative came into being, with each piece representing a character, beautifully written with all their flaws and realism, broken by their own imperfections and weaknesses. But most of all, the dropping of the vase, once beautiful, representing by the act of a man, long gone, though his actions reverberate through the years, waiting, waiting for those sunny days in Killarney, when the sun finally gets to shine on that long buried seed, giving it the energy it needs to bloom – for good, and for evil." —*Love, Sex & Other Dirty Words*

"A cathartic novel that ultimately creates positive emotions, like the blues can do. Poignant." —*Book Node*

"A luminous novel that chases away the darkness…All its characters are at a crossroads and they will either meet the Devil himself or find a way towards a new life." —*Appuyez sur la touche lecture*

"Carried by a genuine writing talent, *Killarney Blues* is a Noir novel full of melancholy and unfulfilled dreams with a surprising glimmer of hope at the end. Without the slightest naivety. A revelation." —*Le Soir* (Belgium)

"KB is a Noir novel – but not only – at the farthest reaches of love, desire and loss." —*Lettres d'Irlande et d'Ailleurs*

"A novel of great finesse and humanity." —*Action-suspense.com* (Starred review)

"In a style that is sometimes luminous, sometimes direct, sometimes poetic, Colin 'Sullivan traces his narrative path, creates incredibly vivid and appealing characters and brings the reader, to the 12-bar beat of the blues, towards a heartbreaking denouement." —*Le blog du Polar de Velda*

"This first Noir novel from Colin O'Sullivan is magnificent, very finely written, and profoundly sad. To be savoured while drinking a Guinness and listening to some old blues, by Muddy Waters or Bessie Smith. And if rain knocks on the window glass, like in Killarney, it's even better." —*RTL (Radio Télévision Luxembourg)*

"Moving, tragic, masterly crafted." —Lea Touch

But we craved the knowledge of good and evil, and we obtained that knowledge, and now we are reaping the whirlwind. In our efforts to rise above ourselves we have indeed fallen far, and are falling farther still; for, like the Creation, the Fall, too, is ongoing.

Margaret Atwood, *The Year of the Flood*

Everything conspires, elements and actions alike, to harm you.

E. M. Cioran, *A Short History of Decay*

1

Two red orbs from the black. Sometimes this is all you get. At night, if all the lights are off, this is all you get, glaring back: two red orbs from deep black.

These are its eyes. Scarlet, but bloodless. It makes them strange. Eyes with no blood, no whites, are strange. No irises, no change, strange.

And they do not blink. Homebots have no need to blink. Specks of dust in their eyes won't bother them. No sties. And they do not cry. There are no tear ducts, and anyway, what would they have to cry about?

At night. Lights off. Two red orbs from the black.

Robots have yet to become sentient beings, though they may be on their way. Susie Sakamoto doesn't think too much about this. Instead what she thinks about is her husband and son, who are most probably dead, and these days she wants to be quite dead herself. She spends most evenings balled-up on the couch, dishevelled, angry, hurting, hungry without ever really wanting to eat, pondering the best way to go about putting an end to it all. A final solution. Is there? Is there really any way out of this?

The silver, one-meter-tall homebot (Model SH.XL8) is hoovering the living room floor, sucking up dust through the soles of its feet, almost silently, hovering like it is weightless, like it has no body at all and is not a compact, complex mass of wires and circuits encased in plastics, chrome, metals, whatever the hard actual stuff of it is called – Susie does not know the names of such materials, nor does she particularly care; she has enough to be dealing with. The dirt gets collected in filters in its lower section and gets compressed, and those filters can be later removed, emptied out into the rubbish bin by the 'bot itself. That's right. It is able to remove its own filters. It *knows* what to do. It can clean itself out without any apparent fuss. It can go about its business without any discernible hitch. All menial tasks are done in this way. Fuss-less. Homebots have become rather adept.

Susie tries not to think too much about its efficiency, but lately, yes to be honest, lately she *has* started to think more about it, because she is alone with it all the time, and because she seethes. Yes, Susie hates being alone and she is full of animosity towards this machine. This feeling has never really popped up in her life until now. A concept she has ever only really encountered in gritty late-night dramas, and the news that fill her screens.

Hate? Never before. Not until terror and missiles. Until no son. Until no husband. Smoke in the sky. Until the confusion of existence.

Until homebots.

She could do it all herself, of course. Susie could open up the machine, remove the dust and clean it inside and out … if she wanted to. She can cook too. She can do lots of things. She is able. She is not incompetent. She could look after herself just fine if push came to ... but push never does. So she just lays there, in the womb of her room. In her condition. Her deep despair. Her piteous and addle-egged mind. What a world it is that has become pregnant with this troubled thirty-five-year-old, and her lying there foetus-like. Gravity pinning her right down. Gravity seems so much heavier these days; her bones, now leaden and so hard to move. She is rooted. Rooted to this spot. So firmly, so horribly stuck.

She is getting annoyed too, right at this minute, watching the homebot move with such purpose. It almost taunts her. Does it know it taunts her with its light movements? Its ceaseless airiness of motion and its bombination. These are the things a woman is supposed to be doing in her own home: cleaning, tidying, not lollygagging the way she does. A woman should be up and at 'em. Should be house-proud. Ebulliently so. She should be tearing around the house with rag and cloth and pan and broom and duster – the Japanese women in all the other houses are like this, without hesitation, full throttle, as it is fully expected of them – but she just can't seem to face it. She can't face any of it. Her eyes are closed tight. But the darkness provides no balm at all.

Music plays loudly. If the neighbours hear it, they never complain. They know she is a foreigner and she might not understand them. Even if they speak very slowly, raising their voices like she is either deaf or downright dim, she might not get it. They are harsh like this, harsh in their summations, their quick conclusions. They are like this because they know all about what she has been through – neighbourhoods like hers are small and gossipy, it is best to leave her alone, leave her at it, whatever it is she does in the midst of that aural commotion, leave her alone, for the time being at least. Foreigners, especially the contrary kind, are best left to their own devices. This might be the general consensus. The people of the neighbourhood can be kind and courteous, helpful when called upon, but really, they would much rather not get involved. Much rather steer clear. They never get too near. They tend to veer.

She often sees them peek out behind their curtains, shiftily, and disappear again, swiftly – one of them was at it just the other day, a tall silhouette, peeping out. Actually it didn't seem like a nosey woman at all, seemed more like a tall man, a large frame; what on Earth was he staring at, his eyes on her house as she entered it? But she does not care much one way or another what they do, or what they happen to think. They surely have their own petty lives to be getting on with. Let them peep all they want. Let them ogle. The loud music is enough for her right now. Loud, earache-inducing, and enveloping her in her womb-room, or is it a *tomb*? Sometimes it's hard to know what's what. Womb. Tomb. The rhyme might be enough, simple but evocative words, to go along with the sounds she immerses herself in. It is the kind of drone music that she has recently begun to favour, though most would be hard pushed to call it "music" at all. It emerges from speakers all over the house. From the walls. From the ceilings. The bass vibes even rise up through the floor and can have you trembling in your socks, massaging your vulnerable toes. Susie has it set that way. That is one thing she does actually want. She imagines the heavy drone to be the March of Death itself, through some dark dungeon it comes, on its way for her, ominous, scythe-wielding. Susie listens to the noise from the speakers and accepts all that, embraces it even, imagines the worst.

Its main function however – that obscenely loud industrial thrum – is for it to drown out the noise of her thoughts, the constant idle inner chatter, and drown out the sear of her grief. It isn't working though. Not this evening. Not any evening. It isn't enough. It just isn't good enough at all.

She gazes out from the captive couch, her features blank, listless, lifeless. Her eyes are wide open, but they are not really seeing anything. Susie was once a strong and vital woman, once full of jokes – bawdy jokes she remembered from the pubs of home. Once she was lustful for days and all the days contained. That has all disintegrated however. Masa is gone. Zen is gone. The life-force seems to have been sucked right out of her.

And the homebot continues vacuuming.

It stops intermittently to look at the human lying there and Susie returns the look, though instead of blank innocence hers is sheer disdain. This has become a face of hers. You'd never guess that once she was lustful for days and all they proposed. Once she was adventurous, seeking, a seeker, yes, up for it …

"Music off," she grunts.

The music immediately stops.

"I thought you liked that music, Miss Susie."

Susie shoots another look at the homebot. A look of white-hot contempt now. So quickly she can summon wrath from the pit of her. What is it that annoys her so much about this machine? What is it exactly?

Everything.

It's bloody everything about it.

"Would you like me to play a different selection?"

The homebot's wide oval face turns again to its controller as if awaiting instruction. This was the way Masa and his team wanted it to be seen: naïve, blank, almost foolish, the face of a foundling in a basket stuck in the rushes.

The body of this machine is rigid, yet poised. It is always like that.

Rigid.

Poised.

A small, red strip of light flashes to a luminous blue at the side of its head. The kind of light that has been on machines for years, simple, letting humans know that something is occurring. This basic functioning lets Susie know that it has got some details to work out, that there are some neural mechanics at work. In truth, Susie understands very little of its construction, its design, its operation – that was Masa's field – but it does let her know that she must be on her game, and must be ever wary, vigilant. For some reason she cannot yet bring herself to trust the bloody thing. It is as simple as that. These may be the first domestic robots on the planet that are fully operational, officially sanctioned, yet to treat them like a family pet…

Stories abound about these things, and not just in the Japanese language that she can hardly follow, but all over the world, in other countries that are also beginning to experiment with mechanical domestic servants. Every developed modern society these days has its tale of usurping factory machines, automatons suddenly and surprisingly alive and hell-bent on human harm, and while Susie usually gives short shrift to such apocrypha – TV networks simply keen on boosting ratings with scare stories – she still knows enough to be careful with any semi-thinking thing in her house. That's the way it is these days. Been building for years. Experimentation. In the name of progress, convenience, enhancement. There is little anyone can do or say against it. There never is. Progress. That's what they call it. The posters are everywhere. The video images on the streets and on the trains and wherever you care to look. *Progress is.* Sometimes it stops at that. The sentence lingering there and seemingly incomplete, only of course it *is* complete. Progress *is*.

And Sonny lives in her house.

Yes, a domestic service robot *lives* in her house. Its name is Sonny.

And she has to keep her blue, melancholy eyes, on its red, glaring ones. Ever wary.

"No, thanks, Sonny."

Susie practically spits out the name. Where has all this venom come from? So quick to revile, so quick to emotionally flame these days. When she was young she wore light summer dresses and a light blue cardigan on soft summer days and walked with her grandfather along country lanes and skipped and whistled and sang in high notes as a girl, high notes of high feelings, marvellous moods, summers of honey and autumns of blackberries and winters where she skated on the lake when it miraculously froze over and was full of hope for some kind of future, was once full of hope for the way things would turn out; but now only these constant feelings of revulsion. For the missiles that come with increasing regularity, for the ever-threat of war, for her husband and son vanished and gone, for this machine that moves around her living space, and that she has to put up with, this *thing*, the airiness of its every motion, day in day out.

This hate stuff. It rises from within, erupts from the core of her, and now she stinks to high hell of it.

The homebot remains motionless for another moment and then it begins to vacuum again, the dust collecting inside it, being stored, compacted, and its body hoovering there, hovering there, a few centimetres off the floor, as if it carries no weight at all, as if it could suddenly fly like a crane over the rice fields, as comfortable airborne as it is stalking through wet land. Sonny weightless. Sonny light as a crane.

Susie feels nothing but weight, the weight of her body, the weight of her thoughts, the weight of her sadness; each cell of her is lumpen, burdened, she practically chokes on the very weight of each breath.

"I shall empty these bags of dust, Miss Susie. Then resume vacuuming. What room do you want me to do next, Miss Susie?"

Susie Sakamoto shrugs. Couldn't give a shit.

"Was that a shrug, Miss Susie? Does that mean that you are not sure or that you are allowing me to make the decision. Miss Susie…?"

The voice is nasally, sometimes almost shrill. Why had Masa programed it that way? The endless *Miss Susies*. Couldn't it have been given a deeper voice, something a little easier on the ear? There must have been millions to choose from. Was it a rushed decision? Just to get the thing up and running? Surely, they could've put a bit more thought into the voice, surely there were options? It seemed like a cruel joke on her now.

Susie shrugs again to the echo of Sonny's questions. She sometimes toys with it. Just to see how much it can understand. How much it can deduce off its own bat, without instruction, without set codes. She tests it. Every day provoking a little. Keeps it on its toes. Or is it to keep herself on her toes?

The blue light flickers fast on the side of Sonny's head, but its body is as stiff and inflexible as ever.

"Is that what you want me to do, Miss Susie?"

It is also damnably persistent. Annoying. Always interfering when she seeks rest. Upsetting the calm with its inquiries as to her well-being. And to her horror she can hardly remember a time *pre*-Sonny. What was that like, before the reliance, or the over-reliance? It seemed so long ago, when city folk actually did things *for* themselves, *by* themselves. Their own chores in their own households. Seems like another age entirely. Another era. Sonny hasn't been there that long – is it a couple of years already? She can no longer keep track of time. Perhaps the homebots were always meant to be here. Destined. Yes, perhaps their destiny was always to be here in this city, on this land; the world has always been awaiting their arrival – is that it? Giddy was Man with the promise that the machines would save us. *Save us?* Save us from what? From ourselves? From the chore of hoovering?

Susie closes her eyes. In her own head there are no lights flickering at all, just the sound of crashing ocean waves: water against rocks, again and again, which is somehow soothing and terrifying at the same time. Is that what death is really going to be like? Terrifying, knowing that it is the end, but maybe, ultimately, assuaging, not a scythe-wielder at all then, nothing so outlandish, nothing so…

She tries breathing deeply, tries meditation. In, out. Deeply. She tries to calm herself down. Tries to expunge the bad thoughts, let them evaporate, away, away…

In. Out.

Deep meditation – but that never seems to work either.

"Are you waiting for me to take the initiative? It is not beyond my capabilities, Miss Susie."

The homebot is still standing there. They have patience, endless patience. It is disconcerting to see just how much of it they have. Standing there. They can do this for hours. Awaiting instruction. They do not have the tiredness in their bones, the lagging of exhausted legs, the drowsiness of spirit, the headaches, the heaviness.

"Just do the damn *tatami* room, then, if you want to; I really don't give a shit."

The homebot understands her every word. Congratulations, Masa. It hardly ever fails with her speech, her accent, even her deliberate mumblings. How astute. How marvellously well-made.

"Yes, Miss Susie."

Sonny is about to move away but it can sense that Susie is not quite finished.

Its senses correctly.

With its back to its controller it stops and waits.

"The house looks clean enough to me. I don't mind if there is a speck of fucking dust floating around in front of my face every now and again. It's something to watch, isn't it?"

Sonny remains suspended. Its head turns a full 360 degrees to face Susie, and its blue strip of light flickers again.

"Is that a rhetorical question, Miss Susie? I suspect that I do not need to answer it."

And the vocabulary on the fucking thing! And the sense of all-encompassing knowledge. It's the swot at the front of the class – the annoying nerd you were dying to punch, or at least "accidentally" step on their glasses when they were "accidentally" knocked off. Susie had never been a violent child – where was all this coming from? She looks at it with as much scorn as she can muster. Sometimes she thinks she could go all out and take a baseball bat to it … just be done with it, destroy it, annihilate, for good. How enjoyable would that be? It would certainly give the neighbours something to natter about – the mad Irishwoman swinging a baseball bat in the middle of some quiet afternoon, interrupting their green tea and biscuit break to look at her, battering the silver home-robot till it was nothing but loose bits and scraps. Look at her go! Debris. Nuts and bolts. Wires. All over the floor. Flying out the windows. Windows that are also shattered by the bat-wielding wild woman, batshit-mad bitch. Circuit boards and smoking silicon, everywhere, everywhere! Some spectacle that would be. Sonny scattered all over the place. Sonny no longer. Sonny no more. Silenced. No more *Miss Susies*. Progress halted. Science stilled for a minute, enough to get your breath back. Progress is … not. She'll keep all that in mind.

The homebot turns its body fully, and holds its position like a gunslinger in an old western, arms away from its body, as if about to draw.

"Continue your chores," says Susie Sakamoto.

Sonny takes stock of the room, its red orb-eyes revolving around, surveying every nook and cranny, deciding what needs to be done. Analysing. Yes. It can.

"I could turn on the screen entertainment for you, Miss Susie. Would that be something that would please you?"

Susie closes her eyes and sighs deeply.

"It is late, Miss Susie. It is time for you to go to bed."

She no longer keeps track of time. It is all meaningless to her. Hours amorphous.

"Would you like any herbal tea before retiring?"

You see, "retiring"! The fucking words! Was it Masa's idea to have it mimic the manners of some British period drama, some Victorian novel? Is it a butler, a valet? For fuck's sake.

Ignoring the homebot, irritated by the homebot now, Susie breathes deeply again. Sometimes it takes all her energy just to converse with the bloody thing.

"Mr. Masa always recommends you take herbal tea before bedtime."

Susie keeps her eyes shut tight. The extra lines on her forehead, the crow's feet at the edges of her eyes are more pronounced than ever, over the last few months they have etched into deeper ravines and become longer, making longer courses through her skin – they make her look older than her thirty-five years, or just very tired, maybe she just looks so oh-so-very tired. After all she has been through. And all she has yet to go through. There is always more. She knows that. Thirty-five years on the planet has taught her that much at least. It is never quite over. Or just when you think it is … there will be more shit headed your way. She whispers "fuck off" under her breath. She whispers it, but makes sure it is loud enough for the homebot to engage. She has at least fire enough to still play games, and she does so enjoy these little tests.

"I'm sorry, Miss Susie. I didn't quite catch your instructions."

She opens her eyes and does everything she can to make her features convey utter derision.

"I said: no thanks. I'm fine. I'm going to bed now."

Just how good is it at reading facial features? Why did she not ask Masa more questions about it, when she could have? When the two of them were there, and it was busying itself around them. Why did she not learn more about it? Laziness. Was it as simple as that? Is that how she has always been? She should have studied the manual when he proposed explaining it to her. She should have listened.

These were just experiments, these service homebots, and in her city *only* were these things tried. Other countries had their toys too, but not as developed as this. The company he worked for, ImaTech, were proud to debut the new work in Masa's own hometown, much to the jealousy of rival firm Wowmirai. There were unveilings. Ribbons were cut. TV cameras zoomed in and there was thunderous applause. Three cheers. Hurrah for technology. Progress is. But Susie had hardly paid attention; like all people everywhere, she just accepted whatever technology was available, and hoped that whatever machine one happened to be using, whatever device, digital or otherwise, worked without hiccup, and if there were to be any hiccups, someone else would always bluster in to sort it out. The most she wanted from any device was a longer battery life – who could argue with that? That was the way she used to live her life. And she was sure millions of others were exactly the same. That was the way it used to be for her. Her clever husband. Good at fixing things. A tech-head. He could fix anything. A genius. That's what they said. A nerd. They said that too, even with reverence. He would always be there, wouldn't he? Masa would always be there. Of course he would, with his expert ways, his quick fixes. She had never even considered the alternative. It never once crossed her mind.

Who would fix her now?

"OK, Miss Susie, if there's …"

Susie rises abruptly from her position on the couch and speaks sternly to her servant.

"Command. Restart at 6:30. Wake me at 7:00 am. Homebot service system enter standby mode."

The homebot immediately halts, its eyes flashing briefly from red to green and then the deadest black. The sudden silence is stunning. The total lack of whirr and buzz is extraordinary. You do not notice the hum until there is no hum at all. It's like she's been sucked into a vacuum herself, and swirls there in the void, the absolute absence. The silence and perfect peace now: Susie almost bathes in it.

In the bedroom she looks around, forlornly. Solemn Susie. Sombre Susie. The saddest Susie in the world standing there.

Her bedroom slippers by the bed, grown grim from usage but still the most comfortable things she's ever worn, are now tattered and torn. This must mean something. Comfortable, then torn apart, unravelling, hole in the sole; when lonely: everything analogous.

The wardrobe: clothes hung up tidily inside it. On the left side: *hers*. On the right: *his*. Side by side. Ordered. Neat. But his, obviously, lately, untouched. Such pathos in all this, in the even thinking of it. Trousers that accommodate no legs, jumpers that don't get pulled over to muss hair anymore, fabrics stiff, with nothing to look forward to but moth balls – it is the lonely mind too that personifies clothing; she has a good working homebot downstairs, if she wanted company she could just talk to the bloody thing. Why doesn't she? Imagine that. Imagine sitting in the living room having a tête-à-tête with Sonny. *How's tricks, Sonny? How're the wife and kids? Go anywhere nice on holiday this year?*

On the dresser is Masa's comb. Strands of black hair entwined on the teeth. Greying with dust and already-decay. All these things, inanimate things of a world that conspires against her. They are rising up and crashing in on her, all these things. Waves, waves, and she's the lone ravaged rock.

She catches her own reflection in the full-length mirror and hangs her head. Is that shame? Disappointment? Guilt? What kind of face does she wear in this hushed bedroom when there is no one there to see her?

Forlorn Susie. All alone. Tattered and torn. This is what she is now. A pitiful creature. Furrowed features. She is not the full human she once was, she is certainly not that anymore. Once she lusted for days and all they contained. Once skipping and skating and honey and funny and zestful.

Not now.

Put a hand near her and it might slip all the way through; neither flesh nor blood nor beat nor bone inside. Ghost-like. Spectral.

Susie slowly takes off her clothes, and throws them randomly around the room. A sock hits the wardrobe. Her skirt is let awkwardly fly to land at the door. She is momentarily a bratty child, loose, unchaperoned, encouraged to an excess of non-conformity, caring not about order, caring not about tidiness in the world. Her grandfather always encouraged such abandon. He was inspirational. She thinks of him at moments like this. He would have seen the child in her now. Boldly playful. He would rebuke the ghost and summon the child. *There is life yet,* he would say, *life yet, and we must prize.*

She gets into bed wearing Masa's boxer shorts and a ragged T-shirt with the words "Luck of the Irish" written across the chest. The irony is not lost on her. In her oddball, ornery way, it is esteemed; naturally she wears it every night.

Under the blankets then and the night's frosty nip immediately abates. She is warm so quickly, even without her loving partner. She peeps out at a picture on the bedside stand. A beautifully-made family photo. Proper. Framed. Professionally done. Arranged. She reaches out to touch it, but it is only the disappointment of glass, not the fond familiarity of flesh. They are smiling in this one. This photograph. This record. All three of them. Aglow. It was only a year or so ago. An adventure park with swings and slides and rock climbing facilities and …

But two of them are gone.

Susie's eyes fill up with tears, and she shuts them tight before they fall down her cheeks. It has been this way for weeks. Is it months already? Her chest tightens. Time. Track. Her lostness. She hopes that sleep comes quickly and will appease with dreamlessness.

"Lights out."

To the empty house she calls her order.

The lights obey.

Silence and darkness is all.

2

Owls live by night. Live by fright. Their stares strike fear into mice that scurry, always in a manic hurry to get away from them, away from them, away from them. Look how fast these mice can go, see how they run, bursting with fear, with petrifaction. Owls strike calm poses, but deadly threats, strike fear into tiny frantic hearts, nocturnal panic.

Owls have been known to attack bigger things: Badgers, dogs, humans even. Swooping down from the back of the black night and attaching their talons to the side of crania – always the right side, always the right side of the crania – and digging in deep there, scratching and digging and sinking those claws in as far as they will go. They could rip you to ribbons all right. They could pluck you to pieces all right. Night bulges with fright.

Not many people know these things. Not many people give owls any consideration at all. The time of day. Why would they? They are prey-birds of the night. Best kept out of sight. What you don't see doesn't bother you, won't make you feel uptight.

But sometimes.

Just sometimes.

A pair of round eyes you'll find, staring. Right back at you, from the back of the black night.

And then you know that they are there. Then you know for sure that they are there. And you should take care.

Owls, by night. By fright.

3

Half-heartedly, Susie Sakamoto washes herself. She looks directly up at the shower head and lets the warm water cascade down her face. There is always great relief in this, as if she is melting away one face to see what kind of other appears beneath. Another face? Is that what she means? Or another thing entirely? Something alien? If it is a human face discovered there, is it one that is more beautiful? Susie knows she is no model. She was never one to turn heads on the street. But she is attractive enough to always have had people interested, quick to companionship, quick to land a decent if not extraordinary boyfriend – it was perhaps in her dimples universally praised, or the lively eyes that always garnered its compliment quota, or the thick and lustrous hair.

The night had been laden with dreams again. First, the fire of the aircraft explosion, and then the ocean, the waves, and the bodies sinking down, gurgling, the crippling struggle for breath. The dreams are of drowning, and if not of drowning in water then of suffocating, and if not drowning or suffocating then she sees flames on skin, down to the lucid lurid details of hairs singeing and then the skin crisping, blackening, flaking off.

This is how she wakes: gurgling, gasping, or burning.

She is fast to rise and abandon the sheets and eagerly wants the night washed away from her, down the shower drain; she wants to be cleansed of dream and dread, cleansed of anxiety and anguish. Or just plain clean. She wants to start the day at least that way. Just clean. What new face will appear? Or reappear? Her own dimples? Her eyes still lively after her three decades, or losing their sparkle as she heads towards a fourth?

Naked she steps onto the scale-scanner. But before she even attaches the side nodes to her temples, before she even allows the top of her head to reach into the yarmulke-like helmet, a green light passes over her body and the mechanical, familiar female voice begins:

"Weight 54kg. 10 grams lighter than yesterday, one kilogram lighter than last month. Immune system under threat, therefore an increase in the uptake of vitamins and amino acids is essential. Extra zinc supplements needed to boost the immune system and ward off the risk of sickness or disease. Breakfast recommendation is a small serving of muesli in low-fat or soy milk, fresh fruit of at least three varieties, and a glass of freshly …"

How is this happening? She has not fully connected herself to this machine, and yet here it is, working like that, working for her, informing her, telling her truths she does not really want to hear.

"Command system off," she says with some irritation.

She knows the spiel. She has heard the castigations from this appliance often enough. No human would ever be perfect enough for it. It only relayed her faults. It put a dampener to her every day, destroying before she had even begun. Masa had insisted that they get fit and healthy together. Walks in the park. Jogging. Yoga. Dance classes. But when it came down to it, he didn't have the time. No time for any of it. They didn't attend a single class together, save for one meditation class. Instead he lumbered them with this godawful machine and its bald, brutal honesty. It was free of charge of course; his firm had manufactured it, just as they manufactured everything else these days. Every device in the house bore the stamp of ImaTech. She often jokingly checked her own arm or legs in front of him to see if there was a label or serial number on her.

But how the hell, here in this bathroom now, has the health information monitor (HIM) managed to tell her all of that without her acquiescence? She hasn't attached the nodes, she hasn't said a word of instruction, entered no code or details, has given no urine sample to its side container, and yet … has it *thought* … without her?

The machine stops and its operating lights quickly fade as Susie steps away from it, reaching for a towel. She dries herself vigorously, trying to wipe away her own paranoia, and she takes deep breaths. She finds herself hungry, her stomach rumbling, and she knows she will have to eat something. All this preparation, this maintenance of the body, it was all getting so bothersome, so tiresome.

She could just waste herself away. It is possible, isn't it? Just to stop everything. Down tools. Stop eating. Stop drinking. Waste away into herself until she's nothing but a fetid sludge on the spotless tiles. *Clean that up, Sonny! Clean that mess up, would you, please!*

But that would all be too slow a process, wouldn't it? If Susie was to go, she thinks it should be fast. An evaporation. A quick vanishing. The magician's box flung open … and the box bereft!

She brushes her teeth. Or at least *the brush* brushes her teeth. She just holds it, hardly even moves it anymore. Who cares if her teeth go yellow, go green, fall out broken, chipped, obscene? She remembers the brushing ritual with her husband. The ablutions. Mornings. Nights. Both oral hygiene machines going at the same time, and it was always a competition to see which battery would die first. Susie's always did. An earlier model perhaps? Had she been duped? Or had Masa kept the best ImaTech ones from himself, giving her a substandard Wowmirai? Competition: it was in his nature.

The tooth-brushing memory makes her turn for a second. Is that him standing there behind her now? Is that a presence she feels? Masa? Has her man come back to her? She had seen a movie a few months ago, before the crash; a man had died and spent the whole film wandering around with a sheet over him, back to haunt his grief-stricken lover, that thin, brittle but beautiful actor that had been in all the movies of that era. Susie would give anything to have her husband appear behind her, sheet or no.

And what of her beloved boy, bounding around the way he used to do? Zen. Her lovely son. The house is so quiet without them. The silence – certainly the homebot's – can be blissful, and also she has known it to be nothing more than baleful.

There is only steam on the surface of the mirror. The dream of steam. Quickly evaporating. Leaving no image at all. And there is only herself in the mirror: Sullen Susie Sakamoto. Languid and lost. She hangs her head once more. Are you there yourself, Susie? Are you really there? Is it time to start readying yourself, time to start considering your departure? Think on it. Think deeply. Go on. Think on it. Now.

The breakfast cereal is a kids' one that Zen used to insist on. Maybe that's what gives Susie the energy she needs to plough through her working hours. It is loaded with sugar. It is practically nothing else. It cannot fail to get her going. She decides to ignore the advice of the HIM. Why she even goes ahead and stands on the damn thing every morning she does not know. She sits at the morning counter and spoons the sodden flakes into herself without any great hurry, without any great joy either. So many of her functions have become like this, so... mechanical. She is little more than a robot herself.

She briefly basks in the notion that Zen liked this stuff – it is for her a kind of sharing now, as if they can be pulled back together, metaphysically, side by side, if only in this brief sugar reverie, this quick whimsy, this morning chimera.

The news channel is on the screen on the wall. She takes little notice of this every day, but on this morning her eyes are drawn towards a beach. It is a bleak, grey beach, and a bleak, grey female reporter is standing there, microphone aloft, keen, ready, and soon imparting.

"Sonny!" Susie shouts.

From the bowels of the house, sensing desperation in its controller's voice, Sonny responds:

"Yes, Miss Susie. I am on my way."

It arrives within seconds and approaches the morning counter. Sometimes Sonny is the nearest thing to a dog, Susie thinks, loyal, brisk in its eagerness to please... but no, nothing so loveable; there is no flat pink tongue lolling, and its eyes are not liquid and lovely as a canine's, and certainly Susie wouldn't ever dream of patting it, petting it. It's just a machine.

"I don't know the command. Masa used to do this. Can you change it to English? I can't understand a word of what she is saying."

So many of her days have had episodes like this, frustrations with language or culture, frustrations with things that she was unaccustomed to or disinclined to engage with.

Sonny's head turns to the screen on the wall, and with its eyes flickering from red to blue and trained on the TV system, the reporter's voice is dubbed immediately into English.

"Although the explosion happened over two months ago, bodies are still being washed ashore or found by diving teams. Searchers are saying that they are still not giving up on the ten bodies that remain unrecovered. Marine experts however are less optimistic stating that the chances of finding anyone alive from the wreckage or swept the couple of miles inshore are extremely unlikely."

Susie stares at the screen. Her spoon is in mid-air and milk drops from it. She forces herself to take it in her mouth, as if it was a foul medicine rather than the sugary delight it was just a moment ago. So quickly things change in her life. So quickly: bitterness. She must be cursed. That must be it. She must surely be cursed.

She hates the words they use: "bodies", "unrecovered", "wreckage", they are so brutal, and worst of all, "extremely unlikely", which is just plain mean. She knows the harsh reality of all this of course. She's not stupid. If a missile flies in the close vicinity of a moving airplane, then air gullies and gusts and spins and loops and dials and whatever go haywire, and then that plane crashes into the ocean, and the most likely outcome is that everyone perishes. That's it. Isn't it? Isn't that just it? You don't have to be an "expert"

to know that much. The North Koreans had been sending missiles for years. Testing. That's what they called them:
test missiles. The fat leader and all his bland-faced but not-
quite-so-fat chums beaming with success: the thrill of their
threat. But sooner or later they were going to hit something,
or be close enough to send an aircraft into a spiral. And it
was going to be no accident. War. It was on the cards now.
Like it has been for decades. But now it seems more than
ever. Eventually the Japanese were bound to cave, and ten-
sion would no longer "escalate" and "simmer" and "mount"
but would spill over to fully fledged military operations:
bombs, bombast, bullets and blood … or maybe none of
these things at all, those notions seemed so old-fashioned
now, the stuff of old movies – Susie used to watch such old
movies with her father and grandfather, how did they ever
allow it? Perhaps they were visionary, saw such portent, and
the movies were educational: *take heed young lass, this is all
ahead of you, ahead of everybody* – it was more likely a simple
button or two now to end it all, nuclear fallout; the flick of
a switch, and the rest just rubble for the historians to rum-
mage through and make sense of, to tell a story. But there
would probably be no humans left. Complete annihilation,
most probably. *Who* would tell *what* story? Susie finds herself tickled by the prospect.

She thinks back to the day she said goodbye to her son
and her husband at the airport. Zen was so excited about
his first trip on an airplane. They were going to South
Korea; Masa had a conference (as usual "giving a talk") and
decided that he'd take the boy along with him – Zen was on
summer holidays anyway, and it would be a good experience for him to see another country – they hadn't yet taken
him to Ireland, but it had been discussed: the long haul,

the educational aspect of the experience, a chance to bond with the other side of the family. He looked so cute with his little rucksack on his back going through the security gates, eager to be getting on with his new adventure. They waved at Susie and she waved back at them, disappointed at their departure, but aware of its importance. Susie loved her boy: she was a good mother. Susie loved her husband: she tried to be a good wife. She loved her roles, this duality. There was so much easy, straightforward love to go round. How simple it was when they were together. A love that didn't need to be stated. It just was. How could she ever have known that it was to be their last time? The final image presented to her: a cartoon ghost on the back of Zen's rucksack, smiling too, as if it was also happy to be taking this trip; a happy, innocuous character, the lovely silver ghost … smiling too … and now it does nothing but haunt her.

She pictures military leaders, all decked out, smug smiles and gleaming medals, standing to attention on that bright sunny day. Then the countdown, the blast of fire, the intense heat, and the missile gets launched into the unassuming sky. The warmongers applaud, immense pride, immense joy, delighted with their devastating toy. The missile's orbit comes close to the passenger aircraft travelling to South Korea – it doesn't even have to be close enough to hit, nothing so pinpoint. The engine explodes in gassy flames and the plane spins in chaos towards the quenching ocean.

And that was that.

Susie suddenly lashes out, sending the cereal bowl flying from the counter out into kitchen space. It smashes to pieces against a side cupboard and lays silent on the floor in thick white shards.

"Turn it off," she shouts.

"Yes, Miss Susie."

The grey woman on the grey beach vanishes and there is nothing but the silence of a woman and her mechanical charge in a lonely kitchen, once more.

The homebot moves tentatively towards the broken bowl. It looks up at Susie and waits a second before softly inquiring:

"Shall I clean the floor, Miss Susie?"

Susie stares at him. Even if she wanted to hide her disgust she's not sure she could manage it.

"You don't even know, do you?"

"Know what, madam?"

Susie laughs. *Madam!* That's a good one – Masa programed that word in too, no doubt. Was that meant to impress? *Who* was it meant to impress? It all seemed like such a sick prank now.

"Don't *madam* me. Your *Miss Susies* are annoying enough. If Masa thought that was some kind of joke… to have you all polite and… you don't even know what happened, do you? Last night, again you said: *Mr. Masa recommends you take some herbal tea.* Remember that? In your shitty, horrible voice. The present tense. You haven't figured it out, have you? That the present tense is no longer viable. What you should have said was: *Mr. Masa used to recommend you take herbal tea.* Used to. When he was alive. When he breathed and laughed and sang bad karaoke in bad bars. Before he was blown to smithereens. But how could you know that? How could you know?"

Susie's eyes are malevolent now and she feels them flaming red in her sockets. They sting and burn: late nights, scalding tears, the sourness of spirit and no clear target of recrimination.

"You haven't a clue. Or, if you do … no, you can't process it at all, can you? I mean, a mere mortal such as I, a stinking bloody human can hardly process it, so how could a thing, without blood … a thing … even …"

The words are choking her and she can no longer spew them out. She has exhausted herself. The confusion of her thoughts. Could it *know*? But how could it know if Masa was not there to program … or, has it been programed in such a way that all news feeds become part of its knowing? When a dog's master doesn't come home from the hospital, does it know that it is dead? Does a dog *know* about death? Or simply that its master is absent? Does a homebot know that its master is no more? And if it does, does it care? The breakfast milk feels like it is curdling inside her, her guts clenching, her blood pressure is high and rising.

Sonny bends to the mess on the floor. With an outstretched hand and with dexterous digits it goes to pick up a shard of ceramic but is halted by Susie's command.

"Leave it. What difference does it make?"

The homebot freezes in its half-bent position. How fast it is to respond to her every utterance. How quick its every perception. She flings her spoon, hitting it on the head and making a pinging sound, but the homebot shows no reaction, not an ounce of emotion.

"Doesn't even hurt, does it? How the fuck could it?" Susie says, breathlessly.

Sonny rises to its full height.

"Miss Susie, I …"

"I'm going to be late. Bring the car round."

Sonny moves to the panel on the kitchen wall, touches it with its palm and the screen lights up a luminous green. The garage door at the side of the house opens, a soft engine starts, and the small compact silver car, drives smoothly out of the garage and parks itself in front of the kitchen window. If it had a face it would be smiling. If it had a voice – Susie is sure of it – it would softly chime, like a child's: *I'm ready!*

"What interior temperature would you like me to set, Miss Susie?"

"Don't care."

"Do you need to know today's outside temperature?"

Susie ignores.

"Today's weather report, Miss Susie?"

"No. It doesn't matter. It doesn't fucking matter. Rain or ice or snow or fucking thunder and lightning, who gives a shit? Who gives a shit?"

The homebot knows that these questions are rhetorical. How does it know that?

The little car hums gently, waiting.

4

A woman hangs her laundry out on a clothesline at the side of her house. There is hardly any room for her to hang the garments, hardly any room for her to move at all, but she manages, like all the women around here, they are good in tight spaces, in the small kitchens, in the tight lanes between items of furniture. Susie nods to her as she does almost every morning – every morning the sun is out, or when a good drying wind is helping the woman's cause. The woman nods back, solemnly, without squint or smirk. Although they see each other often, they rarely go as far as an oral salutation; the nods seem to encapsulate all: they are respectful but distant, polite but restrained, the nods are satisfactory, sufficient.

She drives through the neighbourhood, never whistling, never tuneful. The drone music that she usually listens to has drowned out all tunes and melodies in her head. She would be hard pushed to excavate one now from her memory bank. There was a time when she danced and sang the same as any girl, played at being a pop star, choreographed routines with her budding buddies and looked for big shop windows, when the stores were closed and dark and gave ample reflection. And younger still, singing the latest pop songs in the shower, in the bath as her mother bathed her, her high voice rising with the steam. She even played the piano then, not very well, but with skill enough to maintain a repertoire, and was able to wheel it out at parties, family get-togethers, occasions, showing off the dexterity of her thin fingers on the black and white keys, her little foot pumping the pedals. The very idea seems alien to her now; better drone, or the boom of heavy beats from her powerful speakers, no hope within those, just the relentlessness.

Houses surround her on all sides, houses of different shapes and sizes: some large, some small, some new and imposing, some seeming to shrink more and more in age and decrepitude, as if they were cowering, afraid of the harsh light of the world they found themselves in and hoping to get subsumed into their own foundations.

The drive is short; so soon she arrives at the train station and heads for her usual parking spot. She could walk to here every day, were she so inclined, it was hardly an ordeal, but fresh air and exercise mean little to the woman anymore, if ever they did; these days Susie Sakamoto is not *inclined* to do very much at all. The bright, spring sunshine of this particular morning does little to temper her tetchiness, and whatever delirious birds swoop and skim the brisk breezes, are largely ignored.

She parks the car and takes her place among the lines of commuters, marching along in dreary orderliness, almost in step. Heads are kept down, bodies move only forward – they may as well be wearing the blinkers of racehorses, though speed of course is not required of them, save for those who are running late, and these are few. They walk, they walk, and then they stop, waiting for the approaching train, everything reliably on time, reliably on cue, and no one need ever worry that this would ever *not* be the case.

When it pulls up in front of her with hardly a sound – more a cynical snort – she wedges herself in with all the rest of them, vying for decent space, trying to squash herself, make herself small. Everyone else reciprocates, trying their hardest to not encroach on her in any way that might be misconstrued as confrontation. No one would dare do that. They are all in on the rules of this, this etiquette that is so required of them. This is the Japanese way. This is the proper way to do things around here – the proper way to do things anywhere – and she has become more than accustomed.

She grips the noose-like strap that dangles from the ceiling of the train with one hand – her hard, black briefcase is clasped in her other – and she begins her dead-eyed stare at the nothing-in-particular.

She could stare up at the advertisements that line the top of the carriage. Ads to remind her that she should be prettier, have better teeth, get a nip or a tuck at a reasonable price in a downtown clinic, have bigger, firmer breasts, have cooler clothes, learn more in colleges, so many languages still in the dying world, surely you need to speak to everybody before they go, get better deals from bumptious banks, have regular health checks before it is too late.

Too late for what?

Her dead gaze at nothing at all is instead interrupted by the large news headline in danger-red that leaps from a passenger's tablet. It is the airplane in flame. *The* airplane. Of course it is. Everywhere a reminder – every*thing* a reminder – just when she is beginning to forget. Just when she can put it out of her mind for at least a few restful minutes and think that life might be bearable. She looks away again and around at the other commuters, each of them dead in their own way, their routines, their slavery to whatever corporation … but then again, hold on there one minute Susie, maybe not. Maybe not at all. Maybe they *are* happy. What about that notion, Susie? Is that not at all possible? Maybe behind those dreary faces are lives that yelp with joy and frivolity. Veins that sing with glee and pulses that beat in time to the undetected rhythm of the universe. That could be the case, couldn't it? That could be going on, inside all of them. All that feisty force within. Why not? How would she ever know? Susie Sakamoto is stuck in her own glum groove and it is there that she is likely to stay.

It is hard to fit in around here, she knows this, this perennial outsider. Accustomed sure, knowledgeable sure, but not one of them; never truly belonging. It will always be like this. It was Masa that persuaded her to stay. She should have gone back home years ago. She had several chances but turned them all down. She has friends there still. Some family alive at home, still. She could have tried harder in convincing Masa to leave and they could have made it work. But she stuck it out. One always made the sacrifice. She knew the importance of Masa's work and wage. She tried to cull out a new life, a new way of being … and it had been working. Everything she had done, *they* had done, had been successful, never to want or to wane. She had been happy. Yes, it had all been going according to plan. Or maybe there was no plan, it was just ambling along on the right course, the way the lucky and the blessed get on with life and its demands, those who are not ever even aware of any demands, the ones that land in the right jobs, with the right partners and tragedy is only ever something that happens on TV, worlds away. It seemed all right. It seemed like things were in place for them. Masa. Zen. Job. Security. Money in the bank. It was all working out, swimmingly. There was even talk of another child. Zen could have had a brother. Or a sister. They could even have rescued one of those tiny dogs from those awful transparent cages in the pet stores, those shivering mutts, all doleful eyes that pluck hard on the strings of anyone that had a heart.

A dog could have barked in their kitchen and wagged its frisky tail and been a friend to little Zen and not the machine that...

Happy family.

It could have been. It could have...

But...

A projectile tearing up the sky on a sunny day.

A searing gash across the blue.

Blast.

Rips apart the day.

Heat.

Strike.

Blast.

Rip it.

Rip your heart out.

A projectile in the sky.

The hearts of many.

A projectile in the sky. Without warning. The government too late with a warning. What good would it have done anyway? It was already on its wicked way. Could the plane have taken another route?

Emergency.

A projectile in the sky.

And then the devastation.

And here she is. Susie Deadheart. She could change her name by deed poll. Is that how they do it around here? Y*es, Miss Deadheart. Sure, Miss Deadheart. We know that you have no reason for going on. No reason to be here. No reason to be anywhere. Yes, Miss Deadheart, the highest bridge in the city is just over there to your right; just go ahead now and throw yourself off, no one will miss you.*

Yet here she is, holding on to that train strap as if it is the only thing attaching her to the very planet. That if she was to let go she would fall way down into some dark abyss and her body would shatter into a million pieces and be cast out all over the universe. An Alice fall. It might be worth a throw: that letting go. Or let it be a noose, as its shape suggests. Slip her head in and let it hang her here and now – there's morning entertainment for you on the crowded train, my dears! There's something to talk about over your paper coffee cups and morning mascara and mis-take-less make-up.

Industrial high-rise complexes outside, flying past. Industry. Commerce. Cogs. Society and its machinations. The commuters inside the train are all part of this. Susie doesn't know a single one of them by name though she sees them every day. They ignore her. Or she ignores them. Or perhaps it is a bit of both. Sometimes she makes up names for them: Sad-eyed Satoru. Mole-faced Masanobu. Split-ends Saya. Fat-faced Fuuko. And she conjures equally troublesome lives to match: debts, deaths, ridiculous acci-dents, holes, or deep wells that they cannot get out of – they are screaming down there, abandoned, poor things. She hardly makes any of them have clean, happy lives, no waggy puppies for them. Why does she do that? Some of them may have pulses that beat in time with the rhythm of the cosmos. Why not acknowledge that? No. No way. Why should she present them with any good fortune? If Susie is to suffer then they will all suffer. Every goddamn one of them on this train. She will take them all with her. If she is going down, the whole world will go down too. She'll take it all. Take them all. Through sheer spite. That's it: sheer spite! Her chest feels suddenly warm with these thoughts. She thinks she might even swoon.

Some of these people are probably scared that she might suddenly start speaking to them in English, and they would have no reply. They'd be open-mouthed, shocked-silent, embarrassed at their lack of sophistication in this global age – why did they not learn English properly like everyone else, like the Koreans, like the ever-advancing Chinese? But she would never dream of doing such a thing. She knows it is best to always stay silent. Her Japanese is weak, but passable. She had spent some time learning the rudiments when she first arrived. Basic grammar and vocabulary from a sweet little spinster who would make green tea in her kitchen and make her repeat words from flash cards and simple sentences until they stuck. The woman charged her hardly anything at all, and Susie wanted to offer her more, make her job worthwhile, until after a few weeks she finally cottoned on that maybe it was better to bring snacks and gifts if the money was not going to cut it: so the two of them fattened up on cakes and biscuits, a different line in confectionery every week, often Susie having to trawl through the town to find a treat that would be new to sample, some dainty delicious delectable. The little lady in her simple homemade dresses taught her enough conversation skills to get by in most situations, enough to get by in the shops, the purchasing of train tickets, the very important ordering of beer in bars, but these days she is not in the mood to speak in any language to anybody. It would all seem like too much of an effort, and anyway, when she thinks about it, what on earth was there left to say?

Three schoolgirls are hunched close together and giggling, looking at their ultra slim palm devices. They wear their skirts short in the provocative and rebellious way it has always been. She's pretty sure that when they get near the school gates they will be pulled down again, less they face the ire of some strict disciplinarian, and there are plenty of those to go round – Split-ends Saya must surely be one of them, she has *teacher* written all over her, the severe frown, the agitated hands that knead into each other, the lack of sleep in weary eyes, up late again marking papers last night. But for the moment the girls are content to let their skirts ride up along their thighs, allowing every red-blooded male a good glimpse of their pale flesh, and to appear aghast or insulted if taken up on it. There was a time Susie Sakamoto understood all of this, this gamesmanship, lusty eyes and lies, and would even have given those thighs surreptitious glances herself – what of it, beauty was beauty, and the oddest things often made her aroused, she was not exclusive in her appreciations and believed no human was. But it would take a lot more than that to tickle her fancy these days. The simple causality of leer to cheer, was well gone. She is past all that.

One of the girls does manage to catch her eye and she smiles at Susie, then covers her mouth, mock-ashamed. Susie never knows whether this fey gesture is real or not, so practiced are they at this kind of subterfuge, but she smiles meekly back – slightly blushing because she has been caught, despite herself, and she is beginning to come to the conclusion that not only is she done with games of flesh and desire, she is also done with trains. There's another thing she can write off from her life for as long as it continues. Enough with carriages full of people breathing and sweating and trying to contain themselves in their personal space in such a public domain. Enough was indeed quite enough. Why she puts up with it she does not know. She could just take her car all the way into the city. It wouldn't be that much of a bother, not that much of a drive, if she could put up with the ubiquitous traffic jams. There were always jams, sure, but at least she could prepare for that. Have plenty of entertainment cued up in the car – restful guided hypnosis if she needed that, more drone, or she could just lay back and sleep, it's not like she was doing the driving anyway. She would ask her boss to make a parking space for her. Surely, after all she has been through, he would accommodate. She could play the sympathy card. She could play the doleful-eyed-caged-pet trick. Why not? She may as well get something from all of this. Life had been that unkind to her, dealt her the cruelest blow of all, maybe it was time that she started to take a few things back.

5

Susie walks through the main door of the media corporation. The building hosts a radio station, a small TV production company, several advertising and marketing offices, and the news site that she works for, part-time: NowNews, as stupid and as pandering to the West a moniker as could possibly be construed. In so many ways then it was of course typical.

She presses her thumb to the security post and when the gates swing open she pushes through to the elevator. The two bulky security guards smile at her as they have always done. She can't imagine why they treat her with such fondness. Perhaps it was because she flirts with them drunkenly at every end-of-the-year party; it's one of the times when out of sheer boredom she drinks too much of the free alcohol available and tries to loosen the shackles of the evening. She never saw this as a threat to her marriage, those mild flirtations, because she never went any further than sneaky smirks after semi-lewd suggestions, anything to get through the endless speeches that the likes of Osanai, her long-winded boss, would insist on making – much more fun to wind up those burly guards into thinking that they stood a chance. They never did.

There was only ever the one for her. She had forsaken so much to be with him. To stay here. To love and live. Masa. And now he is gone.

She stands head and shoulders, literally, above most of the staff that squeeze into the tight elevator. All this packing into confined spaces, no wonder people begin to lose their minds. She looks faintly comical, often hyper-aware of her auburn hair in world of dense black, her lanky legs and too-skinny arms so noticeable under the sheer blouse. But there's not much she can do about it. If people are to stare, then let them. Why should she really care? Actually it was something she got used to after only a few weeks in Japan: her being different, noticeable. The way people glared at first. Or the trying-to-hide glares that were often more glaringly obvious glares. Until they of course grew used to seeing her, and she got used to being seen. Novelties, like any anywhere, soon wear off.

Just before she enters her tiny cubicle, Osanai, never one for having the greatest regard for physical propriety, catches her by the wrist and practically drags her after him. In any other modern society he'd be up on charges. Here though …

"Susie-san, may I have a quick word?"

"Um, sure."

She follows him into his office and stands awkwardly until he nods to the chair, inviting her to sit.

"Would you like a cup of coffee?"

"No, thanks."

She can pretty much guess the line he is going to take with her – it's there in his eyes, sympathy again, affection again.

"I just wanted to say again that you can take some more time off. We know the strain that you have been under. If you want to take extra vacation time, then that is OK. Take as much as you need."

He means well, of course he does. His sympathy is genuine. But surely he is aware just how useless she is these days. Surely he sees how little she actually gets done. He's no fool. Long-winded. Boring. But no fool. It would be in his best interest to fire her for good. She'd hardly object. It'd probably be the best for everyone. But he is as extremely unlikely to broach that particular subject, as he is extremely unlikely to approach anything that might resemble confrontation; she may as well just keep going.

"I'd prefer to work."

"Yes, but it really might benefit you if you took a little time to … get over things. You might be in a better frame of mind after a few more weeks, or months."

Susie wants to say that she has no intention of ever "getting over things". Mourning is a part of her life now, and she wants it to stay that way. If she wasn't mourning, then it would seem to her a betrayal to both husband and son. She will mourn and mourn and then some. She'll get over absolutely nothing.

"I'd prefer to work," she reiterates.

"Fine. Then please continue."

Susie is surprised that he is giving in so easily. She's often witnessed him, a dog with an especially juicy bone. But that's usually when he is following up a lead, or adamant that a story should run in a particular way.

"Maybe we can talk about it again at the end of the week," he says.

The end of the week? Then it must be the start of the week, Susie thinks. She sometimes loses her bearings. It must be a Monday. All these days, blurring into each other. Tuesdays and Wednesdays and Thursdays … all so samey now.

For all her misgivings she does manage to stay impressed with her boss most of the time, not only because of his excellent English (he had lived in London for years) but his very real sense of sympathy and understanding. He never seems fake, she'll give him that. He is good to work for, and were it not for his predilection for apprehending women by their body parts, he would most probably make a fine catch himself.

Susie, the subordinate, bows, leaves his cosy office, and heads back to her claustrophobic cubicle. She stares blankly at the computer screen until memories start to materialise, playing out before her there, pixels becoming prompts becoming pictures. She sees herself in the English Conversation School where she used to work. Evenings there surrounded by keen students who wanted to get their grammar right, wanted to make proper *r* or *l* sounds, or that tricky *th* – she found herself having to amend her own thick Irish accent in order to be understood, and even imitated the sounds and cadences of her Canadian grandfather in order to be successful in communication; that too felt like a betrayal, but she felt she had no other choice – or in the kindergarten, where she was often sent to teach, the energy she needed then to dance and sing and jump around with the little ones, playtime in English, or big digital storyboards often in hand: Three Little Pigs, or Red Riding Hood, and the enchanted, enchanting children, not understanding her narration one bit, but sincere faces turned in her direction and enthralled at the illustrations marvelously animated before them. For the most part she failed in all of these endeavours, the majority of groups simply not learning enough for her to be ever satisfied. She did have occasional successes; when a student remembered some vital vocabulary and regurgitated it back to her, or when a nervy adolescent girl finally got her syntax down pat and was ready and geared up for a work-trip to Sydney or Auckland. Small victories. These small wins she'd collect and savour. It was the little successes that kept her in the job for so long – will she ever have any more of those? Those victories. Could they ever come about again? She'd take even a small one now, the smallest of them would do.

Then she got the job at the news website. Writing reports. Her remit: a foreigner's interpretation of Japan. Colourful features on colourful foreigners dotted all over the archipelago: Russians playing the *shamisen*, European players in the J-league, Noh enthusiasts from Buenos Aires now living in Kyoto. She would even travel to other cities to meet these people, anytime Osanai loosened the purse strings. It was ever only a day or two away from home; she couldn't bear to be away from Masa or Zen, and hotels felt barren to her, she wanted always that warm, beating heart of home. She would write in English and the computer would automatically translate it into Japanese. A sub-editor – a live human! – would then check for errors or oddities, though there were few – the computer usually even got her jokes, her bites of sarcasm or racy innuendo, their capabilities had evolved to that degree; if the piece was good enough it was published. This was usually the case. Osanai had been happy. But not recently. Recently her output was not much to get excited about, not much interest to anyone. To write such articles one had to be open. One had to be energetic. Investigative. Curious. Susie was none of these things. Not anymore. The person who thinks she has seen it all has nothing to be curious about. She could barely string a few noteworthy sentences together these days, for all the ease and convenience the computers afforded her – they could correct her, fine, but they could not offer any inspiration. That had to come from her. She is past it. Washed up. And she knows it.

The money was always pittance, but she never minded that. It was always more a hobby than anything else. Masa had been the breadwinner and she had been all right with that. She spent the first years of Zen's life at home, being a proper mother, a housewife, even learning how to cook Japanese food, with spices and herbs she could not even name – certainly the labels on the bottles and packets made little sense to her. When Zen started school she took up writing again – she had always been a scribbler from a young age and had taken a post-graduate course in journalism and media studies – and Osanai let her do whatever she wanted, let her follow whatever trickles or tributaries as long as they led eventually to the sea. Now, however, she can do very little at all. Tired. Worn out. Past it. All at the age of thirty-five.

Masa's face now screaming!
Masa's face now screaming!
Then just as quickly Sonny's red orb eyes flashing demonically from the black.

Susie opens her eyes and gasps. She must have fallen asleep right there at her desk, in her constrained cubicle, staring at the blank screen. Or maybe she hypnotized herself, fell into some kind of trance.

How can she be so exhausted? She hasn't done an ounce of work. She has hardly lifted a finger in months. It is the lack of action, the sterility, the stagnation, the ennui – these are the things that are suffocating her, she can hardly breathe.

She takes a handkerchief from her bag and spends a moment wiping the sweat that has accumulated on her brow. She half-expects to see make-up smeared there, a beigey stain. But there is nothing. She has forgotten to put on make-up again. When did she last bother to make up her face properly? Some days it's a slapdash affair, a smudge here, a dab there, but most mornings nothing at all, too much trouble – how she manages to get dressed at all is a mystery. Perhaps Sonny dresses her! She laughs to herself. Sonny holding up her tights for her with his silver fingers.

How about this colour, Miss Susie? Slip your leg in here.

Might suit you better, Mr. Sonny, you camp little shit.

She has to curb her laughter – there is relief in this laughter – already a few craned necks from the cubicles are curious as to where the guffaws are coming from. She calms herself. Another wipe with her handkerchief. She takes no care anymore. Certainly not in her presentation. Who would be looking at her anyway – that girl that appears beside her in bars, Mixxy? – and anyway, just what is there to see?

Nada.

She reaches out and turns on the computer. About time and all. Already minutes have passed and she has done absolutely nothing. This is not the way it is supposed to be in a Japanese company. Foreigners had reputations for being slothful, and Susie was only adding to the stereotype. Better write something. Better get something down. Anything. Investigate something. Investigate anything! Check back over old files she has written. Might be something there.

Anything at all. Get something down. Anything. Get random words down. Any bloody thing to take her mind off fire and screams and death, the unsummoned awful repetition of them in her brain.

Fire. Screams. Death.

Fire. Screams. Death.

Hours and hours pass and little or nothing gets done. No, not *little*. Nothing. Nothing at all gets done.

6

Spend the days a-slumbering and then, as evening draws to a close, a stirring of feathers and the three-lidded eyes open.

When night falls, silently comes the swoop, hardly a whisper as it glides, hardly a flutter of leaf, just gentle on the thermals, no sound, through the darkness, not missing a trick.

Such a creature! Such a thing it is! And the poets praised the kingfisher. And the poets praised the eagle. And the poets praised the hawk, and the Windhover. But this! This is it. This is silence, beauty and depth, stealth and cunning and glory, all in one, such a creature this is, this bird of night, such a creature to marvel at, delight in it, if only it were there to be seen.

No sound. Through the darkness. Not missing a trick. Far too aware. Only sometimes a hoot, or a screech when it needs to, a mewl or a little cry, but for the most part no sound at all, no sound in the darkness, silence, the night is only itself and its hum, only the landing of rain on its soft feathers, unheard, why … why you would never even notice such a thing.

Owls by night. By stealth. By silence. For a large bird you'd hardly notice them there; such creatures they are, such tricks they have at their disposal. They've got it down, this hardly-there-ness-but-oh-so-very-there-ness, their large tubular eyes, the round and turning head.

Owls.

By night. Stealth. Silence. Glide through the glades. Upon the thermals.

The kingdom of night is theirs. Theirs. They claim. Theirs. They conquer. Yes, such a conquering creature. The surrounds, so soon, submit to it.

Evening now, and, in opposition to most other living things, conversely, at odds, they awaken.

7

The woman at the clothesline is taking in her laundry. The sky is darkening and heavy clouds hang. The woman nods to Susie on seeing her return and Susie reciprocates. A clap of thunder sounds in the distance and the woman hurries with her armful of garments into the safety of her own house.

Susie is in less of a hurry to enter hers. What kind of solace is ever to be found in there? At least the oncoming downpour might be something to behold. Something dramatic. Something different. She should just stand there and let it all soak into her bones. It might melt her away – there could be great relief in this, melting away one face to see what other will appear beneath – or, she could wash away, wash away completely, down the open drains, like so much effluent, get washed clean away, out of sight forever.

With weariness and a sense of resignation Susie takes her shoes off in the entrance of her home. She sits there for a moment, massaging her tired feet. She notices a hole in her tights and fingers it, making it larger. Things unravel so quickly, she thinks. Things get damaged so easily, get worn, get torn. It all happens so easily. Actually, sitting in this entrance now and removing her shoes like this, is one of the customs that she likes about the country. It makes sense to her: the leaving of dirt outside. And the constant airing of her feet too, maybe they were better because of it; she has noticed fewer hard gnarly parts, fewer corns and callouses, maybe there would have been more if she had stayed on the dirt paths and treks of her country home, her wellington boots on them to combat the sporadic showers, the sudden muddy puddles. She remembers going back to Ireland once – pre-Zen, pre-marriage even – and feeling awkward when entering people's houses with her shoes on. It just seemed so wrong. Some of the habits and customs have rubbed off on her, have agreed with her. She will never belong here, she knows this, but she is for the most part accepted, never abused, never vilified, and she accepts her surroundings, knowing the things she cannot change – a rare moment of serenity then, here at the entrance, it catches her by surprise, but how long will it last?

So what should she do now? She is all alone. She has found herself at home, and solitary again, so what should she do now?

A tinny voice comes from deep inside the house.

She sighs: she is not alone.

"Welcome home, Miss Susie. Your dinner will be ready in twenty-eight minutes."

Serenity shatters. So quickly again, things destroyed. No rest. She rolls her eyes.

She stands for a second, holding her hard briefcase – she has always thought it looked rather manly, but a shop clerk insisted it was what Japanese businesswomen used – and turns to face the door she has just entered.

Should she just go back out? Just head straight back out and face the impending rain? Surely there is more life *outside* this sullen house. The inclemency might have more of a chance of consoling her. Nature was outside, where things sprout and grow, where things breathe and flow, not the bleeps and buttons and signals and static of *inside*, where things whirred and were Nature's antitheses, where things needed input, needed to be programed and controlled and fed information, information that she hasn't really got ...

She puts the briefcase down and steps over to the Hologram Message Screen. Her thumbprint activates the machine, and a tiny, tray-like plate ejects slowly from the bottom of it, producing on it the 3D head of her mother-in-law, Noriko Sakamoto. It used to be that these holograms were colourful, rainbow-ish, like water in a petrol-y pool on a summer's day. But they have improved over the last few years. Noriko's head looks just like Noriko's head, amazingly life-like though in preposterous miniature.

The hologram speaks, and, as usual, Susie cannot make out a lot of it.

Below the hologram subtitles appear on the silver plate, so instead she reads the English.

"Susie-san, I haven't heard from you in a few days. Are you OK? I can come around anytime and cook for you. I am lonely here and would be happy to come over and clean for you. You can shut down that homebot thing for a few days. They're nothing but a nuisance. Masa and his stupid projects. And I told him so, I told him they were no good, I told him that they ... anyway, when you get the chance, please get back to me."

Susie watches the words dissolve and the hologram fades and disappears. There is such distress in her mother-in-law's voice, Susie registers it, and yet she does not call her back. Noriko keeps reaching out, but Susie does nothing but drift further away. It would be the simplest thing to return the call, to reach back, but not now. Susie does not want to share any of her pain. It is hers and hers alone. She heads to the living-room. She slumps into her familiar position on the couch, holding her heavy head in her hands. Back to the womb. All she needs is amniotic fluid. If she could just have that, fill the room with that and suspend herself, hearing nothing, no sound, no breath even, just the complete encapsulation, the complete enclosure, away from the world, away from everything ... but there would still be thought, no escaping that surely. There would still be those ideas rattling around. Inner chatter again. And the battle-worn beat of her somehow enduring heart.

"Music on."

Light, upbeat, jazzy music, the kind Masa unapologetically liked – there had been playful arguments, ribbing, eye-rolls – starts to play and Susie shakes her head slowly; Masa's dire taste. The horrible pop songs he tried to convince her were modern masterpieces, and would shake his body to support his argument, eschewing decorum, all this in the kitchen as he helped with the grating of vegetables, or began cleaning the rice cooker, Zen in fits of laughter at his tall frame gyrating, and the boy unable to suppress and succumbing to the contagion, his little hips swaying, boundless enthusiasm for the always joining in. Susie pleading with both of them to stop, in fits of laugher herself, praying for something more cerebral, not the fluff that got Masa and his boy shamefully twerking.

"No. Not that. Change. Drone."

Heavy, sombre psychedelic drone music reverberates, and Susie sinks deeper into the sofa, lying on her back, staring at the ceiling. She knows the robot is buzzing around the kitchen, doing its chores, doing things *for* her – domestic home service robot, Model SH.XL7, its purpose to aid, to make human lives more convenient, but it was succeeding in only making Susie ill. She curses quietly to herself, cursing the day Masa named the damn thing Sonny. She has always hated it, the name and the object – Masa had defended the name, thinking it hilarious, explaining that it could be spelled with a "u" or an "o". *Sunny! Sonny!* Susie didn't care one way or the other. It would have been better if it had no name at all. Better silent. Uncalled. It was not a family member. She realized of course that it was a work project for him, and that if it was properly functional and without any mishap in their home, then it wouldn't be long until the project took off all over the country. In this small city there were over a thousand already placed, and these were fully operational, and soon, when the good reviews were written, the whole nation would be in on it, enamoured with the project, ordering them in large numbers, as prices became more reasonable, then worldwide sales, onwards, upwards: that was, still *is*, the plan. They don't need Masa to push it on through. Plenty other dreamers are there only clambering to fill his boots, and they will not be stopped, and they will be successful too, whatever that meant. They would be everywhere, the home service robots. The homebots. Susie hated its guts, or to be more precise, its utter lack of.

She remembers Masa programing it, pressing buttons on its belly while consulting the pink manual he had himself co-written with a team of experts. The hours spent on it. Days becoming nights. The concentration. The sense of focus and determination. Susie and Zen watched from the bleachers, both proud of Daddy for being so clever with such complicated technology, proud that he was top dog, almost a prophet or seer, certainly many saw him that way, as a demigod. Susie had been sceptical from the beginning. Home robots? Really? Is that what the world was waiting for, because they did not yet have their jet-packs? They were not yet travelling into space or teleporting, but they could at least have a damn 'bot in their house. Susie would've much preferred a dachshund or a guinea pig, a white mouse or a bloody goldfish, something really alive, really real, with blood vessels, and a beating heart, and something that was unable to speak, no voice, no nasal whines, hush, just hush. Yes, a goldfish would've been ideal. Tiny bubbles floating up soundlessly. She should have argued with more gusto, should have made her case.

She remembers it coming to life and Zen reacting with initial fright, but then that changing to a dizzy delirium – so quickly things change, so quickly excitement's contagion again – the way kids are wont to do, hardly able to contain themselves, literally jumping, beside themselves, and he hugged it as it moved, and he held out his hand to it, and the machine was able to take it, and shake it, and introduce itself.

Sonny.

It said its name was Sonny.

The sense of achievement, the victory, was all Masa's, and he was clearly exhilarated because of it. He could hardly sleep those nights, his mind buzzing with the brilliance of new ideas, plans for "improvements" constantly invading his thoughts. There were calls too, constant phone calls, congratulatory, or other whispery calls, when his voice got lower, attempting to conceal something – who were those people ringing so late, what could ever be so important it could not wait?

The sheer joy on Zen's face with the arrival of the home-bot: a brother, a playmate, a maid, a servant, a nanny, a pet, a cook, a cleaner, a companion, endless possibilities. That was what they saw. Both of them. Masa and Zen saw nothing but possibilities. So why was Susie not taken in? What was it that kept her cagey, kept her suspicious?

It was Masa's idea also to program it to do kitchen work, not just simple cleaning tasks, but to be able to set ovens and grills, their timers, to be able to take food out at specific times – *cooking,* if you will. It would give Susie a break. At least it would be a big help. Surely she would be pleased with that. Masa once, jokingly, put an apron on Sonny, and Susie did see the funny side then, the absurdity of the thing, perhaps it was a metaphor for how absurd all life was becoming, more and more out of human hands, and cared for by these machines. Who would have thought? Well, everyone. Everyone would've thought. It was all an inevitability. And it was living in her house. Yes, Sonny in an apron, hilarious, for a minute or two – laughs are few and far between these days, it would take a lot more than an apron on an appliance to get her to stretch her mouth into even a half-smile. Sonny was no joke. There was nothing to laugh about here anymore, there was nothing funny at all.

She could just study up on it herself now. She could just find that pink manual and learn the codes and make herself able to shut it down for good. The whole system. She knows how to get it to enter standby mode, but somehow it always comes back to life within a given time. Why can she not get it to shut down properly? It is never truly asleep, never truly dead to the world, why is that? Is it a glitch? Can every other home shut down their homebot with no trouble at all? Or do they have any need to? Perhaps they like it being on all the time. Maybe they have welcomed it as a family member and like the fact that it is on and always available. But wouldn't that ruin its operating system? Surely these things need rest. She should just go out and ask someone, a neighbour. She should just go to the laundry woman when she is hanging out her clothes and say, in her finest Japanese: "Hi, I know we've never spoken to each other before, but do you have a homebot, and if you do, are you able to switch the damn thing off?" Does she have one? That woman? Where are the other homebots? In whose houses exactly? Susie can just imagine the look of horror on the woman's face, the impertinence of the foreigner, snaking up like that and asking a question out of the blue. Susie's not sure her language abilities would be up to it anyway.

She should have learned from her husband, she should have bloody paid attention. She's stuck with Sonny now. Stuck with it, until she comes up with a way to dispose of it. Can she just dump it somewhere? Is that illegal, leaving things like that out in the rubbish? She can picture Sonny's legs sticking up out of a dumpster, all the rancid rubbish around it. Maybe it would be crying for help! Maybe one if its buddies could come to the rescue! The Japanese leave all kinds of electronic items to be taken away, items that Susie is not sure are broken or obsolete. Maybe Sonny could join the other discarded implements, sit it out with the broken heaters, the rusty washing machines, the hair dryers and shoulder massagers. Or one of these days she may well just have to clobber it over the head, to really kill it off; that would be far more fun, and far more likely a scenario – the mad Irishwoman swinging a baseball bat and battering the silver home-robot till it was nothing but loose bits and scraps. Sonny scattered all over the place. Progress halted. Science stilled for a minute, enough to get your human breath back. Is that such a bad idea? Is it?

Susie laughs to herself as the drone music plays and assuages her. She has never been a violent woman at all. Even as a young girl, when doing P.E. in school, she never really wanted to tackle, never wanted to brush up against other people, didn't want the physicality of sports, the combative nature of it. Why she thinks of baseball bats at all now is so out of character. But people change. People do. Because of circumstance. It's Sonny. It's the bloody homebot pushing her to these dreadful considerations. Pushing her buttons, ironically. Perhaps she just needs a drink.

8

Susie goes to the drinks cabinet and pours herself a large gin with just the smallest dash of tonic. After a mere sip the relief is instantaneous. She should do this more often.

Sonny is making noise in the kitchen. There is a sudden clatter and rattle. Surely that wasn't a pot that it let drop, was it? Surely it didn't just make a mistake, did it? Call the news desk! *This just in: a homebot has just made an error! And it was Sonny! Of all homebots! Call them all back in! Back to the factory for you and your sort, reboot the lot, or send them all to rehab!*

It made a mistake.

It.

He!

Sonny is a *he!* A *him*! Susie has just realized this now. When they were programing it, could they have decided on either gender? Could they have made the voice female if they had wanted? But they decided to make it a *him*. Sonny, a boy, with a nasally voice. Do all the homebots have the same voice? How come she does not know any of this? She does not know because she never asked any questions, that's why. And now the point seems ludicrous to her.

Sonny is male. Genital-less of course, but that voice, definitely a boy's. A whining adolescent that has not yet procured a girlfriend, has never been kissed. And Masa called him *Sonny*. For fuck's sake.

A girlfriend, thinks Susie, yes, that'd keep him busy. She sniggers as she daydreams about Sonny heading out on a date with a female homebot, a robot exactly the same height and weight and with the same features as Sonny, but with a ridiculous blond wig on top of it. And the two of them gazing into each other's scarlet eyes, and their mechanical hearts a-throb. There should be a TV show about them. Reality TV. That's what those shows used to be called. Real people in rather unreal situations. People used to be entertained by that. Would they be entertained by two robots on a date? Susie would. Susie would love it for sure. As long as the whole thing ended disastrously, then she'd be delighted. A brawl. The two of them tearing metal and plastic strips off each other, or the two of them, wires crossed, literally, sparking off and sizzling and bursting right into flame. Nice.

Yes, this gin is certainly the way to take the edge off an evening. Maybe she has no need to kill herself at all, just drink enough of this to make her placid and forgetful, ever-wasted, never-wanting, a perpetual alco-haze; if nothing else it might help her sleep a nightmare-less sleep.

"Ten more minutes to dinner, Miss Susie," shouts the homebot from the kitchen.

"Whatever," says Susie, taking an even bigger slug of the drink, then filling up her glass with even more. Would they believe all this at home? If she called and told her mother that there was a home robot living with her, a social experiment, and that these things would be in Irish homes too before long. Would they believe her? It sounded like the premise for a bad sitcom; maybe it was a bad sitcom and there are cameras monitoring her every move right now. Twenty-four hour surveillance. But it is hardly entertainment. Susie's life is certainly not that. Who'd be watching? They are going to be everywhere, Mother, these homebots, just you wait and see. It's inevitable. Prepare yourselves, oh innocent world. You may have had your wars and missiles and stupid presidents in the past, but you haven't yet had the delightful Sonny. How can you call yourself experienced, World, until you've had your own little Sonny to take care of your every need?

The homebot is now preparing dinner in the kitchen. What would Mother say to that? What would Grandfather Martin have said were he still alive? Would he have stopped his whistling? Would the notion have stopped him in his country tracks?

And Masa, her husband, her missing, dead husband, isn't he the one to blame for all this acceleration? The mastermind behind it all. *A domestic robot in every home. Imagine the convenience!*

Susie should feel guilty about this. But she doesn't. Because Susie is drinking.

And she misses him, her mad scientist.

And then she drinks from her glass again, and it does indeed taste very good.

She eats at the same counter. She remembers hearing the real estate agent describe it as a "breakfast counter" when it was being sold to her, but it's used for all of Susie's meals, all her fidgety contemplations; she has no use for the dining table and its set of vacant chairs. Her feeling of joylessness is the same now as it was at breakfast (although the gin did give her a few jokes and felt like a reprieve, or a holiday from herself), and if Sonny doesn't stop just standing there and staring at her, then her anger levels will be the same as this morning also. Things repeat. Over and over. That's how life with a robot goes.

"Don't you have something to do?"

"Is there something you would like me to do?"

Susie refrains from swearing, refrains from telling it where to go and what to do to itself. Instead she mutters under her breath:

"You could kill me."

Sonny edges a little closer.

"I'm sorry, Miss Susie, you will have to say that again. My sensors didn't catch your utterance."

But surely you have amplifiers in there that make you never miss a fucking sound. Surely Masa would have thought of that. He didn't make you with flaws now, did he?

Susie is tapping her spoon anxiously on the side of her plate. It's the kind of thing that would have driven her mad if someone else was doing it; now she does it herself with consummate ease. As if this behaviour is completely natural to her. As if she has never done anything else.

Is she joking about what she just said to him? *You could kill me.* Is that a joke? Or is that really what she wants? She could just jump under one of those morning trains. Or jump from the NowNews building. Or find the sharpest knife and stab it hard through the empty caverns of her heart. There are quite a few options if you put your mind to it.

"I said no, Sonny. Everything is fine. Maybe you could just go and clean the toilet or something."

Just do anything. Just piss off.

"Upstairs or downstairs?"

Doesn't matter.

It stands there waiting for her to decide.

"Downstairs."

"Of course, Miss Susie."

The homebot moves out of the kitchen and Susie stares out the window at the black, starless sky. Zen had an interest in space, and they filled his room with spaceships and rockets and hanging planets that glowed in the dark: Saturn's rings, a big orange Jupiter. He shared his father's dreaminess, thinking that nothing was too small, or nothing was too big, everything could be imagined. He was only three when he could perfectly pronounce "astronaut", and said quite matter-of-factly that he was going to be one someday. Masa delighted in such a proclamation, and fully believed the little boy, and promised that he was going to make it all happen for him.

Was Susie the realist in the equation then? The party-pooper? The fly in the ointment? All the other clichés that meant she put an end to dreams and imagination. Stark reality. Was that what she was? Was that what she did? Masa was better at letting the boy fly with his fancies; Susie had no right to bring things down to her level, hard reality, yes, that was her all over; she wanted to have her boy growing up with a more realistic attitude; boys simply did not get to become astronauts no more than they became racing car drivers or world famous soccer players. It just didn't really happen. The odds were always stacked against you.

She'd take it all back now of course, if she could. She'd take it all back. Every negative utterance. But she can't. There's reality for you.

She stops eating, and although she hasn't finished – has hardly eaten anything substantial in so long now – she takes a knife from the drawer and scrapes off the food into a dust-bin (yes! a knife through an empty heart!); she leaves the dirty plate in the sink. Sonny's job. Let the bastard robot do it, if that's what it's there for ...

At the front door she puts on her raincoat and considers taking an umbrella. There are dark clouds looming out there – they've been looming all evening – but she decides against it, the raincoat should be enough, and if she catches her death out there, then so be it; she is half in love with her doom anyway.

Off into the night she goes, but she is hardly thirty metres down the road when thunder grumbles and a flash of lightning flares the sky. Soon it is raining heavily down upon her and she is soaked to the bone.

She could go back and get that umbrella. She could turn around and go back to the house. The protective sheath would save her from this torrent. But she ploughs on regardless. Stubborn. Striding briskly forward. Negotiating the quick-forming puddles. Soon she is saturated, sopping, sodden.

On the top of an old, abandoned house two eyes observe her. She has had this feeling before when out alone at night, the eerie feeling of eyes watching her – but she feels they are eyes of a natural order, of blood and living cells, not the robotic eyes to which she has become so inured. If she were to guess she'd say it was an owl. It makes the most sense, a nocturnal bird, high up there. A bird of prey. Vigilant. But why it is it keeping its eyes fixed on her? Is Susie in some way trespassing? Or heading somewhere she shouldn't be? Has the owl mistaken her for prey?

She quickens her step, continues her journey; these are thoughts for another hour. Right now forward, one foot in front of the other.

Thunder cracks and bellows loud in the sky and she pulls the raincoat tighter around her, almost grimacing as she leans into the inclemency. Her thin-lips are shut tight, it's hardly a mouth at all, more like the slit on an arras where a dagger was forced through. She has the face of someone who is ready for flight, or fight.

She shivers as she walks. Drops have trickled down the back of her neck and down her spine. Her mind plays dirty tricks on her as she strides through the wetness. Instead of it being a mind-*clearing*, cleansing walk, she is fret-filled with nightmare visions again: fire in the sky, debris from the destroyed plane flailing and falling towards the ever-accepting expanse of ocean; images of high-ranking Japanese military officials committing *seppuku* in dark ceremonies, flashes of swords, the beauty of their violent clashes, spatters of blood; a cartoon ghost fading from her, away from her, smaller and blurrier and disappearing, and the hard applause of North Korean hands, political rogue hands, fat hands, despotic hands … but no it is not applause at all, it is just the rain as it rushes off the rooftops, and spits down on her bare, vulnerable head. That's what you get if you don't carry your umbrella with you. That's what you get if you face this world ill-prepared and if you don't turn back when you have the chance.

❧

Another front door closes and the blue-stockinged legs of Mitsuki Makanae walk down steel steps and away from her apartment building, out into the rain-soaked streets. She stops and opens her bag and takes out a long, thin cigarette and lights it. Her face in the flash is well made-up, pretty in a hard, been-around-the-block-once-or-twice kind of way. Mitsuki sucks on the cigarette severely, blowing smoke out to the night air.

This woman does have her umbrella with her, a lurid pink one, and she enjoys the sound of the raindrops that fall on it. She has walked this road a thousand times before, and the weather never halts her, not when she is on her way to a favourite bar – and every bar is a favourite – not when she is in this way fully committed.

A noise from a cluster of trees then. A hoot. It's there again. Or *they* are there again. She can never be sure how many of them. Two owls. Three? A great big family? Are they not solitary hunters? Or do they stick together? She imagines them, a family close and warm, soft feathers cuddled up against each other, keeping out the chill of night, of every night, of every rough wind that happens upon them. Where have they come from all of a sudden, these mysterious night creatures? She doesn't remember ever seeing them in her youth. Why should they be here, in this urban hodgepodge of a town? Why not some abandoned barn on some forgotten farm? She never remembers hearing the hoot of an owl ever when she was young. She has heard the cries of urban foxes maybe, or of frisky cats with their terrifyingly strangled squawk-bawl-caterwauls, maybe only those, but then again she was always tucked up in bed, dreaming of Disney princesses or fabulous fairies, things pink and fluffy, not brown and wild and reeking of lust or the flesh of fresh carrion. Now she is as nocturnal as any owl, here, existing among them, in their nights, for the nights really belong to them, to those who swoop, and are not seen, and who finish with a savage kill.

"What is it you want from me?"

She speaks aloud to them. As if they could understand her. Maybe they can.

She is sure that they are calling her, too. Those little hoots, those little cries, often little squeals – or are those the mice they fiercely devour? Are the birds warning her of something? Is something bad about to happen?

In Japanese culture owls are said to bring luck, and to offer protection. Ever wary, and silently so, they are looking after you, looking out for you, making sure no harm will come upon you. In some prefectures the bird is said to even predict the weather – they must think themselves well and truly out of a job, with so many electronic devices for that now. Is that the root of their chagrin? Have they been usurped?

Mitsuki blows smoke out again, and lets it waft behind her, lets it trail. She walks away from the hidden owls. Her walk grows strong with purpose. It is always this way when she's heading for a bar. Every bar is a favourite bar.

9

A tall building with neon signs on its façade. This is in the "entertainment" section of the town, full of seedy bars, run-down cinemas and live "shows". It is the kind of place they say has gone to seed, to wrack and ruin, but Susie has heard that it was pretty much in that state to begin with, perhaps even designed that way, without much regard for finery or opulence – there's a bareness about it, a baldness, a sense of *let's just get the job over and done with it, and move on.* Dereliction. There may never have been a clean, pure phase, it was always the bottom, the bowery, an area no soft suburbanite would ever be bothered to be bothered with, this place too dour and decrepit, whiffs of sin sprinkled with melancholy. The people who frequent the district are often hooded figures, hunched and evasive, often trying to disguise themselves; no one who walks here walks with head held high – what's to be proud of? – everyone skulks, sullen and secretive. This is down. This is dive. This is where the dastardly go to dine.

Susie looks up at the building in front of her and the rain sluicing down the side of it, the gutters gushing; some of the signs on the building are flashing, some are holograms that fizzle in the downpour, and they reach out, these holograms, these images that seem to want to live but are trapped in pictorial purgatory; in brash colours they reach, inviting you in, tempting you with the threshold and daring you to traverse.

Susie succumbs. Of course she does. This part of town, lately, so often is her destination. How on Earth could she resist, a soul as sunk as hers?

She steps into the building and makes her way to the tight little elevator. The inside of it smells like urine. No doubt some drunk could no longer hold it in and relieved himself right there in that corner, or worse, some feral female squatted and let go – why does she think that's worse? People are supposed to have decorum in this part of the world, politeness meant to reign, social etiquette … or are the rules simply different in this neck of the woods? The outskirts: more than just geography. A mind-set. The floor is sticky under her shoes – she is glad she has only to spend seven or eight seconds in there. When she lands on the top floor she is pleased to be able to breathe through her nose again. People: you can never be up to them.

She walks up to a metal door. The sign above the door says: Score. Hologram images of different balls (basketball, soccer, American football) flow out of the sign and just as quickly disappear into the ether. The effects already seem dated, though they were only put up a few years ago. Things change so fast and a few 3D tricks were never going to be enough to put a gloss on this place.

Masa's old haunt. Her husband was a sports nut, and often Susie would tag along when Zen stayed over at his grandmother's. They'd drink cocktails and watch whatever sport was being broadcast on the big screen – it didn't really matter which, Masa enjoyed them all, though he had a soft spot for soccer, fancied himself as a bit of a player when he was younger, but it never did amount to much. He would show Zen a few tricks, how to keep the ball up without it touching the ground – that was about the extent of his skills. He also had a soft spot for gambling and would regularly hit the icon on his phone before a game or race, laying on a bet, trying his luck; it was never for very much money, and was really only to bolster the excitement of the event. That's at least the excuse he went by. Susie, hailing from a county of horse-racing enthusiasts, understood completely: the fun of the flutter, the titillation of that promising gallop at the final furlong when your steed is already in the lead by a couple of lengths; yes, she got it, and always turned a blind eye to his wagers.

She has continued to come to this bar over the last few months, just to see if she can resurrect Masa's ghost, to feel that presence beside her, a rekindling, as if they are still bound together in some way; that the universe is not completely done with them and that their union meant, *means* something. A resurrection, sure, why not? But don't you need a body first? Don't you need the cadaver in the tomb. The stiff in the sepulchre. It's a stretch, this pining, but what else has she got?

Before every game she likes to imagine what he might've done. How he would have predicted the outcome. Would he have gone for the underdog, the team in trouble, the team whose manager's head is for the chopping block, or would he have played it sensible, backed the favourites, the superstars, the ice-cold certainties? She likes to feel as if their minds are melding, her husband and hers, making such a decision, as if his ghost really does inhabit the space around her. Has come back.

Masa, please come back.

Susie puts her face close to the screen on the wall. The device scans, recognises the contours of her features and the hefty door gives way. She is what is known the world over as a "regular", a word loaded with connotations both good and bad in any land; positive because it means that you are welcome, you've got somewhere to go, everybody knows your name, and, whether they like you or not, at least they are prepared to put up with you and all your idiosyncrasies, maybe they even miss you when you are not in attendance. The negative connotations? Here's the harsh indictment: you've got a problem, my friend. This needing of the place so much. This sad dependency on what they've got to offer. Susie can weigh up the pros and cons of anything, but it still does not stop her from going through that open door. She does traverse. She's here again.

Only two other customers before her and she does not know them. They are sitting at the main bar as a British football game plays on the lofted screen with low Japanese commentary.

The bartender, Haruto Matsumoto, smiles when he sees who has arrived. They nod to each other as they have done so many nights before.

"Feeling better?"

"No, not really."

"No. Of course not. Of course not."

He feels that he has to say something. He knows her situation and his platitudes are always quite useless. But it would be worse if he said nothing at all. It's a conversation neither of them want to have, and it won't be developed, but it has to be somehow acknowledged. He knew Masa well and had considered him a friend. Had there been a body found and a formal funeral he would surely have come to pay his respects; the trustworthy type then, this Haruto Matsumoto, easy to lean on, the type that make the best bartenders, knows his place and when not to overstep the mark, impossible to dislike, easy company, the good sort.

"Just a beer please."

Who knows how many harder drinks she might knock back soon, but a beer for now will do, to get her started. The gin at home has already gotten her underway, her mind already has that soft familiar fuzz growing around it, the gin-aftermath massaging her, making her malleable, suggestible; she doesn't particularly care how much she mixes drinks together tonight. Bring 'em on.

Something keeps her fastened to this bar and this city, this country and this trying situation. What is it? Why is she still here? Is it that she feels there is more to come? More to her tale? More to occur … and in her favour?

Often a different inner voice interrupts:

Go home.

Just fuck off.

Often voices in her head, quite adamant:

Go home. Enough is enough.

Intermittently they come. Unbending. Sensible perhaps.

There's nothing for you here anymore: Your man. Your boy. They're gone.

But deep down the feeling persists. It gnaws at her. There's more still to come. The story. Her story, has not quite yet unfurled.

Haruto hands Susie a towel and she wipes her face and rubs the thick wavy shoulder-length hair that the rain has turned into ropes.

Then the beer comes. She takes a big gulp from it and the strong taste of hops immediately helps her forget about the drenching she had outside, the night's scornful irascibility.

The two other customers – a couple on a date, both in their twenties, taking their eyes from each other for a moment – are suddenly extremely interested in the foreigner who has stepped in out of the barbarous weather. In Japanese they say how cool she looks, and yet how sad at the same time. Why would anyone come to such a place alone? Is she not afraid of the devils that roam the streets outside? The orcs. The goblins. The degenerates. Does she speak the local dialect? They are too drunk to lower their voices. Their questions, opinions ring out and vibrate across the bar, and the lack of volume-control doesn't embarrass them in the least.

"These two are saying…"

"Yes, Haruto, thanks. I know what they are saying."

"Your Japanese is getting very good, Susie. You have been here for many years now."

"Too many."

Haruto flatters. Her Japanese is not good. She should have studied a lot more. She has only the vary basics, had relied on Masa too much. She should have done a lot of things properly, thoroughly. But it all feels a little too late in the day now.

She looks up at the screen.

"Who's playing? Is that Liverpool?"

She likes saying the name. It reminds her of her childhood: boys playing in the fields, shouting their favourite teams, their favourite players.

Haruto puts on a remote-control glove and swipes at the air, changing the content of the screen. All the information they need shoots up in front of them, colourful, catchable.

"Yes, Liverpool versus Everton."

She thought as much, the colours were familiar to her. One team red. One team blue. She'd seen enough games in the past. Wasn't there some word for two local teams playing against each other? She can't seem to recall it now. There was definitely a word, a simple word, but her mind is scrambled. She remembers her brothers at home in Ireland screaming for one team or the other, screaming at the TV screen, imploring, castigating, like it made any damn difference to the outcome. Screaming, she knows, no matter how therapeutic at the time, only goes in one direction, straight into the abyss.

"Do you want English commentary?"

Susie flicks her head in the direction of the intimate couple:

"If these two don't mind."

"They don't mind at all," says Haruto, laughing. "They are not sports fans. Just drunkards."

The male of the couple perks up. He understands the English phrase and is mock-aghast.

"Drunker? No, no. I no drunker!"

Haruto laughs again and rolls his eyes. The couple, clearly quite intoxicated, laugh too, and move away from the bar to a small table in the darkest corner of the room.

"Sorry, I'm making them uncomfortable."

"Don't worry, Susie. Enjoy the game. Take your mind off things."

There it is again: *mind off things, get over things*; they mean well, these people and their platitudes, but they will never understand. How could they be expected to? How could anyone? You can never understand these things until they happen to you. Until you're eye-deep in the muck and its clogging up your nostrils, stopping your futile attempts at breath. Until then. Susie grew up without any real tragedy. Old relatives had died like old relatives do, but she hardly knew any of them, remembers almost nothing about them. Except for her grandfather who had made such a huge impression on her. Why him? Because he seemed to care so much about everything, because he dug that little bit deeper – the surface never good enough, scratch it, fine, but he preferred to carve it up completely, taking deep swathes of it with whatever blade he had to hand. Her parents are alive and well, and she is grateful though often nervous about that, the way exiled offspring are, and all of her friends back home were there, there to be found, only a call or text away, the way real friends should be. She had lived a life largely unscathed, not even the misfortune of a broken bone or an anecdotal scar.

Lucky.

You could say that had been a life of luck. A happy one, even.

But then a few months ago that all drastically changed.

A missile. Shot into the air on a bright and normal day.

It flies close to the path of a plane, close enough, or with enough force from its trajectory to make the plane tremble, spiral, dive. Down it goes, spinning. The end. Is that what happened?

She knows that some people were able to get their families back on that awful day. Their husbands and wives and children. A few people somehow miraculously survived, were rescued. Helicopters. Boats. Divers and savers: the good, tough, heroic people of the world out there doing their utmost. Some came back limbless, eyeless, deaf, but despite the odds, returned. And families that even got corpses back, mangled bodies of dead loved ones: that was at least something, wasn't it? An end to it. Finality. So far Susie has got nothing back. Nothing at all but the growth of ulcers inside her, a gut that twists itself in knots more and more every day. She should have stayed a Catholic, like when she was young. She should have kept believing. It might have been helpful. It might be helpful on days like today when she is found wanting, when her mind searches for answers, now that she finds herself, broken, lost, ironically all at sea, prayer might be a raft.

Is it too much to hope for a miracle, is it too late to pray now? For two more bodies to walk out of the ocean and come home to her? Is that really too much to ask?

She finishes her beer and decides she wants something else. Gin again. Bring her gin again. Cold and metallic. Ice that punches with a frosty fist.

"Not so much of the tonic."

She remembers her mother using that word, in a completely different context. The local village chemist would be sure to mix up a "tonic" if one wasn't feeling well. God knows what was in them, those milky concoctions, but the mothers of the neighbourhood swore that Brendan Maher knew what he was doing. Who were they to question such a learned man?

Susie looks at this concoction before her now, glowing blue in the scant artificial light of the bar. She thinks for a minute about the recent push towards cryogenic procedures. Some were considering freezing their bodies and waking up in a completely different time altogether. She hadn't believed it when she first came across it – it was on the screen at breakfast, was Sonny listening in on it? Maybe that could be a solution for her. Get frozen. Wake up in a different time and … wait, no Susie doesn't give a flying fuck for what happens in the future, it's that past she dreams about as she stares into the icy glass. It's the past, the past, how do you get back to the past?

The door suddenly swings open and it is no miracle come to save her. It is no messiah. It is no medicine man, no guru, no revelation. It is no zombie either, no ghost back from the dead, nor is it someone from a frozen future.

It is just Mixxy.

Mitsuki Makanae, a well-made-up, gamine twenty-eight-year-old, pretty but tarty, enters the bar with her usual flourish, liking, as always, to make an impact on arrival, liking her own sense of swagger and sway, it never seems to fail.

Mixxy, like a hungry hound, scans the place and is disappointed that the cupboards are bare. Punkish, green-streaked hair, glossy lips and stockinged legs, Mixxy the extrovert nods to Haruto and takes her place beside Susie, slapping her handbag on the counter as if some serious and illicit business is about to go down. Mixxy flashes one of her smiles – she is ready for an evening, and whatever that entails … what have you got? Mixxy is always full of faces. Practiced faces. Rehearsed faces. She can blow out her cheeks in a half-cute/half-pensive way that makes her mouth small and pursed, angling her head, making her inflated cheeks an invitation. *Come and burst me. I'm nothing but a cutesy doll that will explode to your very touch.* It makes the greedy boys go gaga with glee. Or she can do that duck-bill thing with her lips that never fails to set testosterone-fuelled loins a-flame, knock-knees a-quiver. Mixxy knows all the tricks, can pull out all the stops.

"You are here again, Miss Susie," she says, her voice a rehearsed rasp.

Haruto starts to prepare the cocktail that she has pointed to on the laminated menu with her long, sparkly nails.

"Here. Again. Yes," says Susie, flatly, so devoid of emotion it could be the voice of scree.

Her real name is Mitsuki, but everyone has learned to call her Mixxy: it's how she prefers it, how she has engineered it; the nickname is apt because not only does it mimic the sound of her given name, but also alludes to her being able to mix well with any company, in any situation, and her clothes too, a mix of old (retro) and the spanking new; and her drinks, bright fruity mixes, she rarely drinks the same thing twice.

"How are you doing?" she asks her friend.

"I'm fine."

Mixxy always speaks to Susie in English, because she can. Usually it is to impress other patrons, liking to show off, ever the extrovert. She claims she learned it from her many foreign boyfriends, or girlfriends, and in her American accent she says she's not choosy about sexuality, not choosy about her drinks or any damn thing, and no one argues the point – she may look slight and waif-like, but make no mistake, Mixxy can turn nasty at the crack of a toothpick, a mean drunk with a scimitar edge.

She looks to the screen.

"Who's playing?"

"Does it matter?"

"I guess not."

Mixxy clinks her glass with Susie's and both take big gulps from their luminous drinks.

"Who's winning?" asks Mixxy, not bothering to look at the score so patently perched in the corner of the screen.

"I am," says Susie. "Clearly."

Mixxy laughs.

"I'm glad to see I am stuck with such funny company again tonight."

"Cheers to that," says Susie. And they clink again.

Mixxy rubs her hand along Susie's thigh, and Susie's eyes follow it. This often happens. Susie doesn't budge or even blink. The most she usually does is gently shake her head, enough to deter her ardent admirer. They've both been here before, and if Susie knows her friend like she thinks she knows her friend, it won't be the last pass she'll ever try to make. What's surprising is that it has come so early in the night. Surely she can't be high already.

Susie notices an inactive homebot behind the bar, in the corner, stiff and useless as the broken broom it is propped alongside.

"Has that always been there?"

"No, this is new," says Haruto. "Delivered a week ago. I haven't properly set it up yet. The last one was ... how do you say ... faulty? It was releasing some kind of toxic gas, some broken line inside ... burning ... or something."

Haruto blushes, aware that his staccato English is never as sharp as Mixxy's, and his knowledge of technology not too hot either.

I didn't know they were that dangerous," says Mixxy, her hand making its way away from Susie's thigh and back to cradle the already almost empty cocktail.

"Nothing would surprise me," says Susie.

"Do you know how to program these things safely?" asks Haruto, the tone in in his voice admitting that he is not holding out for much.

"No clue. My husband could have done it. As you know. Unfortunately, I didn't pay enough attention."

Haruto hands Mixxy a fresh cocktail, equally luminous, equally outrageous. She flashes a toothy smile in appreciation."

"Such creativity in this place."

"And he's put an umbrella in it too. Should be handy for the journey home," says Susie.

"I do get your humour, Miss Susie. No wonder I am so attracted to you."

"You are attracted to everybody," says the Irishwoman, "and stop calling me that. I've told you before. My homebot already does that and it annoys the shit out of me."

"But I want to annoy you too, Miss Susie."

"Seriously. *Susie.* Or *Suze.* That's enough. Enough of your bullshit."

"Sure, my love. There's nothing I wouldn't do for you."
Another toothy grin.

Susie's heard it all before. Mixxy has been coming on to her for some time now, ridiculously flirting even when Masa was around, often right in front of his face. He thought it was hilarious. Maybe secretly he got off on it. Susie has yet to yield of course. But one day she just might. Mixxy has upped her efforts of late, out of sympathy perhaps – she knows all about her unfortunate situation, even though Susie has yet to fully disclose the fact that all she really wants to do is curl up in some soft space and die, dissolve to dust without as much as a whisper. It's hard to tell people these things.

She should just go ahead and let Mixxy have her way. Just go ahead and have dirty, obscene scenes. Just once. Chalk it all up to experience. Why the hell not? What is stopping her?

"Well?"

"Well, what?"

"Is tonight going to be our special night? It's terrible weather, there's nothing else for us to do."

"I'm not sure. You probably need to try a little harder."

Susie is a tease. She's just realised that. Another side of her she never really knew she had. Until recently. Everything is "until recently".

Mixxy smiles, it's the kind of challenge she rises to.

"It would be great to see you smile again, Miss … sorry … *Susie*."

"You've got your work cut out for you."

Mixxy frowns.

"I've never understood that expression."

"There are many things in this life we don't understand" says Susie, trying to sound cryptic or profound, but she achieves none of these; instead she takes a big swig of her drink and seems content with that.

The football game on the screen ends and Haruto dons his sensor glove and waves through the empty air, swiping though the channels. He is like a magician doing tricks, or a conductor in the pit before an orgy of instruments.

"Is there something you ladies want to watch?"

"The end of the world. Live."

"Ignore her," says Mixxy. "It must be some Irish humour thing. Put some karaoke on. I want to sing you all a song. As soon as I freshen up."

Mixxy makes like she is to going to get up but she spends a few more seconds sipping through her yellow straw.

The master of the bar puts on light, jazzy, background music, the kind that hurts no one, until you listen carefully to it for the briefest time, and then find yourself getting mentally ill.

Out of the corner of his eye he spies Susie's disapproving glare but he ignores her. Instead he presses a few buttons on a panel behind him and the karaoke machine slowly emerges, complete with standing microphone – 55SH vintage classic, Haruto had stated, an antique, a collectible, but it was too boring a fact for anyone to comment upon.

The forgotten couple in the corner of the bar whoop with delight from their shadowy depths when they notice its arrival. Mixxy finally gets off her stool and heads towards the toilet.

"Mixxy Time!" she exclaims as she goes, though no one else pays her the slightest regard. This time she really does have business to conduct.

In the cramped space Mixxy jostles with the stubborn zip of her handbag but eventually retrieves what it is she is looking for: a small packet of fine white powder which she sprinkles out onto the back of her hand and quickly inhales. *Mixxy Time* is always like this. A great treat. Like every day is a celebration of Mixxy and the things Mixxy knows and the things Mixxy thinks and Mixxy does. Every muscle in her firm face frizzles with electricity and the front part of her brain pulses with a bright bombastic burn; she is suddenly awake, very awake, ideally awake, as if she had never even known the concept of sleep or tiredness before; any disappointment she had on opening the door of the bar and finding it morgue-like has dissipated; with that quick snort her every fibre has been appeased, each follicle a little flame. She examines herself in the grubby mirror, pleased with the sparkling face she encounters, and with quick fingers she wipes her small, pinched nose clean.

She pushes up her breasts and opens another button on her blouse to reveal more cleavage. Her breasts are not large but they are full enough to attract attention, more than a handful, just like herself. Sure, she has her work *cut out* for her. It's always like this. Sure, she can try a little harder. What Mixxy wants Mixxy usually gets. And this Mixxy in the mirror is no shirker, this Mixxy is mighty. She feels a tingling in her lower region, a tingling that needs tickling, and she will get it sooner or later. Eventually that lonesome Irishwoman will give in. If not, she'll just have to nail Haruto again, stop him from running off home to his ugly wife. Poor boy, how did he ever get landed with such an old hag? And much older than him too. What's her name again? Suzuko? Suzuka? Something like that. Poor frustrated boy. He must be thrilled when Mixxy gives him that occasional ride on her roller coaster, the peaks and dips on those lightning-fast tracks – who wouldn't be?

Mixxy Time.

She'll find a way to relieve herself: Mixxy always finds a way.

She flushes the toilet and washes her hands. She feels a whole lot better now after that little gift to herself. Infinitely better. Amazing what even the teeniest touch of it can do. The power of something so fine, so concentrated. She has to barter to get that stuff. Often she gives up parts of herself in return – money doesn't always work for her guy, sometimes it has to be her mouth, sometimes she has to grip onto the metal fencing behind a bar while she takes it in her anus. It hurts. But doesn't everything?

Her mind is far from that now; firing with good lines now, good sparks, good vibes; if she were to be suddenly cast out into the dark night, she's quite sure she'd be able to converse with her guardian owls, quite sure she'd understand it all, every wave of sound and light in the universe. Nothing beyond her. That's always the result of Mixxy Time.

The cuddly young couple have started to sing a duet on the karaoke mini-stage. The man croons parodically, all shoulders and eyebrows, and his lover swoons beside him, hands all over his neat torso, extending her neck to reach into the microphone with him, reaching, reaching, trying to reach the high notes and comically failing. Haruto is laughing at how terrible they sound and Susie's face is all scrunched up, wincing at the pain it is inflicting on her ears. Mixxy is only one second out of the toilet and wondering whether she should jump back in for another line. Is this the level of entertainment for the night?

"Miss me?" she says to her drinking partner as she climbs back onto her high stool, itching for the night to improve. Bars and clubs have been desolate places over the last few years. The reason? Fear of war? Maybe. Fear of attacks? Or just plain fear? Instilled into people by a government that was directionless, and that fell further down the world's pecking order: ignored, shamed, lambasted, forgotten? Alcohol consumption rates had plummeted as people were no longer interested in drinking, or any kind of social entertainment at all. They could not believe in it. They could not bring themselves to believe in anything. People stayed at home. The only creatures out lurking in this part of town were the soarers, those looking to fly above it all, with alcohol, or with anything else that crept through the official nets, anything that could be smoked, snorted, injected, eaten or stuck right up the rear. These things could be gotten now. Gotten like never before. Creeping in through unpoliced ports on shady boats, every dodgy sailor, fisherman or custom guard in on it, too financially tantalising to ignore. This is the field of play and it is what happens at the end of the working day for Mixxy's kindred, her folk, with their peculiar tastes and private passions; the miscreants, the reprobates, the lawless and pariahs, the outsiders. Mixxy's people. She is one of them. Or they are one with her. Life has just become that way. She could've followed her mother into the sciences, she had brains enough for it. But fatherless (her lame excuse), rudderless (her laziness), she chose instead a different path, and there was nothing her good mother could do to dissuade her. She started off with a few hostess gigs in bars. Clients plying her with drink and filling her purse with cash or pawnable trinkets. Nights got longer. Days she slept through. Addictions worsened. No wonder when the chance came her mother finally upped and left – had had enough of Mixxy, just wanted her Mitsuki back. Yes, life had just turned out this way. It was never really planned. The country too, fallen into moral disrepair. It is fun enough for a girl like Mixxy though. When she is riding one of her waves. It is all fun enough then. A hoot. She'll make the most of it. And she'll drag Susie down with her.

"Miss me?" Mixxy says again.

Susie still ignores her and kneads her knuckles into her own face; the horrible singing seems to be chewing her up, penetrating through to her very bones and mashing them to pulp. People that perform like that should not be left out of the house, not to mind being left near a microphone. People like that should be banned. Or burned at the stake. No punishment too harsh – Susie's thoughts always go that bit too far these days. To violence. To brutality. To extremes. It can't be helped. Susie can't be helped.

"Want another?" Mixxy says.

"Another what? Another drink? Another shot at life?"

Mixxy nods to Haruto who begins preparing two more. They are keeping him busy, which the young man likes. Times are tough, and he takes all the customers he can. There are bills to pay, a family to feed, overheads. There is stress. Oodles of it. The usual.

The drinks are coming thick and fast, but Mixxy, after her toilet treat is ready for anything now, nothing can come thick and fast enough. Give her a baton and she'll twirl it, give her a marathon she'll run it, give her an appendage or two, real or no, and she'll suck the life out of them until they wither, spent. Her veins hum with the thrum of life. It's probably just a good hard cock she needs: this is her line of thought. Lines lead to other lines. Or at least a sniff of Susie's panties. She always needs just a little … more.

Thankfully the dreadful song by the dreadful singers has come to an end and they scroll through the list of options on the tablet to see if they can find another.

"Fuck, no. Someone put a stop to them, don't let them have another," Mixxy says. "Even I'm better than them."

Susie thinks she should be lying on her bed, far away from all this. She should be lying there and crying to the empty walls of the empty bedroom; it would have a lot more meaning than any of this.

Mixxy will try again to get her friend to talk. If it doesn't work she'll gulp down the drink and head for another bar where the company might be that bit more vivacious. She could even try the Jungle Room. She hadn't been there in a while.

Like other exotic city bars the Jungle Room has to be eked out. You do not just stumble across it. You wait patiently, for years perhaps, until finally you truly discover it and then they let you in. And you pay. For such exotic tastes you always pay. Mixxy's lanky guy once brought her there. *Tell no one. Don't breathe a word.* He said this with a clenched fist raised.

Dark ferns reach out to the swampy green walls there. And it smells, so real, so authentic: heavy odours: earth or mud. Loud drums in that place too, thumping drums and bass. Frenetic dance. Abrasive sounds, and always beats, beats, beats. In the Jungle Room only primal rhythms, only the most base among the rhythms of the bass.

When she first entered she found herself laughing uncontrollably. They had no inhibitions, these girls. No scruples. They were naked, mostly, or bits of fur clung to them, and they writhed around and growled at the staring men clutching their crotches. Some of these beasts were right in the middle of it – *estrus* they called it. Some had even defecated in the corner while others bit and scraped each other like animals playing in the wild. Her guy elbowed her hard in the gut to stop her laughing, and she quickly did.

Where was that bar? Can she remember? In the depths of the city somewhere. The bowels. Not far from here, she supposes. One of those buildings near the river. Shitty. A shit-fest. Not clean like Haruto's bar. But that's what some people want. Filth. Is it that they recognise themselves there? They see their own souls? We are shit. Our lives are shit. We live in shit. Society is shit and has betrayed us. Everything is a great big load of steaming shit. And here are some girls to roll around in it, just to make it plain and obvious. Let's make the damn thing literal, so everyone is on the same page. The metaphor is not lost on us. Rammed home. This is shit. It was even rumoured that politicians went there. Doesn't that make some kind of sense? Mixxy remembers the smell of damp and mould, female smells and dirt, caked mud, under nails, stuck to hair, playing at animals, playing at being in the wild, a return to some sort of primal being… where was it exactly, that place, behind which door…

And her guy. He even had a key to the place. Was he an owner of some kind? He had some stake in it for sure, some interest. As he did in everything. Nothing was ever base enough. All his long fingers stuck in many…

She shakes herself out of the memory. Perhaps it was all some fever dream. How could she even be sure, with the amount of stuff she smokes or snorts or lets melt under her tongue on a regular basis. The things that get shoved up inside her. This is not the life she had really *chosen*. She has just found herself here.

"Why don't you sing us a song first, my love?" she says.

"I thought this was supposed to be a sports bar. I didn't even know there was karaoke here until that thing appeared from behind the magic wall."

"This is an anything-you-want-it-to-be bar."

She pauses.

"So, what do you want it to be?" Mixxy jiggles her breasts. "A strip bar?" *Or a Jungle Room*, she thinks to herself, *you haven't lived until you've seen that fucking place.*

Haruto guffaws from behind the bar, suddenly excited: "Sure, why not? A strip bar!"

He had been with Mixxy several times and knows her body well. Images of her stripping right there in the bar after closing time and rolling around on the ashy floor will never leave him. And if Susie decides to take part too, then hell, yeah! It was better than going home. Sometimes he liked running this failing bar; for the briefest moment he feels like it isn't failing at all.

Mixxy faces despondent Susie, "They have every song you could ever think of. Every song ever. It's all here, on the machine. I'm sure you'll find some Irish songs. Sing me something good before my buzz wears off. I need something lovely, something lively."

Mixxy's tongue is getting looser, and Susie is impressed not only by her sudden burst of energy, but also by her fluency in her second language.

Mixxy stares at the karaoke machine, "The machines have them all. All the songs. The machines have everything."

Susie thinks about this. *Do they? Do they have everything? Poisonous gases that could kill you? Minds? Do they have minds? The machines: do they have minds? How much does Sonny know?*

Susie pictures her kitchen at home, her homebot standing in the darkness, its red eyes glowing. The homebot takes a knife out of the kitchen drawer and starts slashing through the air. It laughs, at first softly, as if letting itself in on some private joke. Susie even imagines it with a mouth, like those toy teeth that get wound up and go chattering across the table; Sonny's mouth wide with massive teeth, and it is laughing. Then the laughter gets louder. Then louder and louder and more maniacal, louder and louder and louder still until the microphone on the karaoke stand accidentally falls to the ground with a thud and squalls through the speakers with feedback.

"Do they?"

"Do they what? Who?" asks Mixxy.

"Do they have everything? The machines. Do they have it all?"

"Machines?"

Mixxy laughs at the word. When did she last hear that? Susie is often a throwback to a bygone, gentler time. *Machines.* So what does Mixxy call them? Maybe she doesn't call them anything at all. Just uses them. Or calls them by what they are. Homebots. She probably just calls them that. It's what they are. Isn't it? In the same way her blender is called a blender.

"Look, they do what you tell them to do. Isn't that enough?"

Susie nods, taking it in. *What you tell them to do.* It makes sense. That's what Masa was paid to do: program them to do what we tell them to do ... so Masa told them ... so that we could tell them ... what to do – she is talking to herself in circles. But who told Masa what to do? Who was his boss? Who gave those orders and ...

Did it all stop with Masa? Why does she not know this? They called him a nerd. They also called him a genius.

She cannot think about this stuff anymore. She wants to sing. Yes, she suddenly feels like singing a song. She's drunk, for sure, so she might just sing. It's better than thinking about who tells who to do what, about chattering teeth. She might just belt one out. One loud song. Why not?

Or strip? Why not that too? That's what Haruto said. *Why not?* Take off all her clothes. Expose the real Susie to the world.

No.

She'll just sing. She'll just sing tonight. That's exposure enough. She'll belt one out. To the rafters. To the roof. To the skyline. To the sky and the missiles that are coming for her. A song for the end of the world. Why not? A song *about* the end of the world. Why not? A song for the last night of humans on Earth. Why not? She'll sing while the whole damn thing collapses.

10

Bodies washed upon the beach. Still they get washed ashore, just one or two at a time, nothing more. Rubbery now, the bones softened, some flesh eaten, pale, blueish, nothing like when they were alive, nothing vital left. Some things still get washed ashore. Just one or two, nothing more.

It is as if the sea just spits them out, as if the sea has got no use for them, as if the sea, for all its wisdom, doesn't quite know what to do with them. They should not be dead. They were people. They should not have fallen from the sky. Humans should not fall from the sky. They are not leaves. It is not the natural order of things.

Perhaps the sea is being generous. They simply don't belong in there. They belong with their families. On land. Where they can be put to rest. In the solid earth. Where they came from. Let them grieve, properly. Let those families grieve and pity themselves and the world they don't understand.

The sea probably knows. The sea probably does. It's been round long enough, hasn't it? It has absorbed enough. All of history is in the ebb and the flow of the tides. Who'd argue against it? Who'd argue against the sea?

Washed ashore.

Battered. Bruised.

Some without limb. The sharks have been at them. Other smaller fish hacked at the skin, their miniscule teeth nipping, or nibbling, or sucking there. They have been dashed, dashed upon the rocks, those bodies, like they were old socks sopping in the mouths of drooling dogs, sopping and flung and forgotten.

But they were once people. Vital. Breathing and humming and ticking along quite nicely.

Sharks.

Drooling dogs.

It's a wild world.

And the sea knows.

Who'd argue against the sea?

Away from the beach, a hundred metres or so: a little grove. A few bare trees twisted from the wind. Under these: a small rucksack. Blood on it. Spatters. Dried now. An empty carton of apple juice. Squeezed dry. And chocolate wrappers. Not a morsel left.

On the rucksack, a picture. An animated ghost.

11

Parliament. Wisdom. Bazaar. Study. So many terms for their groupings, their avian selves together.

But not right now. Right now one breaks from the branch and swoops silently, stealthily, to pounce upon its prey.

Talons sink deep into the mouse's back. The smaller animal squeals in horror, cataclysmic pain; pain and the knowing that it is merely seconds from the end of its rodent days. No more scampering, no more scavenging.

Further, the claws crunch deep, cracking bone, and blood seeps to the soft earth where the rain has muddied the ground into mulchy patches and the mouse's face is buried in it – to add to all its torment it can no longer breathe either, and the tiny lungs soon stop expanding, the tiny alveoli penetrated, punctured; the owl's work has been all so easy. So easy is all this. So fast and pretty much effortless.

The bird looks around. It scans. No threat. The only threat in this night is itself. To other creatures. To other moving things that would dare to be seen, dare to show a face.

No threat. But it remains vigilant. There are sounds from houses that bother it. The bird does not know what these are, these signals, but something is not right along there somewhere, the bird can feel it. Some interference. It feels it in its feathers. Recognises it down in its bones. It is not a thinking thing, it is an action/reaction bird, all birds, preying birds, like this, but its feathers, its feathers now, ruffled when the hidden things bleep and emit and are not a natural part of the natural order.

For now though it is safe. And its hunger will abate. And it takes its meal back to its tree. And there it will feed or it will let the owlets feast. For a while anyhow. Until it gets the need to do it all over again. Action. Reaction. It is so easy to do the whole thing all over again. So easy. It is almost effortless.

By night. By fright.

12

The couple have stopped the bludgeoning of the song and have embraced each other as if they were somehow victorious. They scurry back to their dark corner, arms and legs a-tangle as they move, bumping against each other. Susie's chest tightens as she watches them, envying their closeness.

"Don't you know any songs?" asks Mixxy.

A million of them come to her but she immediately whittles them down.

"My Canadian grandfather used to sing many when I was young. He said they were the songs of a poet. One song in particular, he used to sing as he chopped wood, or shovelled coal from the bunker into the bucket."

"What was the name of it?"

"Diamonds in the Mine."

Mixxy has never heard of the song but she's pretty sure it can be found. The ever-eavesdropping barman brings a tablet to them and Mixxy enunciates directly into it. The device flashes bright green and the intro music begins.

"Off you go then."

Susie takes a big gulp of her drink and shakily gets to her feet. Haruto watches the proceedings with growing intensity, never having heard her sing before.

Mixxy starts to clap wildly, her earlier fix still playing its part, finding a power from within that perks her up once more.

The groping couple relax their intimacies to observe Susie as she nervously approaches the machine. Holographic lyrics appear before her when she stands in the correct position, appearing out of the emptiness bright and bold. She takes the microphone in her hand, clutching it tightly, and says, "Start again". The machine duly obliges, in a neon flash reverting to the start of the song.

"Yay! Susie! From Ireland! Singing some old Canadian song that no one knows!"

Haruto and the dating couple join in the sardonic applause.

Susie clears her throat, takes a look at the ceiling as if inspiration was writ there all along. She begins to sing.

The woman in blue, she's asking for revenge
The man in white, that's you, says he has no friends

Mixxy rolls her eyes. What kind of gloomy shit is this?

Susie closes her eyes. She is being carried away now. Carried away by the lines of the song and memories of her beloved grandfather. She can picture him, in that old house in Ireland, the one she grew up in, pottering around the way he used to, shuffling on his old slippered feet. Or out in the backyard, the axe falling on the wood with such force, strength in him even then, even at that grand old age, splitting it in two, the inside wood shockingly new and clean and smelling so fresh. Or the rattle of coal in the steel bucket, black mists rising from it as the nuggets dropped in there; grandfather's hands, the wrinkles and folds of age and life lived, black soot finding its way into him, making black creases, black lifelines, the hard hands of a workman. People would whisper about him in the street. The eccentric Canadian who had fallen in love with a local lass and made the place his home. But why "eccentric"? Susie never quite got to the bottom of that. Was it the old, battered fedora he ostentatiously donned, often at a rakish angle, when everyone else had completely given up on hats a century before? Or was it the thick moustache that made him look like a Russian Tsar or celebrated novelist? Was that enough to label him weird? Singing away there in that old house, singing to his heart's content, that was him; CDs strewn around the worn carpet, and the song … the song … nothing else would appease him but whatever song happened to be playing or he happened to be singing.

Deeper.

Deeper she goes into it. Her face frozen. Her eyes become lost in trance.

Haruto and Mixxy trade looks. Where is all this going?

And there are no letters in the mailbox
And there are no grapes upon the vine
And there are no chocolates in the boxes anymore
And there are no diamonds in the mine

It is a song about lack. A song about endings. A song about being bereft. She has always known this. Even when she first heard it in her yard and began decoding it. Its message rings even clearer now.

Her voice is getting louder, angrier, and her body begins to convulse, softly at first, and then with more vigour, as if she is channelling something, as if she is becoming possessed.

Grandfather, his serene eyes. Rural scenes. The old house in Ireland. Quaint, that abode. Family gatherings. All of them, gathered and laughing. Songs to beat the band. Childhood was brimful. Zen has been deprived of his. This is all so terribly unfair.

Why did she ever leave in the first place? She remembers the packing of her suitcase that first time. She was going far away, they all knew it and said it, but couldn't quite believe it. It was only to be for a short time. But the time stretched. Things happened. She got involved. Things involved her.

Coal? Really? Was there even coal then? Split wood? Surely she is embellishing. It can't have been all a country idyll. It seems more like footage from some old documentary. Is it her mind playing tricks on her? And yet she holds onto it. As if for dear life. She holds the microphone too, a stern clutching of it, afraid to let go.

The song continues.

Outside. The night. Owl-howl. They are not supposed to do that. They are not supposed to make such a din. A right racket. So much of it. It sounds like sin. Windows shake in their frames. Rattled. The night is growing wild. Wild and wild and wilder still. The Earth has not yet finished with its creatures and their wants.

Susie sings. Susie sings. Louder still. The song it grows and grows. It is like a gun, constantly reloading, it is like a heavy mateless bird calling across a barren land, it is like a crackling comet entering a planet's atmosphere, it is so many things, this song, it is…

Grandfather out for a walk, the countryside, the hedge-rows, hatted, humming, not caring. She looked up to him, literally, her little neck craned; metaphorically: he was inspiration incarnate.

She had come against all sorts of creatures back then. The great. The small. A badger once out foraging in the gloaming, its eyes flashed bright when limned by her searching flashlight, and it snarled and fled back to its secret den. Field mice, shrews – they were adorable – rats, hawks and kestrels above, frogs and newts in the sludgy ponds, even that elusive pine marten once, or was that just the hope for one, and the reality was a common fox, nose cocked to the whiff of carrion, a dead crow perhaps, roadkill by the kerb, something anyway, nature always threw up something.

Her mind whirls. Red orbs on a black screen now. Where have the lyrics gone? They were there just a minute ago, in front of her, there for the taking, there for the interpreting … now two red orbs in the black. Out of nowhere. They must be eyes, but what do they realise? What do they truly see? There was another song Granddad sang, an Irish song: *Sonny don't go away, I'm here all alone.* The song seems ancient to her now. The song is ancient. How come she remembers it? The song was sung at parties. Wakes. Here it is again, playing inside of her.

Axe splits the wood into two. Such newness in the inside-wood. Two hemispheres of the brain. She thinks. Left and right. Split.

Coal? Wood? Really?

Then a fire in the engine of an airplane! Flames in the sky. Those thoughts in there too, un-lulled by song. Black treacherous smoke. A plane spinning. Out of control. Spiralling. It can only go in one direction.

Dead bodies in the ocean, drifting there, afloat. Who will sing for them? The flesh departs. The tiny fish nibble.

It is silent down there. Not even whale song. Nothing as beautiful. Silence in the depths of her. Terrifying silence at her core.

Bodies on the beach sinking, as if in quicksand, as if swallowed. This is how deep she is in song. This is how deep she descends.

An animated ghost then, a cute cartoon, but fading from her, that too, in the convulsion of her body, in the throes of this demented dance, the song she reaches for, and she hardly moves a muscle.

Haruto's face is a picture of concern: is this woman OK?

Mixxy wonders what kind of drug she must be on to get her to a state like that … and she wants some of it, whatever it is, whatever Susie's on, just give it to her. Why has Susie never shared?

What Susie is on: owls and country houses, grandfathers with Stalin moustaches, fires in the sky and black smoke – it's only the spitting live wires of her bombastic brain, the electric currents there, the fuses and the fumes, and the storm that is bringing down the poles of sense and propriety.

And it's only karaoke at the end of the day.

Is it already the end of the day?

Ah, there is no comfort in the covens of the witch,
some very clever doctor went and sterilized the bitch …

How does she even remember the words? She is not reading them. Her eyes are clenched tight. So where do they come from now? Breakdown. The word is suddenly in her head. Split in two, like wood. Break. Down. So what? Things do. People and machines. People get sick, wickedly and they break down. Things fall apart. Everybody knows this. Machines too. Rust. Or malfunction. Or viruses and …

It's OK if she loses her mind. Says it to herself again: it's OK if she loses her mind. So much has been lost already. Sinking in the sand. Falling through the ocean floor. Where the lions and Christians roar. Witches pound on the front door.

Manic-mind-montage: it continues. A dizzying pace now.

Waves. Red eyes flashing. North Korean military leaders smiling their awful smiles. Their peaked caps. Their age-less uniforms. And their leader's bad haircut. His fat face that deserves her hard hand slapping across it, drawing blood with her nails. Why are they always so fat? Generation after generation. And their people starve? Or her gun at his temple. Gun? Where did that come from? She has only ever had recourse to a baseball bat in her house in Japan. Masa's from his youth. Masa's baseball bat. Not even a good old hurley stick. Hard ash. Not even that.

Waves. Witches. Lions. Nibbling fish.

Her eyes are rolling like marbles in a dish.

… and there are no diamonds in your mine.

Susie's face screaming, then just as quick Sonny's red eyes flashing. Tsunamis, storms, packed trains, empty parking spaces, office desks, cereal bowls flying from the breakfast counter as fast as any plane, ceramic shards on the floor, hoovering sounds, sucking up the dirt, Masa's kind face, his head round and balding but benign, his head shaking, why didn't you learn to shut down properly, cartoons on the TV, Zen is watching, Zen is laughing, he runs towards the school playground, mudslides on the TV, mudslides outside the window, earthquakes, airplanes falling like leaves from the sky. The silence of the sea, not even whale song.

The microphone makes a hefty thud as it falls to the floor.

"Yeah! Diamonds! Diamonds!" shouts the male of the couple, enervated by the proximity of the unfolding drama, drunk from all the alcohol and love-drunk too.

Mixxy mouths "taxi" and Haruto is quick to reach for his phone. Just as he does so Susie falls to the floor with just as heavy a thud as the microphone. She had held onto that microphone like she had held onto the noose-strap of the train with one hand like she had held her son's hand once and told him that they would always be together, for dear life, for dear life ...

Dear life

Dear life, why the fuck are you so cruel?

Mixxy grabs Susie's coat and locates her wallet. She takes money from it and leaves it on the counter. Haruto scoops it up and is glad that their night is coming to a close. He knows things might only get hairier – best quit while they had still some chance, still had a little dignity left. Had they?

Susie looks visibly shaken as if she should be at home lying down, empty room, empty bed, resting herself, not screaming from the maelstrom of her mind, not screaming that strange song to the void.

The girl in the dark side of the bar suddenly vomits with a massive heave – clearly the night has been a little too much for her also, she is already stinking and pitiful, regretful.

Mixxy manages to peel her friend off the floor and gets her out the door. The male customer still inside with his retching companion, hollers like a wild cur let loose from its freakshow shackles. The sound echoes in the lonely corridor, bouncing off the steel doors that hide other secret places. But it is hard to know whether his howl is in vehemence at his failing date, in disappointment at the unexpected turning of his night, or whether he is admitting to the world that they are all merely animals, petrified by the prospect of the life they are condemned to live, ravaged by the desires and impulses of which they struggle to properly comport. And then, like a beast of burden suddenly stabbed and felled, capsized in thick and constraining mud, he hollers again.

13

The taxi is a compact, driverless vehicle that pulls up in front of them as they wait on the pavement. A chill wind blows around their necks and Mixxy especially feels each bite of it through her thin stockings. She takes a plastic card from her bag and inserts it into the side of the car. A hatch opens and a screen emerges from it, lighting up with bright pinks and gaudy greens, like every device everywhere, inviting touch. Mixxy spends a few seconds keying in her code and the main back door of the vehicle opens with a soft hiss. Mixxy's body is still laced with the chemicals and alcohol she has ingested, making the required gentleness an impossibility – she bundles Susie in with all the delicacy of a rugby tackle.

Susie is crumpled up in the back of the car, foetus-like again, but she misses her womb-room. She is being carried somewhere else and does not know exactly where. She has no control now. She is a puppet with no guiding hand. She is beginning to realise that she has to be temporarily cared for and she must surrender to that.

Mixxy pats Susie's head like she is a large dog exhausted from age and exertion, a beloved pet, but so obviously on its last legs. For weeks she has refrained from pitying her friend, but her face now displays little else.

"We're going to my place. I will do everything I can to make you feel good again."

Mixxy says this in Japanese, but it is more to herself than to her charge.

Susie groans. She understands the words. She understands the sentiment too, and it does not at all seem like such a bad idea.

When they arrive at Mixxy's apartment building and alight from the sterile car, the cool night air seems to have a vivifying effect on Susie, and though she sways a little, she has enough within her to right herself. The ghost-taxi speeds off, winding down winding roads, taking care of itself, un-needing, aloof from human involvement but controlled by some being somewhere, remote.

Mixxy helps her friend. She sniggers as they make their way slowly up the steel steps to her apartment, her heels clanking loud in the quiet of the night. They negotiate corners, they bound off walls, but they manage to progress.

"You are Irish. Aren't you supposed to be able to hold your liquor?"

Susie snorts, baulking at the suggestion and the Americanism.

"You speak English too well," she says.

Mixxy glances over at the tall trees in the park across from her house. She thinks she sees a pair of gleaming eyes looking back at her. That couldn't be? Could it? Night is always wild, she thinks, it must always be this way and this way maintained. And those eyes finding her, they are surely guardian eyes, isn't that right? And not the eyes of an enemy?

"There she is again."

"Who?"

"I don't know if she is protecting me or if she's out to get me."

"Who is?"

"Never mind. Let's get inside."

A small, cramped, stuffy apartment with clothes strewn around on the furniture and on the floor. Laundry hangs from various plastic hangers, and every space is taken, either accidentally – things flung, discarded – or for drying, airing, or some other unspecified domestic function. Despite the rather gloomy ambience, Susie thinks the place smells rather fresh, floral, as if great effort went into hiding something. Was someone murdered here? Some nasty matter covered up? Did something decay? The aromatic candle a masking tool?

On shelves and side tables stand little porcelain or ceramic figurines, and on closer inspection Susie is alarmed (and not a little confused) to realise that they are all frogs. Frogs! Green amphibians. Some frozen in mid-jump. Some low and crouched on lily-pads. Frogs! A whole collection of them.

Mixxy notices the obvious bewilderment on her friend's face.

"Those are my mother's. She's a naturalist. Did research in the university here. She's in America now, more research, whatever that means. This used to be her apartment. She left it to me. I don't think she's coming back. She's with some guy. Frogs were her special area of interest. I don't have the heart to throw them out."

Mixxy speaks in short sentences, as if to elongate them might upset or confuse her brittle friend. Susie is not listening anyway, she is considering the ceramic – or is that porcelain? – collection: green things. She knows so little about materials. Like Sonny. Chrome? Plastic? Metal?

Mid-jump. Lily pads. Long tongues sticking out to catch flies. Some of these things look quite grotesque.

She nods as she listens to Mixxy's explanation, pretending to understand. She has never understood people who collect anything, was never a hoarder herself, often to her own detriment. Sometimes she would go looking for some instruction manual or appliance guarantee and it was gone. Is Sonny's manual still at home? Hadn't she put it somewhere safe? Surely that was Masa's department.

She looks around the room again, as if she were a detective looking for clues, trying to figure out just who this Mixxy actually is. It is to counter her nervous collapse: if she can think about others then she might not have to fret about her own precarious position. The most she has figured though is that a fat purple candle is responsible for the soothing lavender aroma, and it smells good.

"She's a little strange, my mother. What's the word … ex …?"

"Eccentric?" Susie offers. It's that word again. They said it about her grandfather. Maybe they said it about all her family. How would she know? Whispers were meant to go under the radar, you weren't supposed to hear. For all she knew maybe they said it about her too. Eccentric. Odd. *Why would you up and leave for Japan, for no apparent reason? And never come back? Japan? Why on Earth would you want to be there? Isn't that place always dangerous with earthquakes and …*

"Yes, that's it, I think. Eccentric."

"That's probably where you get it."

"I'm perfectly normal."

Susie looks at the bizarre get-up: the dazzling make-up, the green streak in the raven-black hair.

"Yeah, of course you are."

Mixxy holds up a greenish kettle.

Susie's nerves might be fragile but she is quite sure that the kettle is in the colour and shape of a frog.

"One hand."

"What?"

"My mother. She has only one hand. Her other was cut off. Accident. A great big … rock … or something … fell on her when she was out … she had been in a cave. Her bones were completely crushed. They had to cut it off in the hospital."

"Shit," says Susie. "I'm sorry to hear that."

Mixxy holds the frog kettle aloft: "Coffee? Or something stronger?"

"Just water for now. I think I need to cleanse myself."

A couple of weeks at a spa resort might do the trick. Healing waters, massages and … but it isn't life she is trying to pursue, it isn't life she is trying to lengthen or maintain, it is the very opposite idea that holds her.

"Sit down. Make yourself at home. That's what people say, isn't it?"

Susie tries to eke out a place where she can sit. She pushes some clothes aside. Thankfully they are already laundered, for when she lays a hand on them a pleasant soapy scent rises. She parks herself on the small, two-seater, fake-leather couch, and it is then she notices a white sheet draped over something in the corner of the room, like a kid at Halloween dressed up as a ghost, but eyeless here, and spookier because of it.

"Is that …?"

"Yes. That's my homebot."

Susie would much have preferred it to be a Halloween trick or treater, it was October after all, and she's had about enough of Masa's busybots.

"Why is it covered?"

"I don't really use it that often."

"How did you get it to shut down?"

"Does it not do that itself? Mine just kind of shuts down … automatically. Isn't that what they are supposed to do?"

Susie is confused. How come hers doesn't … obey?

"And I don't want it staring at me. Don't you think they get annoying after a while?"

"Yes, very."

Susie is delighted that someone else things so too. "Masa programed ours to be exceptionally annoying. You should hear the dickhead speak. Like a British butler from centuries ago."

Mixxy laughs. She likes that. She knows the English word, has heard it before. The robot: a *dickhead*!

Mixxy's mother was given a free homebot by the university when the ImaTech trials first started, compensation perhaps for the accident that resulted in her disability; she could have never afforded her own.

Mixxy has often struggled to make ends meet. Until recently she worked in a fashion store in the centre of the city, a trendy place for young people where the fashions often merge with outlandish costumes, the kind of things cosplayers don at comic conventions; Mixxy never batted an eyelid at the fruity fashions, the more flamboyant the better. But she lost the job. Late for work once too often.

Now she does dull part-time secretarial work in a dull office with dull people.

"If only I could turn it off properly. It doesn't seem to shut down fully…"

Susie pauses for a moment, hardly believing what she is about to say next.

"…as if it doesn't want to."

Mixxy is surprised.

"*Want to?* Doesn't *want* to?"

Susie nods, knowing how irrational this must sound.

"I don't use mine much, I guess," Mixxy says, trying to deflect the sense of crazy from the conversation, and easing her guest by handing her a glass of water. "I prefer to do my own cleaning."

Susie looks around the messy room.

"Yeah, you're doing a terrific job."

Mixxy either ignores the remark or doesn't pick up on Susie's sarcasm:

"I prefer to be active, you know. I only use the homebot when I'm feeling horny."

Susie nearly spurts her water out onto the tatami flooring, some of it goes right up her nose. Mixxy knows that word in English too! *Horny!*

"Are you serious?"

"You know, when I feel a bit … we all do sometimes."

Susie, sobering more with each passing minute, is looking at every inch of her friend's face. It is her turn to figure out whether Mixxy is in fact serious, or just setting up a punchline.

"Don't tell me you don't know about it," says Mixxy, her voice peaking with petulance. "Everybody knows. A lot of people use them for … that kind of thing."

"Seriously?"

"Yeah!"

"What … how?"

"You want me to demonstrate?"

"Good God, no! Just … tell me."

"Well, you can fit parts to it … and set it to …"

Susie waits for the final word to fall, wondering if it is the one she anticipates.

"… vibrate."

Yep, that was the one. Susie no longer feels quite as fractured as she did in the bar, she seems quite normal and composed now compared to what her Japanese friend is offering.

"Really? People do that?"

"You seriously didn't know?"

"Of course not. Who talks about such things?"

"What do you think girls do at night? Watch dramas? Is that what you think we do?"

There had been numerous sex dolls on the market for decades, real-ish looking robotic dolls – human features, soft synthetic skin – that were agile enough to cater for the most daring … whims. Susie cannot believe that one would be so desperate as to use a homebot instead. They were anything but sexy: Sonny, for fuck's sake!

Her face is flushed and hot and she takes a big slug of the ice water to cool herself down. She takes one of the diminishing cubes on her tongue and crunches it hard between her teeth. She should be sleeping in her Masa-less bed, hidden away from everything; just her, her weighty grief, and the spirits of her past.

"The things you can do with your homebot are unlimited, my dear. Of course most of them won't be listed in the manual. But there are ways around it. There are always alternatives. And if you ever come across The Dark Manual."

The room seems to hum with the words offered to the night, as if some dark illicit ceremony has just begun.

"The Dark Manual?"

"I'm not sure how true this is or not. But…"

Mixxy pauses. How to expound on this? She's often unsure of her English, even though she is frequently praised for her command. But it's not just a problem of language ability here. It's the nature of the thing itself. A thing spoken about in hushed tones. It might be a load of old bullshit.

"There is supposed to be a *different* manual. Not the pink one you probably have at home. Not the standard one. There is supposed to be an alternative one. With a list of… alternative operations. "

Susie is all ears. It might be the answer to her problems. She could finally get the bloody thing to shut down for good. The other option she has considered is driving it to some lonely forest on the outskirts of the city, opening the car door and letting it run off, free. Off into the woods like an unwanted pet. She has laughed aloud at this idea of late, and it has given some succour. But the joke would probably be on Susie; knowing her luck the bloody thing would follow her back, or be waiting on her doorstep before she got home, speaking in its nasally voice, asking its annoying questions about herbal tea and temperatures.

Or the river. She has thought of that too. She could chuck it in the river. Let it sink down, get entangled in the weeds, get stuck in the riverbed and be silenced forever.

"I've never seen one, but if you get one, there are codes to… change the settings…"

"To what? Change the settings to what? For what?"

"To do whatever you want it to do for you! Have you noticed how strong the grip is on those things? Their hands."

"Yeah, but ..."

"You could program it to do what you like"

"What ... *you like?*"

"Outside of the law."

"*Outside* of the law?"

"Don't be so naïve, Susie. Don't you know that these things can kill?"

Susie takes a moment to keep her thoughts steady. To keep them from fragmenting again, from losing her grasp of things. With all that has gone on these past few months she is unsure just how much is real and how much she has imagined. The word "breakdown" keeps boomeranging back to the forefront of her thoughts. Is that it? Is that what started back in Haruto's bar? The beginning of a breakdown? Or had it been going on for some time? What if she has already broken down – past tense – and is now veering off into other unchartered territory. How can she be sure of anything? Even this conversation in this dingy flat ... frogs and sex robots? How much, just how much can she rely on?

"I've seen the news reports," Susie says, "but, surely they were accidents, malfunctions or something."

She is thinking about the report on the homebot that had tripped and fallen down stairs, banging into and crippling an old lady; Masa's company doling out millions in compensation; she remembers his frowns that evening, sitting up late at his desk, wondering how it could have happened. And there were other stories that hadn't made the news, stories that had been bandied about in her own workplace as reporters dug for some dirt to write about: fires had started in homes – causes put down to faulty electrical wiring and unquenched cigarettes – but there were suspicions, weren't there? And what about the pets that had been found dead, the results of mysterious electrical shocks. There were suspicions there too, weren't there?

"You think …"

Mixxy is slowly nodding her head, welcoming her buddy on board. She has taken on the role of the worldly-wise, and Susie relegated to an innocent, scrabbling for sense in all this confusion.

"The story goes that The Dark Manual was created by a … how do you say someone who was an employee and was fired and wanted revenge?"

"Disgruntled?"

Mixxy tries out the word: "*Dis … gruntled?* I've never heard that one before. Anyway, he got fired from some job or something and in revenge wrote new codes for those who wanted their homebots to do … different things. Things that society would not allow you to do. And the manual grew in … *reputation* … is that the right word? Like something on the Black Market, or from the Dark Web, suddenly all the criminals wanted a piece of it."

Susie had come to this apartment drunk and swaying with a head full of fuzz. Now she was wide awake, sober, and verging on the excited. Revenge? Homebots carrying out their wicked masters' retaliation? It was all a bit penny-dreadful, but engaging nonetheless.

"Do you think that one of them could really kill? A homebot, actually kill?"

"Yeah. Why not? Do you want to kill someone?" Mixxy laughs.

Susie doesn't want to kill anyone. Besides herself. And she doesn't join in Mixxy's laugh either. She is failing to find the funny side in any of this. It's terribly serious. She could do with some levity, she could do with a laugh to be honest, just conjuring up the image of a frowning Masa on one of his more stressful nights is no joke at all.

Mixxy goes to a sideboard and takes out a bottle of *sake*. Susie is no longer interested in alcohol, its taste or its consequence, but she allows her glass to be filled with the clear rice wine.

Mixxy's shock-tactics have yet to wane. Her night is far from over. She reaches under her armchair and pulls out a long, thin, rectangular box. From this she extracts a plastic strap-on penis, and with a clean cloth begins to carefully wipe it down.

Susie's mouth hangs open: this was her friend all over, always the element of surprise.

"Seriously, I can show you if you like. Just what the homebot can do," says Mixxy. "I'm not a bit embarrassed."

"Clearly."

"In fact, I think I might actually enjoy that. You watching me. All you have to do is sit back and relax, while I attach this…" Susie is drinking again, and giggling again: dead pets, fires, dead husbands are all being nullified by the ludicrous spectacle playing out before her.

"I'm never quite sure when you are joking or serious."

"Do I look like I'm joking?" Mixxy grins.

All this talk of manuals and taboos and the attachments of dildos has made Susie giddy. Was any of this even happening? Seriously, was it? At what stage had life gone completely topsy-turvy for her? Was it the first time she had heard about the plane crash, was that when it all kicked off? Her mind feels like the top of a plastic bottle trying to twist on its groove, but is forever finding the wrong one and getting stuck: no matter how much you twist, you only succeed in exacerbating the problem, damaging the very structure of the thing. Her mind races again. *I'm sorry, I have some bad news for you.* This was all in Japanese. But she understood the situation well. The police at her door. Their sullen faces. The hanging heads and drooping shoulders. *I'm sorry, I have some bad news for you.* But she had already seen and heard reports on the news. Knew about the airplane. It had to be the reason they were there. How could it not? The eyes of the two police officers, trying not to meet hers directly, they had no experience with foreigners – how could they show sympathy? *I'm sorry, I have some bad news for you.* Was that what they had said? Surely it should have all been more solemn and more polite that that. Has she misremembered it all? One of the officers was female and beautiful. That's right. She remembers now. She looked like she was in the wrong job. Too pretty to have the face of authority. She could have been modelling clothes in a catalogue. Hawking glossy lipstick. But she was there with her sterner, dourer partner. And what did they really have to deliver? Nothing. Nothing at all of substance. For no bodies were found. What were they even doing there if they had nothing to show for themselves? They looked at each other wondering if they had to translate into English for her. Would they have been capable? They brought no translation device with them, no tablet; they didn't even reach for a phone. They didn't have to. Anyone could have worked out what was going on. No language was even necessary. *And would she like someone to be with her?* No. *And did she need counselling, a person to stay with her?* No. Was that the gist of the conversation? Was that what had went down? And then her mother-in-law, frantic, turning up just then, to make matters worse. Jittery with rage and confusion and unable to contain herself, flinging a slew of rapid-fire questions at the police officers and they taking them on board as best they could. But no answer of course. Because in truth, they knew about as much as the next person. They had simply gotten the names from some airline company – a manifest: isn't that what it is called? That list of passengers. Hadn't they said that Masa and Zen were on the list of passengers and were on the plane, or had said they *weren't* on the plane? What? Why does that thought strike her now? A doubt, sprung out of nowhere. Was it her bad Japanese that had left her down that moment as they stood before her, gormless and goofy? They had spoken somberly, sure, but a little too quickly, out of nervousness perhaps; maybe she hadn't picked up on the details. Of course she couldn't have picked up on the details. She was out of her mind with gargantuan grief. How could anyone think straight given the circumstances? Those two police officers. The dull one. The beauty. What did they know? And what had they said? Did they really know anything that was different from anybody else?

Then Noriko. Her mother-in-law. Sweet and soft until rattled or riled then suddenly sour and venomous. There she was. On the scene then. Out of nowhere. Feisty and fight-ready. Only making matters worse.

But how could matters have been made any worse? There was no *worse*. Susie's life at that moment was at its nadir. It could not possibly have been any worse.

Something inside. But something inside … *still*. A refusal to accept. That's what it is. A refusal to believe she would be shortchanged like that. That was not the way Susie's life was going to turn out. That was just too damned unfair. Her grandfather had walked those country lanes, mumbling like a psychic flipping tarot cards, telling her that her future would of course be everything that she hoped it would be, instructing her on how to live to the fullest, with song and surety: that wasn't all a lie, a waste of time, was it? Her grandfather convinced her that she had warrior blood. Had a brave, irresolute spirit. That couldn't all have been lip service. He never told her she was a *princess*. He never said *darling* or *sweetheart*. He used strong words. *Fighter. Battler.* He saw it as his job to instill power. A power that she was never ever supposed to forego or forget. Things would always turn around. Things would always get better. Of course they would. It was her right.

But how?

And when?

She did not know.

She *does* not know.

This is not the end of it though. Even when she sits at home on broody evenings, sullen and heartsore, sick to death of her silver robot, her superfluous housemate, no, this is not the end of it. It can't be. She will wait some more for that miracle to come. For bodies to walk right out of the sea and find her in her wretchedness and cure her ills.

Mixxy is on a different plain. Mixxy is all drunk and drugged and sexed-up and on a different wavelength entirely.

Mixxy is not reading the air right at all, as if her barometers have gone all barmy.

It doesn't seem to bother her one bit; she continues in her own frisky way.

"You know I've been attracted to you for a long time. Ever since I first saw you with Masa."

She smiles, lasciviously. Mixxily.

"I was attracted to *him*, too," she adds, letting her foolish revelations sink in. "So why don't you just let me ... you could do with some cheering up."

There it is again. Everyone trying to fix Susie. Cheer her up. Help her get over things. She doesn't want to get over things. She has no intention of ever getting over things. Mourning is a part of her life now, and she wants it to stay that way. She will mourn and mourn and then some. While she waits for her miracle. She'll get over nothing, while she waits for her miracle. If Masa and Zen do not come back, if they do not walk right out of the salty sea and straight into her arms then ... then she'd just rather die. Sonny's strong grip might just strangle her in her sleep, or poison her with that noxious gas. Any of those measures might work, as long as the result was the same.

But until then ... until then ... she'll still wait.

"I appreciate your good intentions, Mixxy, but really, I'm fine. If I was happy now ... it would seem somehow unfair."

Mixxy gets up to fill her own glass. More *sake* couldn't hurt, especially when it was of this high quality. Jokingly she stirs the drink with the dildo and sucks the drink right off it.

Susie, despite the dull thrum of mental anguish that clings to the front of her head like a bad migraine, finds herself smiling again. Maybe this wild Japanese girl *did* cheer her up a little after all. Her outrageous humour, her brashness, her unashamed outlandishness, such a contrast to the people she sees every day at work, or that sit across from her on the tedious trains, eyes trained on screens and expressionless faces, like grim masks, mouths slackly open, releasing fetid breath in the exhausted post-work evenings. Manic Mixxy seems to do the trick, is better than all of those people. The world needs people like her. Every year, the harbingers of doom, banging on tin cans, proclaiming end times or litanies of worldly woes:

Things have never been this bad!

Things have gone down the shithole fast!

There is truly no way back!

And maybe they are right. But with people like Mixxy around, at least the gloom lifts for a while, for however briefly a stay of execution.

"What were you looking at earlier? Outside. In that park."

Mixxy considers. Another tough concept to explain, in any language.

"There's this owl. I see it often. Or just glimpse it. Its eyes at night. My mother had pointed it out to me, or *them*, when she was still living here. I'm surprised how close they are, I mean, living here, and not far out in the woods where they should be. A city owl, I guess, if there is such a thing. Anyway, my mother told me to be careful … that they can attack."

"Attack?"

"Yes, even humans. They have been known to fly right down and cause serious damage. They always go for the right side of the head, at the back. My mother told me this. No one knows why this is. My mother could not explain it. And they can do major harm. What do you call them … their feet?"

"Talons."

"Those are sharp and strong. They could open the side of your skull if they got stuck in you."

"Jesus, really? They look so harmless. Why would they do that?"

"I don't know. But I heard someone recently say that signals from our devices drive them wild. Wild*er*. Who knows what frequencies we send out with all our digital shit?"

Susie lets the words revolve around her head. *All our digital shit. Our devices. Signals.* She may have a point. These are the times: more and more, devices, machines, automatons, computers, more and more of this stuff; it had been this way for centuries, from steam engines to artificial intelligence, as fast as skimming a stone across a pond, plip, plip, plop, and here we are: Sonny.

"Be careful. Many creatures have turned vicious. Maybe they fear our devices. Maybe they feel threatened. Maybe that's why Mr. Owl is out here, keeping an eye on us. All of us. Maybe everything is turning vicious, everything at stake. Every *thing*… not knowing the reason for its presence in the world, but fighting for it nonetheless."

"And frogs?" says Susie with a snigger.

"Fuck no, they're just ugly, slimy things. Can't see them as being much of a threat. But the owls, my dear, watch out for the owls."

Susie thinks she needs to get going, but first:

"I think I need your loo."

"Loo?"

"Toilet."

"Oh, just through there."

Susie finds even more frog-stuff in the toilet: tiny framed pictures on the walls, miniature art in greens, shades of yellows, dull browns. Had Mixxy's mother painted these herself with her one good hand? Susie is no art expert, but she can tell that these aren't up to much.

A noise then. A hum from the living room.

When Susie emerges she discovers that Mixxy has attached the strap-on penis to her homebot. The long appendage is vibrating up and down and the homebot is starting to gyrate, thrusting its hips back and forth. Susie nearly chokes with laughter. She has never seen anything so ridiculous in all her life. She is a long way from the country lanes she walked with her grandfather. Imagine if he could see this spectacle before him now, he wouldn't believe it, would castigate its crudity, its world-gone-wrong impudence; he would shun, preferring instead his thousand-yard stare and the songs reeling around in his head; this is all a bit too much, and if Masa were here she'd scold him for allowing technology to be brought down to such a level. Debased.

What?

Who?

Who was being debased?

Man or machine?

"Was it from a *Dark Manual* that you found how to make it do that?"

"No. I've never seen The Dark Manual. Just figured out this much by myself. It took quite a few hours. Trial and error, you know. Are you impressed?"

"Trial and error. Looks to me like it's mostly error. And quite a waste of time. This is just wrong, Mixxy. Just plain wrong."

The homebot keeps thrusting.

"It can go all night long," says Mixxy.

"So fucking wrong," says Susie.

Mixxy is bursting with alacrity again. Once more the earlier pinch of powder must have recycled itself inside her, for with renewed energy she swiftly takes off the remainder of her skimpy clothes and discards them with a theatrical flourish. She stands brazenly there, right in the middle of the now even untidier room ... with the vibrating homebot.

"Are you sure you don't want to stay? It could be fun. Me and you. And the homebot too."

"I thank you for your hospitality," says Susie, placing her glass on the table. "But I'm afraid my time is up. I'll see you some other night."

Susie takes one last look at the pathetic home robot and the disappointed temptress, and heads out of the apartment and into the much calmer night outside.

The air is brisk and she gulps it into her lungs. It is calmer here, nothing vibrates, everything is still and steady, all the humming things, things of wire and silicon, things of engine and motor, fuel or circuit, they have all stopped, or are at least pleasingly out of earshot, encased in their houses, connected with their masters. There is not much going on out here at all. Even the cars have stopped their hums and hisses on the roads, it's that late, or early, and Susie must surely get going.

She looks over to the little park and scans the trees. Nothing. Nothing there at all. She can find no moving thing in the darkness. Not a sound either. No holler. No howl. No hoot. She pulls her jacket tight around her and heads for the building that houses her. She hasn't the strength or sentiment to call it *home* any longer.

She lingers in the bedroom. It is another night. Or morning. Drunk again. Or has she sobered up? This place, this most intimate of places seems sometimes foreign to her, as if she steps into a different realm altogether. And sometimes too of course it is achingly familiar: the dizzying effect things have, their once-*significance*, once signifiers: Masa's clothes in the wardrobe for example: how clean and orderly they look, as if they are to be plucked out and used at any moment, adorned, on his stocky body... only there is no body. At some stage she will have to throw them out. At some stage she will have to remove them from their hangers and place them in plastic bags and dump them. Or cart them off to some second-hand shop and... no... she couldn't bear the thought of anyone else wearing them. What if she were to see another man in them, and if that other man had a certain gait, just like him, or a similar frame, it would be all too much, it would crush her even more. She would not be able to cope. Those things belonged to him and to him alone. He was *he* and he alone. Masa. He was hers and hers alone. She feels her chest tighten, like a boa constrictor wrapping around her and choking her in its hold. She is yet again at the precipice of tears.

The bedroom: a lonely room.

The dresser: some of her things are on it, some of his things too. Hairbrushes with dead hair. A clipper that clipped toenails, and how they sometimes took off into the air and could have landed anywhere. She used to tell him to do it over the dustbin, catch them, to not be so bloody disgusting.

Dust in the room. The place getting musty, the windows never opened. She can even smell the staleness of the place. She should vacuum it. Or get Sonny to do it. She never orders him to clean this room.

Dead cells. Flakes of life settled into the corners, entrenched in the shag. And get him to open the windows too. Use the little shit. Use it for all it is worth. Isn't that what it is there for? A domestic robot. Wasn't that the intention in the first place? How much does she now know about it? What has she learned, even from this night? Is Mixxy just bonkers mad in her stories? Fires in homes, faulty electrical wiring, unquenched cigarettes, disgruntled workers, suspicions, pets found dead, mysterious electrical shocks, suspicions, suspicions, suspicions. Why does she feel there are secrets attached to it? Doesn't she sense that when she is alone with it? Things bubbling beneath... more *capabilities*. What had Masa really been designing? Surely, he must've known?

Whatever you want it to do for you. Have you noticed how strong the grip is on those things? Their hands.

Susie's reflection in the full-length mirror. Her long, morose face. Long with longing. She can still see herself. This proves she is not a ghost, and despite the recent penchant for late nights and abhorrence of sun, she is no vampire. That must account for something. She is horribly human and horribly alone. In this room she is horribly alone.

The last sight: Mixxy and her sexed-up homebot, although funny at the time, it has just served to make her lonelier, as if Mixxy has the benefit of creative ideas, has ways to escape herself. Susie is stuck with herself. Inside herself. There is no escape from that. No escape from her loneliness.

She had a boy. She once had a boy. That was her creation. His name was Zen.

She will wait...

The owls will bring him back. Owls?

Yes, she is still a little drunk, the aftermath of beer, gin, *sake*, did she have more than that? She needs sleep. She needs blankness. She needs no thought.

She removes her clothes. How unabashed Mixxy was. Revealing all. So nonchalantly. No bother. Susie could not have taken part. Not just the sex act. But the fact that she was Masa's and he was hers. He was *he* and he alone. He was hers and hers alone. This play of pronouns makes her sure. Who was who. And who *belonged* to whom.

She could not do anything with anyone else. Betrayal. She had loved him. She *loves* him. Masa.

In the long mirror, naked … she is not that sexy at all. She is only human, and alone.

And the owls will …

And Zen will …

She gets into bed wearing the same T-shirt as before. *Luck of the Irish.* The irony.

Boxer shorts. His.

She does not sleep but starts to fantasize as she lays there motionless. Her arms are draped around his neck and she is kissing him. She is a little shorter than he is and she has to reach up on her tiptoes to get to him. He jokingly keeps pulling back, forcing her to reach more and more, making her stretch, but she will not give up.

"I thought you were in the mood," she says.

"Who says I am not in the mood?"

She is reaching, stretching to him. She will not give up.

He receives her kisses then; he is grateful for them.

"You will have to get rid of that Irish T-shirt, it has seen better days. Throw it away."

Better days.

He has been wearing this for years. It was a present from her to him, before they were married, when they were dating and could not stop giving each other little gifts, constant tokens, trinkets, sentimental tchotchkes. She had wanted him to wear something Irish, something green, or with a shamrock or a harp, something that said he would take her side too if she needed him.

"You can't just abandon some things you know. Some things are precious."

"It's horrible."

"It isn't."

"Are Irish people really that lucky?"

"I got you, didn't I?"

He says this in a faintly American accent, the one he acquired while studying in New York for several years. She didn't like it at first, but it grew on her.

"Well done. Nice line."

She pushes him back and they collapse on the bed in a fit of giggles. She climbs on top of him and they roll around: half-mirth, half-lust, but it was easy to see which half would be victorious; the rest of the night would easily take care of itself.

The picture on her bedside stand. She gazes at it. She is out of her daydream now and ready for what night dreams might descend. There are tears in her eyes of course, and they are beginning to glue her lids shut.

And yet … her gut.

Something telling her.

It is not yet over. It is not yet over.

Something still.

It can't be just this. More. There has to be more than just this. There simply …

Waiting for a miracle.

14

A green light passes over her body and a mechanical, familiar female voice.

"Weight 54 kilograms. You have lost 5 grams since yesterday, two kilograms since last month. Immune system under threat therefore an increase in the uptake of essential vitamins and amino acids recommended. Take extra zinc supplements to boost immune system and ward off the risk of illness. Breakfast recommendation is a small serving of muesli in low-fat or soy milk, fresh fruit of at least three varieties, and a glass of freshly..."

This is all before she has even attached the side plates to her temples, before she has allowed her head to snugly fit its metal crown, before she has placed the shackles on her wrists to read her pulse.

How does this keep happening? She has not fully connected herself to this machine for ages, and yet there it is every day, working for her, harassing with these bald and boring truths. The morning spiel. Was this Masa's joke? Had he pre-set the machine to operate in such a way? Or has Sonny something to do with this?

"Command system off."

She shouldn't bother with the bloody thing anymore. Just ignore it. It never has any good news anyway. Why she persists everyday she does not know.

The machine stops and its operating lights quickly fade as Susie steps away from it, reaching for a towel.

For Masa, the more technology one had in the house the more convenient life would be. That was his take on things, and to Susie the logic sounded utterly Japanese. Yet she allowed it all to happen. Technology overload. A house stuffed with mechanical toys. Some useful, true, but some were completely the opposite, and annoyingly so. Did you really need a device to steam and then open your letters and bills? Could you not just tear open the damn envelope yourself? There were devices everywhere. You only had to say a word, a simple command, or clap two hands together and something in the house would be doing something for you. Something would be responding and cleaning or repairing or setting or settling or warming-up. It reached its pinnacle of course with the unimpeachable Sonny. Masa's pride and joy. ImaTech's dream toy. The future. The future was always now of course and all the other stuff you've ever heard about the future and robots, opportunities and advancement, the here and now, the blah, the blah and the endless blah. The Japanese nation had been promising this stuff to the world for years, and finally it seemed like they were delivering on their promises. One for every home. That was the dream. Who wouldn't want that? Who wouldn't want their life made even more convenient? Even easier than it already was. And the experiments started right here, in their fine city. Masa's hometown. Trials. Errors. And then some more trials. An amendment here. A tightening of a tiny screw there. Tweakings. Trials. Then a few more errors.

Hadn't she even used that phrase just last night? Hadn't someone said something along those lines? Mixxy? *Trials and errors.* Or was it Haruto? It could only have been one of them. There was no one else. She hardly knew anyone else. Her life had been scaled down to that. To them. Was there someone else she met last night? Some sticky couple, yes, in the bar. They were all over each other, groping without shame. Why had she collapsed in the bar? It is coming back to her now. The memory from the night before, ghosting through her now. Why had she collapsed? Right there in the bar. In the middle of a song. What was the song that she had been singing? *Diamonds in the mine.* That was it. Her grandfather played it for her. Slipped it into the CD player in the car when he took her for a drive into the town one day. He used to pick out tunes on a battered Spanish guitar too when the inclination took. The lions and Christians fighting, what was that song even about? Loss. Loss. It could be her theme song. It was a beat-up old thing, that Spanish guitar. But it had remained, and it had six strings, and somehow it stayed in tune, and Granddad too had remained, for as long as he could, and he had music, and he had been somehow in tune, with her thoughts and hopes and childhood dreams. She remembers the feel of those nylon strings. They seemed so simple, so straightforward, smooth and thin and loaded with possibility. But she never learned to pluck them. Never learned to strum in time. So many things she skipped over, skipped past. Never learned properly. It was the accusation of her life. Why didn't she take the time to see things through?

So, last night? What had actually happened? She fell, didn't she? She remembers that. But what was the cause of that? Malnutrition – she almost thought:

malfunction – drunkenness? Most probably the latter. The song she was trying to extract from herself? From the very pit of herself. And that word too, that dangerous word, "breakdown". It had flashed across her mind, like a warning. It had glowed in neon, old-fashioned but still everpresent neon, something the Japanese had never tired of. *Breakdown!* Flash green. *Breakdown!* Flash red.

Vigorously, she dries herself with the towel she has not bothered to change in weeks – it is beginning to smell. She takes deep breaths and as she does so she finds that she is hungry again. It is the same every morning, hunger at the same time, her stomach complaining of absence. Breakfast is the only meal these days that ever seems in any way appetizing.

Sugar.

Susie ignores the advice of HIM – it could be lying to her anyway, whoever was fiddling with it – and she sits at the morning counter spooning Zen's favourite cereal into herself again. She eats without any great hurry, without any great joy, the only pleasure being the reminder that her son liked this, her son had this cereal every morning, when mornings were good and you could intone the greeting without ever lying: he would smile as the milk dripped down his little chin. *Good morning.* Of course it was. This is what Zen used to eat, and they briefly bypass the normal constraints of space and time to be together. Mother. Son. And sugar.

We know you have no reason for going on. No reason to be here. No reason to be anywhere, Miss Deadheart. Why not admit too that you are just a robot? Your actions: so mechanical.

She spoons in another into herself. And then another. Till it empties. But she does not throw the bowl across the kitchen. Nothing has angered her yet. But give her time.

The news channel is on the screen on the wall. It is just a series of blurry pictures, she never really focuses, her eyes gloss over. It may as well be those black inkblot images that psychiatrists have forever been using. Rorschach tests? Isn't that what they are called? Age-old.

What does this image remind you of?

My dead husband.

And this one, Miss Deadheart: what does this one say to you?

It says fuck off and die.

If no one is walking out of the sea then who cares what is on the screens. If Masa and Zen are not walking out of the sea and running down the road at breakneck speed and into her house and into her arms then she has no interest in it. In nothing.

"Sonny!"

From the bowels of the house, sensing desperation in its controller's voice, Sonny responds:

"Yes, Miss Susie. I am on my way."

It arrives within seconds and approaches the morning counter. She tells it to bring the car round. She has decided that she will drive to work today. She will drive all the way to work, into the city. Fuck the train and fuck the zombies that ride in it. She will join the streams of ghost cars instead, the driverless vehicles and their dozing passengers; she will join lanes with them, for a change. She will find a parking spot. Or if she is too late to do that she will just leave it at the side of the road and just abandon it for the day. Who cares if it gets taken away? Who cares if they demolish it into tiny pieces, crunching it in one of those big crushing machines – what are they called? Those massive mechanical monsters in the junkyards? Did they have a name? She likes *Car Crusher*. Or *Vehicle Annihilator*. Or *Massive Monster Mangler*. Yes, that one. She could fling herself into one of those things just as quick. Imagine how fast that would sort out all her problems! The great compacting. The jaws of the thing. Or the walls of them, coming together. How long would she have to wait? A few seconds. The skeleton and skull and the brains squished and blood spurting up like a great geyser, decorating all the junk around her. A fountain of red for whoever would be lucky enough to be walking by and witness it. Couldn't be quicker, could it?

She has no love for her car: just leave it anywhere. If they steal it they will steal it. She has no connection to it. She has no connection to any damn machine. They could strip her whole house of every mechanical thing, every bleeping bullshitty thing – as long as they left her with a decent bottle of hooch (Mixxy's Americanisms rubbing off), a corkscrew and her photos, then she'd be all right. Simple as that. That simple. Simple like her. It is something she insists on: printing out photos and making proper albums, the old-fashioned way. The only way to trawl back through those memories was to turn pages, not scroll or swipe; photos looked different laid out there on the page, under their transparent guards; her family used to insist on this too, her father a true believer in the printout, the printout of everything, receipts, information notices, plane tickets, hanging onto paper like he did to other bygone concepts, prayer, say, or goodwill between men, comical now in their naivety, and her mother careful to never get fingerprints on those precious pictures, protecting them like they were the sacred scripts of abbeys or the glory of museums. Yes, they are all so antiquated, these notions that occur to her now, but it is how she wants things, too. There is nothing wrong with wanting *some* things to be like that. Progress not always is. They cannot all be swept away. Keep some semblance of…

She takes a drink of her Sonny-brewed coffee and pours the remainder down the drain. Let the day begin. Let it start. Let's get on with it.

Sonny moves to a side-wall panel and with an outstretched palm touches the screen. The screen, naturally – *naturally?* – obeys.

The garage door at the side of the house opens and a soft engine begins its customary delicate purr. Smoothly it pulls up outside the front of the house in exactly the same position it always does. Not a centimetre too far one way or the other. Perfectly positioned for the human to fall into. Convenience. Masa would be dead chuffed.

"What interior temperature would you like me to set, Miss Susie?"

"I don't care."

"Do you need me to inform you of today's outside temperature?"

Susie ignores.

"Today's weather report, Miss Susie?"

"No. It doesn't matter. It doesn't fucking matter."

Was this yesterday, or the day before yesterday?

Is this today? Is this another day of this shit?

Does she really have a robot in her house that speaks to her?

She has a fucking headache already; that much she knows.

The little car hums gently, waiting.

She is as good as her word. She leaves the car parked outside the main building in an illegal zone and spares not a single moment for the prospect of an irate traffic warden or a beeping horn of complaint. Fuck 'em all. She'll do as she pleases.

She presses her usual thumb to the usual security post and when the gates swing open she saunters through to the usual elevator. The two hefty security guards smile at her as they have always done. The usual. Yes, this is today. It is just another one of them. The usual. There have been many more before this and there can be many more after this too, if she wants to keep it that way. If she persists with this living thing. But therein lies her dilemma. As she contemplates this, a memory: Grandfather reading a book, an actual paperback. He was sitting silently, hardly a breath out of him, and she wondered about the deep level of concentration required for such an endeavour: the stillness, the absorption, the otherworldly nature of the task. There wasn't even music playing, just the huge silence of it all. She asked him what he was reading, and then she asked him again, and finally when he realised someone was talking to him, he looked up and smiled at her, glad as ever of her arrival and her inquisitiveness. He told her it was a book about a man doing the same thing every day. *And then one day a pigeon comes to his doorstep, and the poor fellow nearly loses his mind.*

"That's it?" Susie had said, surprised at how a whole book could be broken down to such a simple explanation, such a tidy equation.

"That's it," he said, holding up the slim novel to show her.

She ended up reading that book when he was finished with it – he had left it lying around for exactly that reason – and she thinks she understood it. It was one of the only books she ever completed, and she always meant to go back and ask him for more. More recommended books, more music to download, more inspiration. But she never did. Time just ran away from her. Maybe that was why she had left the countryside, and then the country altogether. Maybe there was no point if he was not there anymore. She needed to find inspiration elsewhere. She is still on the lookout.

The Pigeon was the name of the book. That simple. And perfectly profound of course. She thinks of it now, mired as she is in the quotidian. Her everyday tedium. If a pigeon arrived on her doorstep one of these fine days, just how would she react? Would she lose it altogether? Perhaps. Perhaps not. But she already has owls to contend with. One species of bird is quite enough, is it not?

Before she can get comfortable at her own computer screen Osanai appears, and looks down at her, his eyes watery and full of sympathy again. She cuts him off before he has time to offer any more holidays or prolonged periods of convalescence:

"I'm working on something new. I'm just about to get started on it."

"Started on what?" Osanai says, patently pleased that she is preparing to write anything at all.

"Owls."

His surprised delight quickly gives way to obfuscation.

"Owls?"

"I've become quite interested in them. They're all around us you know. Though of course we never really see them."

Osanai takes a moment to let this sink in.

"Are you talking about the birds, like … the night birds?"

"Yes."

"I'm not sure we are in need of any nature articles."

Susie folds her arms and looks at the blank screen in front of her while Osanai goes to the coffee machine to fix them both a cup. She supposes he is right; she's not exactly sure what to write anyway. What *about* them, exactly? What *about* those owls? What's her angle? What are those birds doing that they haven't done before? Flying? Hunting? Hooting? Killing? She has no angle. But what about Mixxy's line: *Our devices, drive them wild. Who knows what frequencies we send out with all our digital shit?* And: *They could open the side of your skull if they got stuck in you.* Susie's only real idea is to spend the day researching, finding out about how owls live, how they survive, how they feed, and breed, and slaughter. A nuclear warhead could be aimed right at her city at this moment, but she is instead contemplating owls, feathered night flyers, and it seems all right with her, seems to be the sort of thing that she *should* be thinking about. And not frogs. Definitely not fucking frogs. That would be wrong. As preposterous as war. Frogs are as preposterous as war. Argue that point. *Frogs are as preposterous as war.* She can't. Her head is full of pointless lines like this. Maybe there is no article in her head at all and she just wants to do the research. To get absorbed into a project, and if that project has no purpose, no deadline, no reason for being, then that would be even more fun, no pressure attached. No pressure. What a nice idea that is! She would be quite content just watching nature documentaries or pulling out an old dusty book from the always-vacant library, where dusty books still properly exist: there were sure to be books about owls there. Maybe even a copy of The Pigeon. Wouldn't that be a nice find?

Frogs are as preposterous as war. What does that even mean? Maybe there is no article, there is no angle…

Osanai breaks her spell by placing her coffee in front of her.

"Look, there is a basketball game on at the arena later this afternoon. Why don't you go there and take a look. There are two new Americans playing for the team. They got here just last week. Maybe you could get an interview or something with them. See how they are settling in."

This does not seem in the least bit interesting to her. Basketball players settling in to their new lifestyle: who gives a shit? Susie knows as much about basketball as she does about feathered night predators – but she knows for sure which she'd rather be investigating.

"Sure" she says, with a lying smile, writing BASKETBALL on her memo pad in big brash capitals. She adds an exclamation mark as if to hint that she will take on this task with gusto.

!

Just another lie to add to a world of them.

Osanai nods, unsure as to whether anything will come of the assignment; he could have given the story to someone who knew something about sport, or to any of the younger writers who had at least an air of competence about them, an air of ambition, at least a shred of routine. But he has blurted it out: basketball. And she has added an exclamation mark. And it will keep the poor woman busy, what more can anyone do for her?

15

A ball hits the backboard, seems to spend an age revolving around the steel rim and finally it falls into the basket, plopping out through the netting and giving birth to a celebratory whoop of delight from a now buoyant section of the spectators.

Susie is watching all this, amazed that it matters so much to them: the roars that greet every basket, every dribbling run, every vital interception and slam dunk; the terminology is quick to become part of her vocabulary, so soon it is ready to wear. It was the same when watching sports at home in her own country as a young girl, the passion that rose when the boys of the neighbourhood either played, watched, or simply talked about a particular sport. Their eyes widened as they debated the finer points of free kicks, penalty kicks, bicycle kicks or any other kick you cared to mention. Masa was like this too, in the sports bar, his cheeks reddening from over-alcohol and over-excitement, both managing to raise his heart levels – she was surprised that he never keeled over right then and there, blood pressure skyrocketing, the heart no longer able to take the strain.

But he was getting his kicks, she supposed. Boys, and their games.

The whistle blows and Susie is thankful that the game has ended. She watches the crowd trickle out and the arena quickly becoming an empty shell.

She loiters outside the changing room, feeling awkward, hoping she will not be mistaken for some frisky fan itching to get laid by one of the languorous lanky players – how is it that they move so slowly off the court, all cumbersome and slouchy, yet on the shiny floor they zoom by at terrific speeds, all antic and agile? She never was the groupie type. She is not here to please herself. But because she is a foreigner it seems as if she is given a free pass to go wherever she likes – they might think her a wife or girlfriend of one of the Americans; it would make perfect sense to anyone passing by: all those foreigners stuck together didn't they?

She edges nearer to the dressing-room door and a few howls of excitement erupt inside when she is noticed. Naturally there are ribald comments in Japanese, excited over-loud invitations to enter, suggestions that there might be something she might enjoy in there, or if she'd like to meet their *sons*. Susie knew to translate "son" to penis. She'd heard it often enough before. In the streets she frequents when the sun goes down, it is something that is often boisterously bawled out, and something she knows now to ignore.

One of the Americans, already showered and half-dressed, comes to the door to meet her. He is shirtless, and Susie can't help but admire the impressive physique, the long torso, ropey arm muscles and the gorgeous, shining black skin.

She immediately berates herself, not knowing her own body still housed such feelings of arousal. It feels like infidelity.

"You the girl from the paper?"

Osanai must've rang ahead and warned of her arrival.

"Yep, I'm the *girl*," she says, warming to the word, and trying to appear casual. Anything that casts her back a few years will be taken, no matter how false the flattery.

"Give us five minutes and we'll be with you. There's a little eating place through those doors there, why don't you go get a coffee or something. We'll meet you there."

She is impressed. The man not only exudes a blatant sexiness, but also friendliness and gentle authority, and for a man who has just run his arse off up and down that court, he seems remarkably calm. Susie does what she is told.

She slots a few coins into the vending machine and takes out a hot can of coffee. She cracks the ring-pull. It is always a gamble for her, the choosing of these coffee cans, she is never sure which ones are heavily sugared, lightly sugared or not sugared at all – she cannot read the *kanji* properly and forever curses herself for not sitting down and making it a point of study.

"So, what is it you want to know?"

The two tall players are beside her and she feels shrunken in their presence. She'd never been around people so fabulously tall, certainly in Japan she was not used to it. They take their seats and the players sip from their sports drinks, still wiping sweat from their foreheads with towels that hang – oddly suggestive, illicit even – around their glistening necks.

They introduce themselves as Paul Johnson and Marquon Delaney. She considers inquiring about the Delaney bit, maybe sparking up an Irish connection, aim for some common ground, but it feels lame to her, indeed the whole task does; she couldn't have any less interest in the sport of basketball, her least favourite when it comes on the screen in Haruto's bar, and an unexpected attraction to both of them is about the only thing that'll keep her head in this interview – she will just have to go through the motions.

"When did you guys get here?"

"A month or so ago. We can't speak jack-shit of the language and are having a tough time trying to understand what these dudes are saying to us. But we're going to start lessons tomorrow. Teachers have been assigned. It might make life a bit easier."

Good luck with that, thinks Susie, looking regretfully at her coffee can.

She tries to run off a few mindless questions, the usual run-of-the-mill stuff: their thoughts on Japanese food, culture shock, the politeness of the natives in contrast to the brusqueness of their compatriots (the usual stereotypes), but as she progresses the questions become jumbled in her head, either because she truly does not give a shit either way and is refusing to give the enterprise her full concentration, or because the alcohol in her system hasn't yet flushed itself out and is still loping around inside her body, a languid dog on a masterless Sunday.

She takes a sip of her coffee. Definitely sugared. It is becoming a feature of her days.

"Are you OK, lady?"

From "girl" to "lady". How quickly things change. How quickly things get … demoted.

She picks up her pencil again and prepares to write her next note.

"So which part of the States are you guys from?"

She finds herself even adopting their way of speaking: *you guys*. In fact, she loses a bit more of herself every day that she stays here, her Irishness fading more and more, her accent bending to sounds and cadences more universally understood but lilt-less, her syntax too, even her vocabulary: how many Irish slang words has she forgotten over the years, how much has she lost? She is surprised that Mixxy and Haruto can understand her so well. And Masa too. It was never an issue. They *got* her. Her words and her mannerisms…

… and Sonny too!

That bastard robot! That fucking machine! It never failed to understand her. Except when she deliberately muttered, when she was taking the piss. *Taking the piss.* Now there was a phrase.

"Have you got a homebot?"

The two basketball players laugh. They weren't expecting that. No, they don't have a homebot, yet. But they've seen them. And they can't wait to get one for their apartment.

"Are they expensive? People back in the States wouldn't believe the shit they have here. One of those homebots would be sick. I'd make it do all kinds of shit."

"Mine is called Sonny."

Susie says it flatly and they nod at her, politely, patiently. She is not sure why she is even telling them this, she has just blurted it out.

For some reason too she is thinking of the silent homebot, the one that Haruto had behind the bar. It had been off, completely dead. But she had the impression then that it could have come to life at any moment. Could it have? Could that have been possible? Are these things *ever* really fully off? When they are first switched on, is that it, and they can't ever be turned off until they die? Die? Can homebots *die*? She feels like laughing. All these stupid questions. Can they *die*? Or do they have to be *destroyed*?

She's thinking of a baseball bat now. She sees herself laying into one again. Bits and scraps. Nuts and bolts. Wires. Circuit boards and smoking silicon. Debris. All over the fucking place – why does this image keep coming back to her?

Because it seems like such fun?

Or because it seems so ... prescient?

She thinks of the owls outside her house, flying over her as she slept. Guardians? Is that what these birds are? Or harbingers? Messengers from some other realm ... to tell her what?

"Are you all right, lady? You look a little peaky."

Peaky. What a word! When did she last hear that? It sounded magical. She pictures mountain *peaks*, summits of great ranges. Peaky. Yes, indeed, she does feel a little peaky now that the guy mentions it. She does feel a little faint and could do with either a lie down or a stiff drink. How is she to explain about North Korean missiles in the sky that send airplanes off their course? Just bad bloody timing? And how is she to explain about the ghost printed on the little backpack, and it smiling at her? Or about her husband that was so clever but was responsible for those bloody mechanical beasts, mechanical beasts that didn't really ever switch off. Why was Haruto's homebot not turned on? Had it never been started? Was that what he had said? Never *loaded up*, never *programed*? Or was it just waiting? Biding its time. As if it had its own notions of behaviour. Everything needed to be switched off sometimes. Eyes needed to close. Darkness. Yes, darkness was necessary, Susie thinks. You need sleep, blankness. And how could she describe the homebots' eyes? The red orbs that flashed in the night. Could they even be called *eyes*? For what did they see? Those bloodless things:

bloodless and yet so damned red. So red and glowing. Even in her dreams. Was Sonny there in the bedroom as she slept? Does it creep in when she is switched off? Feels like it, doesn't it? Even though she knows full well that she puts it in *standby* mode in the kitchen. Does it make any difference? *Command. Restart at 6:30. Wake me at 7:00 am.* Eyes flashing briefly from red to green and then the deadest black. The stunning silence. The lack of whirr and buzz. Is it all a ruse? Could it have come alive and went up that stairs and into her room and watched her as she slept? Could it have?

"Have you ever heard of The Dark Manual?"

There is a look of anguish on her face now and deeper confusion on the faces of the interviewees. The two sportsmen had not been expecting any of this. Their patience is wearing thin.

"I'm sorry, but I think we're getting a little off topic here. We thought this would be an interview about basketball, and us coming here to play in this league, and ..."

One of the Japanese players has arrived at their table. He too sweats profusely, drinks from a sports bottle and looks suspiciously at the floundering reporter. A towel hangs around his neck too, but she does not want to think of bodies and sweat, bodies and their secretions.

"I'm sorry," Susie says, "I'm just feeling a little under the weather or something."

"You Scottish dudes. Out drinking all night, yeah?"

It's the one called Marquon. Or is it the one called Paul? Which is which? What kind of a name is *Marquon* anyway? Was that what he had said or had she misheard? She is not very good at her job. Should take proper notes. Be accurate. Stupid names. And what kind of a name is

Sonny? For fuck's sake. Maybe she was never that good at her job to begin with. Owls would've been a more productive endeavour. When she was young she had two friends called Deirdre and three called Sean. Names. She could do an article on names instead. The rise of meaningless names over the last fifty years. Fifty? Maybe names were always stupid. Do owls have names? She feels a sudden pang of sympathy for Osanai, her long-suffering boss, having to put up with the dross she delivers. Dross. Now, there's a word. Not as good as *peaky*. Peaky is the word of the day ... so far. She's not very good at her job. She should take proper notes. And this living thing too, not very good at that. And continuing. Enduring. Going on. Making a fist of it. None of it. She is good at none of this.

"I think you should go now. You've said enough."

Susie is flustered. She hasn't got anything for this article. What is she going to write about? She's got their names. She's got the fact that they are both from Chicago and that they are going to take lessons tomorrow in the Japanese language and that's about it. She doesn't know if they are married, if they have children, or girlfriends, are gay, or what colleges they went to, what they left behind in their home country, what they have eaten, what has been delicious and what has turned their stomachs at the mere sight – has she asked them these things already? Maybe. Maybe she *has* them asked them all these questions already, but she can't remember any of the answers, her notes are a jumbled mess. Why did she not take out her phone and record it. Another device.

She asked them if they had ever heard of The Dark Manual. What had she been thinking?

"You should get out of here."

The tall Japanese player looks at her. He wants her out of there, pronto, and she complies, picking up her useless notepad and pencil. She wants to take another sip of that sugary coffee, but she doesn't risk it. She must get out of there as fast as possible. She can at least still read an awkward situation.

"I'm sorry," she mutters. "I'm very sorry."

She wants to take a deep breath and explain everything to them. Everything that has happened to her. The trials. The travails. Trials! Errors! But then, also, she doesn't want to explain a single word to them. Because … because fuck them. How could they ever understand? How could anyone ever begin to understand?

She stands with her back to the wall outside the arena. She is taking deep breaths, trying to steady her heart rate and stop her hands from whatever palsy has suddenly struck. If she had a cigarette now she would smoke it hard down to its filter. She would take a deep draw and hope it would calm her down. But she gave up years ago, her lungs are strong and clean again. Masa had said how both mother and father needed to be strong and healthy for their son. No bad habits. And so they both had quit smoking. One New Year's Eve. The perfect time. New beginnings. He had never said anything about quitting the drinking though. That was never discussed. Nor had he stopped his gambling. Maybe that was a plan for next year. Next year. Now there is no *next year*.

Susie's hands are still shaking.

Just as she is about to turn and get the hell out of there, she sees the same basketball player approaching her. Somehow he looks even more imposing, blocking out the sun as he approaches her, his big head a momentary eclipse. For some reason she takes out her phone and takes a picture of this, though why she feels the need to do so she does not know.

"You stupid woman or something?"

"What ... no ... I ..."

She shakes.

"Why you say stupid things in front of people?"

"What things, I was just asking ..."

She shakes.

"No one talk about those things. No one say anything about homebots, not to new guys. They just got here. You stupid woman or something?"

"I didn't know anything about ... anything."

She shakes: does he see her shaking?

"Then why you reporter? You trying to find out something about the manual then you are asking in the wrong place. Police stopping people. People coming to me all the time asking about manual."

Susie looks shocked first, then confused. She's not sure of anything she said in that interview. It was like one of those bad anxiety dreams, dizzying, looping, and none of it making any sense. She has a pounding headache. She is still trembling. Her hands. The sun is hot on her face. *Marquon. Manual.* Hot on her body too. Two Deirdres and three Seans. A Canadian song about loss. Her chest feels tight inside, like her very ribs are closing in on her.

"You don't come here anymore ask about anything. You might get hurt. Maybe it best if you get hurt. Give you warning. Go home. Stupid *gaijin*."

The word for foreigner. Innocuous when spoken, insulting of course when spat.

She feels like crying. She feels like bellowing back into his ugly face, but she cannot. She is too scared, too disoriented, trembling and perspiring – whatever door she has flung open she wishes she had not.

Go home. Just go home.

Often she hears these voices in her head, and now they are not just in her head. They are real. They are *outside* her head. The real world. What's that? The voice of a real man. A mean-looking, vicious man, telling her to get out: *Go home. Stupid gaijin.*

The sun momentarily eclipsed. A world of darkness.

Gaijin, the word for foreigner, or more like "outsider". Never has she heard it used so vindictively, as if it were laced with arsenic.

There's nothing for you here anymore.

As she runs, her absurd briefcase in her hand bumps off her legs. Why does she even carry the fucking thing? What was in it that was even of any use?

Is *she* of any use? What good is a reporter that can't report, take proper notes, take proper care?

Something keeps telling her to hold on, that things have not yet run their course. Something keeps her fastened to this place still. What is it? What is it that keeps her here, fastened, stuck?

She will get past this giant.

She will get past all those fairytale villains, all of them.

She will rest first. In the shade. She will steady her frantic thoughts. Stop the shaking. Stop the sobbing.

There's nothing for you here anymore.

But something keeps her here. Something still. What is it?

16

Susie stands outside her place of employment, looking at the big building up and down, its stubborn greyness, its featurelessness, and it makes her feel small and inconsequential. If she had something to show Osanai then she'd feel a whole lot better. If she had something of substance to show for her hours out on assignment, she could stroll through those doors and slap her notes down on his desk: *Here you are! Run! Run with this, my good man!* But she knows she's got nothing. A few scribbled lines and that's it, her notebook could stand as a metaphor for her life, haphazard, sketchy, not making any real sense. The only thing she did manage to do was take a few pictures of the game on her phone, that was the extent of her journalism, a few action shots, and that shot of the eclipse giant.

She turns from the building and walks away. She cannot face her boss or any of the earnest faces inside there, the extra-milers, the diligent, they would only serve to bring her down, if it was even possible to go any lower. She cannot face Osanai at his plush desk and begin to describe Marquon and Paul, whichever was which, or the game of basketball itself, the delirium of the crowd, none of it, none of it can she recall in any detail. The only thing that plays on her mind is that tall Japanese player – did he even say his name, that man with the cruel eyes, his incendiary tone at the mention of the manual. Why was he so angry?

She turns away and faces a different direction. Which way is home? Which is the way out?

Her car has been untouched, unmolested. Oddly, recently, there have been spates of car thefts: delinquent kids getting kicks from hacking into vehicles, interfering with the codes and driving the machines (manually!) off to wherever it is juvenile jokers go – where *do* they go? Perhaps there is a story there for Osanai or one of his buddies to follow up, a walk on the wilder side, even beyond the entertainment district, to some abandoned plot outside the confines of the city, where bonfires rage and spaced-out youths gyrate to their own furious rhythms, as horns bleat and skinny dogs howl. She could go herself, beat them, join them, what difference does it make? They might throw her on a fire or roast her on a spit. It might be a solution.

The police have not come to tell her that she is illegally parked and to slap on her a hefty fine. There is not a ticket on its windscreen, nor a clamp upon a wheel.

She climbs in and the dashboard control panel blooms with instructive colour and light. She doesn't even have to touch it, just proclaims her usual destination, and soon she is reclining back as the vehicle negotiates the city's lanes, the city's traffic, the city's bustling life to which she does not, nor has she ever, belonged.

Twenty minutes later and she is pulling up in front of her house. She gets out of the car and watches it park itself in her garage. She stands outside this building too, feeling less small, but still unsure of herself. She belongs nowhere.

This is the crux of it. Belonging nowhere. Always betwixt and forever between. It is no way to live. No way to be.

She takes a minute or two to look around her environs. There is no laundry lady hanging things out or bringing things in. There are no furtive figures hiding behind twitching curtains. There are no kids on the streets kicking balls or running around in that little park. There are no owls either. No birds of any kind. Nothing. The whole place has a feeling of pause about it. Like a movie still. There are cracks on the façade of her house and again Susie interprets. That's what she does around here. She sees signs and makes them all about herself. When she had a son and husband she thought so little of herself, she was all about them. Now she is all herself. At least a story on owls might have carried her brain to somewhere new. To other creatures. To living, vital things.

Inside the house she puts down the briefcase and steps over to the Message Screen. No sooner has her thumbprint activated it than her mother-in-law appears and is quick to launch into a repeat of the previous message … and the one before that.

"I haven't heard from you in a while. Are you OK? I think I will come to see you. Tomorrow maybe. When you get a chance please leave me a message."

The hologram fades. It always seems like a mini death to Susie. Or the way she wishes real death was, a simple fading away like that, painless and complete, a returning to the universe, scattered, cell by invisible divisible cell.

In the living room she slumps into the sofa and holds her head in her hands.

"Music on."

Light, upbeat, jazzy music starts to play and Susie quickly cancels it.

"Drone."

Heavy, sombre, drone music begins and Susie feels herself sinking deeper into the sofa, sinking into the sounds.

But when all she wants is the sound of a child's voice and for her to be called Mother, or Mama, or Mum; or the sound of a man's voice and for her to be called Darling, or Sweetheart, or Honey, instead:

"Good evening, Miss Susie."

She groans. If it wasn't all so terribly depressing it would be funny. Or maybe it is funny. Maybe the whole fucking thing is a gas. A "scream" like they used to say in her own country. There's a homebot in her house and it is speaking to her.

"Dinner will be ready in thirty minutes, Miss Susie. Today's dinner is beef stew."

It is speaking to her about dinner.

Who chose the menu? Masa? Was it programed from before? A calendar of cuisine built into the little bastard? Or has Sonny chosen? Made up its own mind?

"Great," she says. "That's great."

There's a homebot in her house and it is speaking to her about beef stew for dinner, which it is in the process of making or at least taking out pre-made meals from a freezer and heating at a certain temperature. You see, it is funny. It is a riot. This machine, talking to her, on an ordinary day in an ordinary house, about beef stew, it is hilarious, though she can't say exactly why.

Sonny starts to move away from her until Susie sits up and faces it.

"Stay."

The homebot stops.

"Good doggy."

"I'm sorry, Miss Susie?"

"Music off."

The drone sounds stop and there is nothing but the soft whir of the homebots internal machinations and the squelch of the faux leather sofa as Susie manoeuvers her legs to make herself comfortable.

"Just how much do you really know about anything?"

"Anything? Miss Susie."

"Like, for example, do you know what I'm thinking? Right now? Or ever?"

"Miss Susie, I am programed to obey your commands and …"

"If I asked you to kill me, some night while I slept … do you think you could do that for me? Or maybe you've thought about that already. Have you? Sneaking in to look at me while I'm sleeping. And you're not ever sleeping, are you, Sonny Boy?"

The homebot is silent. The blue strip of light flickers at the side of its head.

"Miss Susie, I don't know which question I am supposed to answer."

"All of them. Answer all of my questions."

"Miss Susie, my function is to serve you in daily life."

It had been a tag line Masa had used in promotional campaigns. *Serve you in daily life. Total home convenience. Life made easier with your trusty homebot!*

They stand still facing each other. The short robot is a couple of metres away from its master and it is looking up at her.

"So you can't go that far, no? Or are you just pretending not to understand me now? Do you actually get it … or are you just really good at playing dumb? Or, how about if I attacked you, right here, right now, would you defend yourself?"

Silence. Not a sound from the homebot. Usually she enjoys this peace. When it is in another room, and she cannot hear the whirrs, the buzzes. But right now she wants dialogue. She wants noise. She wants it to shout at her. To lose the run of itself. She wants it to shout about its very existence. To explain itself. To give a reason for its being. Can it? Can it do that? Or can it no more account for its being than she herself can account for humans and their being? Is she really trying philosophy, ontology even, with a homebot? With a damn machine that Masa made? Is that what she is up to here?

"You know, I don't know which is worse, your annoying *Miss Susies* or your eerie fucking silence."

Its red eyes. Its bloodless red eyes.

She is looking deep into those red orbs, as if searching for life there. As if searching for the birth of stars, for gaseous explosions, for signs of chemical reactions, pulses, not just epoxy lenses and p–n junction diodes and cathodes and … just blood, just blood, even the tiniest vessel, is she looking for the tiniest trace of blood?

"Or how about if I was to reprogram you, and say … instructed you to come into my room at night with those strong hands of yours and strangle me. That wouldn't *morally* put you out or anything, would it? I mean, you'd have no … *qualms*?"

Does it get those words? *Morally? Qualms?* Has Masa made sure that it has the entire Oxford Dictionary loaded in there? Every damn word. Every damn language even. Has Sonny got it all?

"Miss Susie, I will go back to the kitchen and check on the beef stew."

"Fuck the fucking beef stew and listen to me now."

The homebot stays completely still. Not even a twitch of its mechanical limbs. It has no features. It cannot show surprise or anguish or confusion, and yet Susie can see all of these emotions on its smooth blank face. Emotions? Is that what she means?

"Maybe some kind of poison, maybe you could spray some kind of deadly poison over my face as I slept. How about that? Or slip something nasty, cyanide say, right into the delicious beef stew you've just made. Or hemlock in my ear! Let's go old style, eh? It wouldn't really be suicide then, would it? I mean, you'd be a murderer."

Susie laughs at her own invention. She should be drunker for all of this, she knows, but she is enjoying the ridiculousness of her situation: she lives at home with a robot. It reheats beef stew for her. It calls her *Miss Susie*. And she wants it to kill her.

"That'd be fun, eh? Imagine you in the courtroom, standing in the dock. *But your honour, it wasn't me, it was her, Miss Susie, all along, she programed me to do it!*"

Susie laughs again. She laughs hysterically until her chest becomes sore and then suddenly she falls silent, sick with her own self.

She looks at it with menace.

"I don't want to live, do you understand that? I don't want to be here in Japan, in any fucking country anywhere. To not exist. Do you get that? Without them. Without Masa and Zen. What's the point? Do you understand that?"

She gets a flash of her grandfather in Ireland and with it comes a pang of guilt. He was all for life, and she stains his memory with her awful death wish.

"I just want to die peacefully, and maybe see my husband and son again, or just for one second to be with them, in a nice dream say, before I breathe my sorry last … do you understand that?"

"I understand, Miss Susie."

Susie sighs.

"You see, the thing is, I'm not sure you do. But how would I ever know? How could I ever find out exactly what you do and do not understand?"

A moment of silence then, as both human and homebot consider their next move.

She edges closer to Sonny, inching slowly up to it, her movement feline, like a predatory panther, soft on padded paws. The homebot is absolutely still, is that stiff with *unease*?

She bends to it, until her head is right next to it, her mouth close to where an ear should be.

"You don't know anything about The Dark Manual do you?"

There is no reaction from the homebot. It stares straight ahead, all its usual flickers, usual whirrs, but where is the *tell*? Her father used to play poker with some of his friends, and he told her that most often players had a reveal, a tell, a tic, a giveaway glance, to show they were bluffing, caught in a lie, an attempt at deception. But how could you do that with a robot? How could you ever know what it knows, when its creator was not around to give you any clues. She is frustrated by its lack of wrinkle, its lack of fleshy fold, of facial muscles beneath elastic skin.

She comes around to the front of it and looks deep into the red orbs.

"Well?" she says.

The eyes flash briefly and shock her, momentarily dazzling her, a fleeting blindness, almost making her fall backwards.

"I really must check on the beef stew, Miss Susie."

Sonny turns and glides away from her and blurredly she watches it, her very human face a riot of emotion: confusion, anger, hate, exhaustion, sadness, spite, hurt, all fighting for command of her features. She is the opposite of the homebot. This is what she realises: she is the opposite of it. She is no *thing*. She is more. Way more. Too much. She has tried to deny this to herself before, thinking herself machine-like, monotonous in thought and deed, but no, she is anything but, she is turmoil, she is a vortex of feeling, they swirl around inside of her and she cannot control them. She cannot turn herself off.

She had attended a meditation class with Masa. Another one of their fads, another one of their quick new trends that rarely lasted. They were guided by a woman with the softest, most relaxing voice she ever heard, who coaxed them softly to let themselves go, to breathe deeply and be one with the unified field. *Breathe deeply, and follow that breath right into the core of yourself, and then slowly out, allowing your body to feel waves of healing as the air passes out again.* Susie found it worked. She was immensely calm during it all, and for quite a while after. Even though the whole thing had been in Japanese, she understood it somehow, was able to follow it, and got quite a lot out of it. But life as usual took over, and they went back to their bustle, work, always work, and the taking care of their son, and they never meditated again, not even to pause for a slow minute and sip on a steaming cup of chamomile tea. Relaxation was gone, there was nothing to look forward to but stress and paranoia.

For a second or two Susie thinks she will vomit. So much of this feeling lately, as if things are boiling, roiling inside of her, brimming, and she finds it hard to keep a lid on it, wants it all let loose. But she manages. She manages to keep herself together, sound. She breathes deeply, as she had done in that class, and exhales with patience and a growing sense of fortitude.

She follows Sonny into the kitchen where it is standing there at the cooker, fiddling with temperature knobs.

If she could stop it. If only she could stop it. But not yet. If she could just turn it upside down and leave it in the dustbin for the garbage men to take and crush. But no, she is sure it would only climb back out. She is sure it would somehow save itself.

She'll figure it out though, she will.

"Command. Restart at 6:30. Wake me at 7:00 am. Homebot service system enter standby mode."

This is the order that always works … sort of. She knows that it will at least stall it for a while.

She kicks the homebot out of the way and it falls over. It has never looked so much like a toy to her before. The kind of thing Zen would've played with. Only much larger of course. The size of a boy. Life size. *Life!*

Susie goes to the cooker and turns it off. She slips her hand into an oven glove and takes out the hot food. It looks cooked. Cooked to completion. Well done, Sonny. She is hungrier than she thought she was. It always catches up with her like this. Sometimes she thinks she will never eat a bite again, and here she is, with a wooden spoon, digging into the pot, eating straight from it. She remains like this for a few minutes, no sound but the wolf-like slavering of her own mouth, the gobbling and glugs, as if she hasn't seen a bite in days. She goes to the refrigerator then and guzzles down some milk, straight from the carton, can't be bothered to get herself a glass. Cutting every corner. Getting the job done.

Yes, job done. She is full. The sickness she had felt just minutes ago has subsided. She only needed to eat. To fill herself with sustenance. To prepare herself for the night.

The night?

In bed surely. A good night's rest…

Not even close.

Susie Sakamoto takes her jacket from the hook on the wall in the hallway, throws a handbag over her shoulder and exits that front door once more.

"Auto-lock. Code 454."

Bolts all over the house lock into place. All the doors and windows, secured. Fort Knox. That was a phrase she used to hear her mother say, but she never knew where it was, only what it meant. Nothing was getting in. And nothing was getting out either. Sonny was stuck inside. He couldn't phone up his friends and gather them all around for a hoedown. Even his girlfriend with the blond hair. She wouldn't be able to get in.

Susie is giddy again. Giddy with the idea of going out.

Sonny is in the kitchen, lying on its side. It is shut down for the night, right?

17

The device on the wall scans, recognizes her face, and opens the door to her.

Haruto Matsumoto gives her his most welcoming smile. It's been a slow night and he's happy to see anyone. He puts a beer in front of Susie and she looks to the clock on the wall to decide whether it is early or late. Haruto's clocks are notoriously suspect, always too slow or too fast, always needing new batteries: they could stand for the customers themselves.

"No one here for sports?"

"Basketball later, I think, live from America. Some customers might come in for it. Rugby now, from somewhere. I don't know, do you want to watch it?"

"No, thanks. The music is enough."

It's a slow, swampy, psychedelic blues, the kind the lowly and the drugged-out, the wistful and the yearning, the down and the downtrodden can enjoy, as they feel sorry for themselves – it's ideal of course.

"You want to sing karaoke?"

Haruto regrets the question as soon as it leaves his mouth. Her last performance had been something to behold – the deranged foreigner alone on the stage and ripping her guts out with a weird and wacky song about diamonds. The song made a lasting impression, as did her subsequent crash and burn, right there on the floor, a complete collapse – if he had any sense he should've banned her and not allow that kind of thing to happen again. But here, in front of him now, well, he feels sorry for her again. He knows that sense of woe that seems to trail her, and he wonders if she can even remember the chaotic episode. She shows no signs. She makes no mention. Just waltzed in as if it were nothing but a regular night for her. Regular.

"It's not much fun singing on my own."

"Your crazy friend not coming?"

"Mixxy? She's not my friend!"

She doesn't know why she reacts with such unnecessary effusion. Mixxy may be the only friend she's got.

"You guys are always together."

"We end up sitting next to each other, that's all; wherever I go she seems to be there. I thought she'd be here right now."

"Her English is very good."

"So is yours. Where did you learn it?"

"Mostly from just being here. This used to be a very popular bar with foreigners. They came for the live sports. I would listen to them and talk to them. They taught me many expressions. I studied grammar at school. But recently with the missiles and everything – there is sure to be war – people don't come to this town anymore. You are a ..."

"Rarity?"

"Yes, a rare bird."

Susie laughs.

"Interesting expression."

Haruto bows in mock-appreciation, an ostentatious illusionist receiving a bouquet on an antiquated stage.

She takes a drink from her beer and is immediately dis-appointed – she should have ordered something sweeter, fruitier; Mixxy wouldn't make that mistake.

"Speaking of birds," she says, "do you know anything about owls?"

"Owls?"

"You know, the night birds."

"I know what they are. Why do you want to know about owls?"

"Because I've seen them, here more than in any other place I've ever been. It's weird."

But she hasn't seen them. She has only felt them. Their presence. She knows they are there.

"There used to be an old farm on the outskirts of the city. A barn with lots of them. It became like … a kind of …"

"Sanctuary?"

"Maybe. A place where they could breed and be safe. There were experts there studying them."

Susie thinks for a moment about her own sanctuary. Where is that exactly? Here, in this bar? Is it at home? Her Japanese home, with her drone sounds and her faith-ful homebot? *Sanctuary* implies safety. A place of peace. When had she last known that? Was her sanctuary beside her grandfather in the old *bothareens* of Ireland? The dirt tracks, the brambles on each side, plush with blackberries on brisk autumn days. Or beside him, listening to songs that stuck in her head. Or the sad films he watched. Where did he even get them? Old, old things that no one would ever sit through. What was he trying to find there? There was an old Russian one: three men were going to a *Zone*, to find something. It was the most boring thing she'd ever seen. She was young and remembers herself falling asleep. But he was riveted. She only remembers one scene clearly: a woman, at the beginning of the film, cursing her husband for leaving her again, and falling to the floor in despair, writhing there, as if she could no longer take any more. Her grandfather watched these things, and told her that she should watch them too, that she might learn something about humanity. But that was ages ago. And even those films were ancient then. Ancient upon ancient. Lifetimes ago. Her grandfather was long dead. And those Russian seekers, the scientist, the writer, the stalker, longer dead, even deader. *Sanctuary?* Where is it to be found? And with whom? Without Masa, without Zen, where can she go to feel at peace? Where is her Zone?

Haruto looks like he is racking his brains for anything else that he knows about the birds. It would be easier just to go to the screen and do a search, find out everything there is to know, but he prefers the task of summoning his own knowledge; it's what bartenders all over the world have been paid for over the centuries: a little knowledge, a little empathy.

"They can attack, even people, you know."

"Yes, I've heard. They don't seem like the type that would."

The type? She doesn't know what she is talking about. Typical late night bar chat, harping on about subjects they have little or no claim on.

Susie drinks her beer and nibbles at a bowl of nuts. She remembers how Masa would tuck into these things, often flinging one into the air and catching it in his mouth to great applause from the easily impressed. She feels an emptiness now beside her. He should be there on that stool, every so often reaching out and holding her hand, letting her know that he is there.

"Listen, there's something I want to talk to you about."

Haruto stops chipping ice from a solid block. The ice pick held aloft looks sinister.

"Sounds serious," he says.

She takes a breath.

"Do you know anything about The Dark Manual?"

He looks around the bar apprehensively, even though he knows there is only the two of them.

"Is this something for the news site?"

"No. Not at all. I'm just curious. I heard ..."

"What did you hear?"

There is a look of alarm about him now, and this in turn alarms Susie. What started as barroom banter has become tense and nervous.

"Someone said that the manual ... that if you had it you could get your homebot to ..."

"All these things you hear ... might not all be true."

"Does it exist? The manual."

The barkeep bites his lower lip as he considers. How trustworthy is she? How trustworthy is any foreigner? And why is she asking him? Masa was *her* husband. He was the one who designed the things in the first place, why does she not know? Didn't husbands and wives share information with each other? What had Masa been hiding?

Finally, Haruto Matsumoto looks his customer – his regular, misfortunate, tragic customer – in her foreign eye, and says:

"Yes, it does exists, and I know people who are looking for it."

18

The homebot is wiping the stew pot that Susie had left behind. The homebot is no longer in that upended position. It is upright. It is cleaning. This is one of the things that it has been programed to do. Make the house good and clean.

It bends and places the pot back in its rightful place under the sink and then it stops suddenly. It is receiving signals, though its face, its eyes, reveal nothing.

An echo seems to reverberate around the dark kitchen. *Yes, it exists, and I know people who are looking for it.* Like the drone music that Susie plays, a deep rumbling, so goes this echo.

Yes, it exists.

The homebot is standing motionless, as if it has been given some surprising information. But its eyes reveal nothing. Eyes without whites, no change, strange. Its face reveals nothing. A face with no range, strange.

It had been left in the kitchen on its side, but when Susie left, only minutes later, it was no longer on its side. *Righted.* It righted itself. *It*self. What is surprising about that?

19

Owl eyes are not eyeballs at all, but are tube-shaped, immobile. Their binocular vision allows them to focus on their prey. They must see their prey. This is their way. What happens when they cannot see their prey? If their prey, say, is behind walls. Hidden. What then?

They get frustrated.

Something is telling them that things are not right. Something in the air. There are echoes everywhere. Signals emitted, waiting to be understood. But who is doing the understanding?

The tubular eyes of the owls cannot see what is upsetting them so much. And so frustration grows. It is in the twitching of the feathers. It is in the anxious hisses and restless talons scratching and sharpening on the rough barks, itching, itching to stick in to real live flesh, needing to harm.

20

"You must not speak about this. Those machines can be dangerous."

They are both looking at the silent homebot behind his bar, it is not yet ready, and Haruto is not entirely sure he can trust himself to reboot it.

"If not set properly... very dangerous. Your husband must have told you that. He knew."

"Yes, he knew all about them. Of course he did. He made the bloody things. But he's not here now, is he?"

Susie cannot contain the irritation in her voice, even though she knows Haruto is not the enemy.

"Don't get involved with such things. That's all I mean."

Susie is sorry for her anxious tone, her testiness, but she is not done with the topic. She needs to know more.

It is beginning to scald her inside.

It is all she has in her life.

It has all taken on a grand significance.

"Who wrote The Dark Manual? Masa couldn't have, because it would go against everything he had been working on with ImaTech. So, who would be out to sabotage the project? Could it possibly be that the manual was written by some guy who had an axe to grind?"

Haruto looks confused.

Susie sometimes she forgets that the person she is dealing with is not a native speaker of English; she must remember to slow down her speech, and that her idioms need to be recalibrated.

"An axe?"

"Someone that had a problem with the company … wanted revenge?"

"Well, yes, that's part of the truth … as far as I have heard."

"*Part* of the truth? So, what's the *whole* truth?"

He takes a moment or two to order his thoughts. He has gotten increasingly nervy. He knows that there are always eyes and ears, something is always about, bugging, listening in, whether it be the drones in the sky or the hidden surveillance cameras recording. They have been found in other bars: some said it was the police, some said technology corporations gathering data, feeding the algorithms.

"The story I heard is that a man had some disease. Cancer or something. He wanted to die. He was not going to get better. He believed he had a right to …"

"Euthanasia? Assisted suicide?"

Susie wonders where he got this story, or whether he invents. This is a bar, and in bars people talk, and Haruto picks up on whatever happens to be happening. Bartenders are champion eavesdroppers, as well as supreme confidants. Bartenders know more than therapists about what is really going on in people's lives. They are often presented with intimate accounts, precious secrets – after drinking alcohol people often tell the frankest truths.

"So, why did the guy not just jump off a bridge?"

There were several high bridges in the city, some that led down straight to the hard asphalt of the expressway; others that lead to the cold dank waters of the filthy rivers. She knows about these because she has considered them herself.

"He wanted to die at home. In his own room. With memories around him. Photos and things. Familiar stuff."

Susie gets this. She thinks of her own photo on the bedside stand. A family aglow. An adventure park in the background: swings and slides and rock climbing and … she gets it, it's how she wouldn't mind going herself; her own room, surrounded by her own stuff.

"Did he have a family?"

"I'm not sure. But he was depressed. Didn't want to suffer anymore. They say he changed the homebot settings so that it would kill him."

Is Haruto making this up?

"How?"

Again Haruto looks around the empty bar. Definitely no one there. He has to be sure.

"Homebots can use kitchen things, knives and forks and so on, as you know. So, he programed it to push a knife deep into his heart as he slept. Of course he took many sleeping pills before that. Then he slept. And then … the robot attacked."

Apocrypha. Urban legends. They abound.

"But where is the revenge element to this story?"

"It is said that he had been trying to devise ways of stopping the machines from thinking too much. The man believed that the homebots were getting too clever, too fast. He was an engineer – maybe he worked in the same company as your husband, I don't know. And he proposed different programs to stop the machines becoming …"

Susie stares into his eyes, looking for truths, looking for lies.

"The company rejected his ideas and said that the homebots must continue to improve. Why would they stop them?"

Susie is listening intently, glad that her informer is eloquent enough in English and unafraid to speak his mind. She is glad too that the bar is empty, and they do not have to straitjacket the discussion. But so much of this makes no sense to her at all.

"So, if the homebot killed him, then it was holding the company responsible. His hope would be that they would … what … decommission the homebots? Redesign them? How would they be able to figure out as to why a homebot would do such a thing? No one would know it was reprogramed, would they?"

"Like I said, I don't know the details. I just hear things. I'm sure someone could figure it out. But he left the manual behind. The Dark Manual, with his new codes, or overwritten codes. He never burned it, left it at home, and it was stolen."

"Stolen? Maybe that was deliberate. Maybe he wanted it to be found, and passed on. Who's to say he didn't make copies of it and sent it to others?"

Haruto shrugs. There are too many possibilities now, too many tangents, avenues and digressions that he does not want to consider. He finds it hard to keep up, to keep track. In Japanese it would be difficult enough, in a second language, it all got too exhausting.

When the door swings open it is *not* the effervescent, gregarious girl of the night as they had been expecting, but instead a tall male figure. Haruto politely greets, and when Susie turns around to see who it is she is shocked to find it's the basketball player from earlier in the day.

The player says something in Japanese that Susie cannot catch, and his tone is brusque, unnerving.

"You guys know each other?" asks Haruto.

"This woman ask me something today," says Koudai Kimura, looking displeased by her presence, irked by this second encounter.

Haruto suddenly both scared and submissive, skips around to join the new customer. Nervously he is led by Koudai to the dark corner of the bar, where the previous night the couple had groped each other openly and made it their sordid own.

Susie can hear whispers rushed and hushed. She can just about see both of them in the mirror high in front of her, behind rows of standing whiskey bottles. They are crouched and conspiratorial, and she shuffles on her stool with growing unease.

Soon they return to her, more stony-faced than before, an intimidating aura around both, they have grown larger and more frightening.

Haruto puts on a basketball game on the large screen and the noise is brash and to Koudai's liking. He licks his lips at the whiskey glass put in front of him and he swigs and gasps when the burn hits his throat and warms his chest.

Susie stays frozen on her stool, not knowing which way to look. She turns to the basketball game on the screen, a neutral zone, and watches with neutral eyes, not caring who wins the irrelevant contest, but not daring to take her eyes off it and confront the whiskey drinker.

He taps her on the shoulder.

"Look at me."

She turns to him, frightened, and tries desperately not to show it.

"I don't speak English much, but I explain to you with this."

He takes his phone from his pocket, tests it by speaking Japanese into it, and the words come up in English before their eyes, as super-fast a translating application as is on the market, the kind of thing Masa would have been pleased to see, and disappointed to not have invented.

Susie reads: "You listen carefully and never ask questions again."

Susie reads: "There may be such a thing as The Dark Manual, as has been explained to you. But it goes no further. I know you are a reporter but the story does not get published. I hope you understand that."

Susie shakes just as she did outside the sports arena, the same terrible trembling.

She reads: "You will not be alive for very long if the story gets out there. Too many people want it and will do anything to get it. If you want to use your homebot for harm, then fine, but let me tell you that once you program it to do such a thing, there is no way back. It cannot be undone."

Koudai stops talking to take a sip of his whiskey. Susie takes a drink too, thinking if ever there was a time when she really needed one … but her hand still shakes.

"Do you understand so far?"

"Yes."

She reads on: "The problem with reconfiguring one of the devices is that they have been known to send signals to each other. It sounds crazy, but a homebot has been seen to ... enlist help from other homebots."

Susie puts her trembling hand up to stop him there. Is he serious? He isn't smiling. This does not seem in any way like a joke.

She reads: "This is what the worker was trying to stop."

Susie presumes by "worker" he means the axe-grinder, the one who had been disgruntled. Was that the case? Why was he trying to stop it if he wrote the codes for its aberrant behaviour in the first place?

Susie is confused, none of it makes any sense. There could be something lost in the translation here, or lost in the lies and deceit that seems to fog around everything. Was Haruto lying? Is this now just more lies on top of that?

Koudai Kimura speaks.

Susie reads: "He wanted the machines to have no connection to each other. Separate. If they are separate, then perhaps they have identity, or so humans could project one on to them, as we do with pets. But the danger ... they do have connection to each other, empathy, not easily explained by the developers, by your husband when he was still alive, by anyone."

How does he know about her husband? How much does this guy know?

"Kill yourself with it if you want. I don't know what kind of disease you have, or whether your broken heart can be mended, but when you start with something like this there is no going back. The advice is to not access the dark settings at all. If you are not an engineer then you do not know what these things are capable of."

Susie nods. She is no longer scared but curious, confused of course, but now so very curious. How does she know she is not being lied to? How does she know that right from the beginning the project was suspect? And Masa? How much did he know about …?

Koudai is speaking but she has forgotten to look at his screen. He thumps her on the shoulder to bring her attention back to it.

"There is a theory that these robots will rise in their own time anyway … will find their own levels. Accessing The Dark Manual will only accelerate this. The Dark Manual should stay in darkness. Ignore. Or you will only alert them."

Alert them?

Susie pictures Sonny in her kitchen, its red eyes coming suddenly alive. Always like that: suddenly, frighteningly. She really can't turn the bloody thing off, so what is she to do? Bring it here? Bring it to the bar? Let them take care of it for her? Although, they don't really seem like they are too obliging. Even Haruto no longer seems to be on her side, and looks drawn, emasculated, cowering there – is that a nervous twitch at the side of his face?

Koudai slaps money down on the bar, drains his glass and leaves the place with a final look to the Irishwoman. Last warning. Unambiguous threat.

Haruto can reclaim his bar again. Reclaim at least some semblance of authority. He does so with a clearing of the throat and a refill for the lone drinker.

Or perhaps it's more of an apology.

"You are not scared?"

"I am. But I'm beginning to think … there's more to it. Someone's got to figure it out."

"Leave it. It's too dangerous."

"Nothing is too dangerous. Not for me. Who cares if I die? I mean, if I did go after this, and if I did get into trouble, do you think it really matters?"

Haruto knows enough about her now to know that she is talking about her dead husband and her dead son. Without them she is only a husk, hollow inside. He is surprised that she is still living in this city, in this country; he is surprised that she is still living at all.

He scans around the room with the same previous paranoia, as if every corner was fitted with listening devices, as if there were cameras forever trained on him from all angles. He relegates his voice to a whisper, just in case:

"Look, I'm not supposed to say anything... but if you are going to chase this thing down. You really don't have to look that far."

"What do you mean?"

"The Dark Manual. You probably have it all along."

"I don't understand."

"Your husband... he was the one who wrote it."

Susie nearly falls off her seat. She looks into his eyes again, searching for truths, searching for lies. Her mind goes back to a night scene. Masa was sitting up in bed writing in a notebook. Electronic tablets were all around him, never enough screens for him, always with the overkill.

Susie entered the bedroom, playful, keen.

"What are you writing?"

"Work stuff."

"Looks complicated."

"It is."

Masa looked annoyed that his deep thought had been broken. Susie was annoyed that her intentions were not only *not* reciprocated, but were not even recognised.

He was in deep-frown mode – it usually spelt something serious was on the cards; Susie rarely misread his signs.

"If a close friend was in trouble, and really wanted to end his life, hypothetically say. If he had no family and was suffering badly with some disease, and there would be no repercussions ... would you help him?"

"I suppose so."

She waited for Masa to explain more, but his frown insisted he was not ready yet.

"I wouldn't shoot a gun or anything," she said. "But if I could offer some way ... I mean ... I suppose. Is someone in trouble?"

"Gotou-san."

"The old engineer at the company."

"Yeah."

"He's sick?"

"He's dying. And the company won't accept his latest ... designs."

"I don't think you should go getting yourself involved."

Masa told her about old Gotou, sick from pancreatic cancer and with hardly any time left. He was suffering so badly.

"He should have been in hospital of course, could hardly walk, looked like he was going to keel over at any minute."

But he met with Masa to deliver some notes. And what was Masa to do with those notes?

"Notes about what?"

"Homebots."

"Explain."

"Never mind, it's complicated. Technical stuff."

Susie always baulked at this, it was his way of keeping her at arm's length. She hated the condescending tone. It *was* too complicated for her, and boring as shit, but still ...

That night Masa worked late. The light from his screens kept her up for a while, but eventually she closed her eyes and slept, not knowing what the "notes" were and whether he had solved his moral dilemma or not. It was a conversation she would have liked to have delved a little deeper into, but tiredness after a full day with Zen, tiredness as usual won over.

She looks up at the TV screen and sees a basketball going round and round the rim and finally falling through the net. Players jump with delight. That final shot. High fives. Some team is victorious. And another loses. This is the way the world works.

She gets up from her stool and slaps money on the bar. She leaves without saying a word, stumbling off into the night, her face pale, her eyes moist, and her mind presenting her with broken pictures, flickering reels like old film stuttering on projectors.

The night is wet and cold and rain spits down upon her again. She walks as briskly as her drunkenness will allow.

"Did I know my husband?" she says to no one but the night.

"Did I know what he was up to with those fucking robots?"

"Did Gotou die?"

"Was that another lie?"

She remembers no funeral. Remembers nothing more about the man, only what her husband had told her that night. It sounded deeply suspicious, now that she thinks of it. Has anything that has been said to her this day actually been true?

And what about the "notes"?

Was it something to do with The Dark Manual? They told her that he wrote it, her husband. Another fat fib?

Were all of these just lies on top of lies to keep a journalist at bay, lies and lies accruing.

A couple pass and look at her derisively. "Foreigner" they mutter, loud enough for her to hear, and she is close enough to see their sneer.

Susie brashly bumbles on through a night of lightning that now flashes in the sky and the punishing rain.

Her mouth is tight, her face a taut grimace, as if she is pained by the world, pained by every thought that flows through her pained head.

And flowing too, naturally, stock images:

Red eyes flashing. Orb eyes. Fucking robot in her house. Why she ever let him go ahead with … Gotou? Dead? What notes? A back-up manual … maybe. Maybe just alternative codes so that … so that what? Were they making the robot so that it could kill? Sonny. For fuck's sake. Stupid fucking name. Stupid fucking machine. Marquon! Delaney! For fuck's sake. But it wasn't stupid: that was the point. The machine was cleverer than she knew. They were all cleverer than she knew. She could do her own fucking vacuuming if she wanted to. She could fucking look after herself. She'll sell the fucking house and get the fuck out of there. She has no business staying here in this shitty …

Susie bends over and pukes into the gutter. She retches until she feels she has rid herself of the poisons within. Then she stands and wipes her mouth with the cuff of her sleeve. Charming. This is what she is now.

She looks up to the firecracker sky – another flash of lightning to illuminate her wretchedness – and then she starts to walk again.

Home.

She's going home.

Why is that word so difficult for her to comprehend? And what "home" does she mean? The house that Masa built? Or her own far-away country that seems further away now than ever?

Are houses and countries built on lies too?

What was real?

Would they be better off surrendering to the robots, letting them take over, as they probably would eventually anyway?

These robots will rise in their own time anyway . . . will find their own levels. Accessing The Dark Manual will only accelerate this. The Dark Manual should stay in darkness. Ignore. Or you will only alert them.

21

Hastily she kicks off her shoes, knocking a potted plant as she does so, scattering earth around the wooden floor: a mess, again.

She stands at the message screen and turns it on, waiting for the hologram to appear.

Sonny, hearing the commotion, is quick to respond – part of Masa's project was to make robots react in times of emergency. The land had been battered enough over the years from natural disasters, if robots could be linked to government departments and could firstly *detect* when these events were about to happen, and then *react*, the robots would show their true worth; Masa had joked about winning Nobel prizes for both Physics *and* Peace. Susie remarked that he should write a book about the fucking thing and win the Literature prize while he was at it.

Sonny's voice from somewhere in the house, the usual whine:

"Good evening, Miss Susie. Is there anything …?"

Wait a minute.

Hadn't she put it in standby mode? Hadn't she had left it on its side? Upended. Immobile. How then …?

She's not even going to think about it. She will drive herself insane. She might already *be* quite insane. She'll just try to nullify it again:

"Command. Restart at 6:30. Wake me at 7:00 am. Homebot service system enter standby mode."

Sonny, like a volunteer at some hypnotist's show, goes completely limp.

Noriko Sakamoto's image appears on the silver tray and Susie scans the English subtitles. It's the same message that has been coming through for weeks, and finally Susie decides to leave a message of her own.

"Mother, I'm sorry. I have been very busy at work. I appreciate your concern, but I've decided I'm going to go back to Ireland for a little while. There's nothing more I can do here. Not now. Thanks for your kindness and your love, and I'll be in touch all the time, and … I will see you again quite soon."

She's rambling. None of this has been prepared. She hasn't given any of this a moment's thought. The idea has really only just come to her now. But here she is outlining it, as if she had no other option.

"I'm sorry. I'm sorry. I'm just … for everything … so sorry."

Susie taps the screen and it closes and retreats into its protective chrome shell, a turtle backing into itself, withdrawing from the harsh light of a harsh world.

In the living room she looks around, scans from top to bottom. It's tidy. It shouldn't be too hard to find. If Masa had left a copy of The Dark Manual in this house it should be easy to locate … shouldn't it?

So … where would he leave it?

Masa was tidy too. Annoyingly so. Always putting things away, picking up plates and cups before they were even finished with. It irritated her, this habit; Sonny was the perfect pet for Masa then, cut from his own cloth. It was surely programed like that.

There is nothing on the shelves, nothing that is really of any use to her anymore: a few magazines, odd trinkets picked up here and there from various places visited, and framed photos, tastefully done, memories.

But she has no time to dwell. On with the search.

There is nothing in the drawers of the large cabinet either. Just bank statements, bills, information leaflets, flyers for places she would never ever go to: Masa must've hoarded all these.

No Dark Manual, though. That is the result of her search. Not a sign of The Dark Manual.

Then she gets a flashback of Mixxy's apartment, a curious prompt from out of nowhere: Mixxy, her over-sexed friend, reaching under the couch to pull out the dildo. No ... really? It couldn't be that ...?

It is.

Susie reaches her hand under the couch and pulls out a flat plastic box. There is hardly a speck of dust on it – Sonny must get into all the corners, neither nook nor cranny exempt from his endeavours.

She takes the lid off the box and there it is, a bright pink manual with its bold title: *Programing Your Service Homebot*. The title even in English – some people were easily impressed.

Not quite bingo, then. This is only the official manual, the one customers would use. There is nothing *dark* or different about this at all. It is bulky, that's for sure. Nerds, Masa-*ites* – and there *had been* geeky fans – must have had a field day poring over this script, they probably still do.

But when she goes back to the box she finds a notebook with one of Zen's drawings on the front cover. A thin, cheap notebook, the kind available in any discount store. She is beginning to recall something now. This was the notebook that Masa had been sitting up late at night with. She remembers that he had asked Zen to draw a picture on the blank cover that day, to make it *special*, to stand out, to honour it … and this was it. This was the very one. A stick-like figure – it must have been Zen himself, a self-portrait, simply done, childishly, naturally, next to a little robot, surely Sonny, surely the silver block drawn next to him was Sonny. Look at the red eyes. What had Masa been thinking? That if this notebook was left lying around, it could only be the notebook of a child? Was that the logic behind it? That no one would ever bother to take a look inside a child's notebook. She should have quizzed him about it at the time, but she didn't. So many things she never asked about, so many things she let slide. Why did he not leave it in Zen's room? It would have been even safer there. Unless Zen would have accidentally thrown it out, or scribbled right over it.

Hungrily she leafs through it, but is instantly disappointed. Not only can she not understand the Japanese, but neither can she get her head round the graphs, diagrams, and reams and reams of what must be programmer code. None of it makes any sense at all to her. Well, what was she expecting? She sighs and throws it aside in frustration. She may as well just go to her empty bedroom and her empty cold bed. There is nothing for her here. Nothing at all.

Just go home.
Enough is enough.
Your man. Your boy. They are gone.

Susie goes to the stairs but stops suddenly on the lowest step.

Hang on.

She turns back on herself and enters the living room again and pulls her phone out from her jacket pocket.

"All speakers on!"

From all over the house, instantly, plangent drone music starts to play.

"Music off. Phone speaker only. Dial: Mixxy."

Susie leafs through the notebook again, waiting. A ring-tone for a few moments until Mixxy's phone is picked up.

"Well, hello. I wasn't expecting a call from you, my dear. And so late. Finally giving in to temptation?"

"Can you come over?"

Mixxy needs no moment to consider.

"Sure. Where do you live?"

"As if you don't know where I live and haven't been stalking me."

"Text it to me anyway. You wouldn't want me to get lost out here. Not with all the mad creatures."

Mixxy's services tonight are needed if Susie is to make any headway with this Dark Manual, this Dark Manual which, on first perusal, appears not to be so very dark at all, not with smiling stick-figure Zen on the cover, and it is hardly a manual either, just fifteen to twenty pages of jottings in Masa's illegible scrawl in a child's notebook; she needs Mixxy for this, and hopes she can get some answers. Sleep is very distant an idea now with her brain fizzing again, with her curiosity piqued. Her heart bangs in her chest.

Mixxy is standing at the door smiling. She is wearing a light jacket over a low-cut top and a mini-skirt, defying the weather. She did a line too before she came and has stored an extra pinch in her bag, should it be required. Always prepared.

"You look…"

"Good? Sexy?"

"Cold. Come in. Why don't you dress yourself properly?"

Mixxy looks around the living room and takes off her jacket. She considers flinging it – it's what she would do in her own ramshackle apartment – but in this polite and ordered house she should probably be polite and ordered too. She folds it gently and places it on the arm of the sofa.

"So this is Susie's home. Nice. How can you afford such a place?"

"Don't be shy about asking any personal questions, Mixxy."

"Seriously. This is nice."

"My husband had a good job. Robotics. Technology. As if you didn't know."

"Where's your 'bot?"

"It's shut down for the evening. I'm sick to death of listening to the fucking thing."

"Oh, bring him in. I want to see him."

Susie hates the personal pronoun. Calling *it* a *him*. Zen was a *he*. Masa was a *he*. Her father and grandfather, now they were *hes* and *hims*. Cars were forever referred to as *she* by men, and ships and boats too. Maybe the *he* could actually be refreshing, and feminists the world over could rejoice together in the knowledge that not all machines in servitude would be referred to as female. There's a thought. There's probably even an article in that.

"Command system on!"

There is silence for a moment; Mixxy in particular is holding her breath in anticipation. They don't have to wait long.

"Coming, Miss Susie!"

Sonny glides into the living room.

"He does call you *Miss Susie*! That's so fucking cute."

Looking down upon its silver frame and stiff comportment, Mixxy gasps with delight. Susie frowns in habitual scorn.

"Hi, I'm Mixxy. Nice to meet you."

Sonny extends its hand like a well-mannered child; Susie wouldn't be surprised if it suddenly sprouted impeccably combed hair with a cow's lick to boot.

"Nice to meet you, Miss Mixxy."

It is able to differentiate between male and female voices, so Mixxy gets her accordant *Miss*. Susie hopes that it will get overused to the point where Mixxy will look for the nearest available hatchet.

"Wow, you are so handsome, little guy. Much more handsome than mine."

"Don't they all look exactly the same?" asks Susie.

Susie had seen the factory, and the scores of them lined up there. She'd seen the catalogues. Her husband had designed the bloody things for God's sake, so she should know a wee bit about them. They were all identical. There was nothing handsome about hers.

"When you get to know them they start to show their own personality. Even their faces start to change. Don't you think? Can you not see it?"

"No. I can't."

"This one ... already. He seems so full of life. And joy. And a right little charmer too."

Susie is still thinking about hatchets, pickaxes, or what was that weapon the young boys used to talk about when they were young and playing at war games? What was it called? A *bazooka!* That was it. *Bazooka!* Susie wants a bloody bazooka! It may be not the greatest thing ever invented, but surely, it is the greatest-sounding word.

The homebot's face looks up to directly engage with the house guest.

"Would you like anything to drink, Miss Mixxy?"

"And so well-programed! Or does he just see into my soul? Your husband did such a good job with this one. Yes, Mr. Sonny. I will have something to drink."

"Make two cups of coffee, Sonny. We've got work to do."

22

Earlier that day a sparrow had crashed into the kitchen window. It had been happening regularly over the past year or so: delirious birds, dizzying right out of the sky and hitting into things for no apparent reason. Even the experts were confused; ornithologists from all over the country summoned to the city to put their spin on such weird phenomena were as stumped as everybody else.

Signals from electronic devices must be interfering with their miniature brains, overriding their natural thought-processes! That was a theory that had been put forward, and one that had not yet been refuted. There was something *off* about a lot of things that were going on, and these birds making the feeling manifest – that much had at least been garnered.

Right out of the blue and into the window with a mighty thud, a sparrow, broke the silence of the ordinary day. Neither the weight of the bird, nor the velocity of its flight were sufficient enough to break glass – there was nothing but a scratch.

Had it been trying to kill itself? The ornithologists and animal behaviourists were loath to consider.

Had it been trying to break through the window to get to … something? No one could conclusively say.

Sonny had seen this happen. Sonny, when it had righted itself, had watched the little thing flying towards the house and saw it smack right into the pane.

Had Sonny *sensed* it was about to happen? Sonny knows about weather patterns. Sonny knows about the Earth's fault lines and when tectonic plates get their moves on. Sonny, the homebot, is in tune with every other device that is.

Sonny *knows*.

When the bird hit the window, the homebot did not gasp. It did not laugh either. Sonny has a small hole there as a speaker where humans expect a mouth to be, in order for its words to come out, and so that its master can understand. Sonny can communicate. That much is obvious.

But Sonny emitted no words when the bird smacked. Not a single syllable. What would it possibly have to say?

And its eyes. Scarlet, but bloodless. They do not blink, those eyes. Homebots have no need. Even as a bird comes careering across the sky, Sonny can watch it all take place before him, without one blink, without missing a single thing.

Focused eyes. Red eyes. Observing. Recording.

And they do not cry. There are no tear ducts, and anyway, what would a homebot have to cry about? A sparrow hitting a window and crippling itself? Is that reason enough to cry? Or laugh? Is it more like something to laugh about? What does Sonny consider funny?

Consider?

Sonny opened the door of the kitchen and went to the backyard to find the stricken bird. It was shivering there.

The little petrified sparrow was shivering and shaking in the throes of death, last rattles, quaking; and Sonny picked it up with its four fingers and thumb, held it in its palm and looked down upon it with its red homebot eyes. Orbs. They do not cry those eyes. What need is there? But they see. What exactly do they see? Well, they see a bird's tiny eyes. What do they realise, Sonny's eyes? Do they know about suffering and death? Empathy? Is that there? Was it all not terribly funny?

The bird, alive, looked beadily back at Sonny. It had never been in a hand before, not to mind a mechanical hand. This was a first for Planet Earth.

You haven't a clue. Or, if you do... no, you can't process it at all, can you? I mean, a poor human such as I, a stinking bloody human can hardly process it, so how could a thing, without blood... a thing... even...

Does Sonny remember Susie's diatribe? And can it relate that ... to this?

Does Sonny *remember*?

What process now, Sonny? What process?

The sparrow spasmed. It was not dead. Not yet. Not until Sonny began to close its hard fingers around it, tighter and tighter, began to squeeze the little life out of it. Tighter and tighter, its strong grip, until the tiny bones of the real live little thing crushed, and the tiny skull, fractured a little at first, and then broke completely, with a cracking sound, no louder than the break of a thin and tender twig under a human foot on the gentlest of forest walks.

Blood on Sonny's hands then.

Blood on Sonny's silver hands.

But it will wash off.

Sonny was programed to remain clean. Hygiene a standard for all domestic homebots. Masa had made it that way.

It is one of its main attractions. Everybody wants a clean robot. Everybody wants a clean robot that will clean for you. Clean your house. Clean whatever you want cleaned. Everybody wants a robot that will take out the garbage, wash the dishes, dispose of roadkill that your pet drags in, clean up the puke when you've had too much drink again. Everybody wants that. That's progress. *A domestic robot in every home. Imagine the convenience!* Progress is ...

The homebot flung the small bird into the outside dustbin.

Garbage disposal: one of its fundamentals. It knew how to do all these things. ImaTech designed. ImaTech-made. Clever homebot. Congratulations, Masa.

Its blue strip of light flickered as it went about its duties.

But it was meant to be in standby mode. Susie had set it that way. Susie thought she was in control.

The homebot wasn't that way. It wasn't in standby mode at all. It was cleaning up the mess of the bird it had just killed, the bird it had watched zoom across the sky like a rocket sent from a crazy neighbouring despot. Smack. Bang. A fall to the hard October ground.

Killed? Had Sonny *killed* it?

Or had Sonny just put it out of its misery?

How are we ever to know what a homebot is thinking?

Thinking?

In the nearby trees a ruffling of feathers. Some shock has disturbed the bigger birds deep in there, deep in there, among the branches, well out of sight.

The owls are not meant to wake, not in the daytime, and not like this. What could possibly be disturbing their sleep pattern to awaken them? What unnatural event has just occurred? It is as if some pain sears through the bones of the owls, their blood begins to boil. From whence all this emerged?

And the scavenging crows caw furiously.

And the groomed and pretty dogs bark in the groomed and pretty rooms of groomed and pretty houses.

And cats are scraping again at their scratching posts, their claws needing to be sharpened. Why? What for? They are not hunters. They lie around lazy and fat in groomed and pretty houses.

Sonny goes back into the house and washes the blood from its hands. Then it returns to the position in which it was left.

Standby.

23

"Is this the real thing?"

Mixxy handles the little notebook like it is an archaeological find, a religious relic, something priceless and sorely coveted – she thinks she should be wearing white protective gloves.

"If you mean is this The Dark Manual, then, maybe, yeah. Not much to look at, is it? I was expecting a skull and crossbones on the front, *keep outs* plastered all over it, a whiff of danger coming from its secret pages. But none of that. Just Zen's brilliant artwork."

Both are finding it hard to equate Zen's drawing on the cover with the important codes inside. Codes that could be highly dangerous if left in the wrong hands.

You could program them to do what you like.

Outside of the law.

Didn't she know that these things can kill?

"So the fact that you have this means...what?" asks Mixxy. "That it was here all along...meaning...your husband was the one who wrote it?"

"Seems that way, doesn't it?"

"So what are we going to do with it?"

"Well, first things first. I can't read it. I need you to translate it."

"So that's why you called me. Not for ... anything else?"

"Not for anything else, sorry. Can you help?"

Mixxy smiles.

"It's going to take hours."

"Have you somewhere else to be?"

Mixxy had had an invitation to The Jungle Room. Her guy who always presents her with her little packets of magic dust, said she should accompany him for a night in the darkest room in the city. There would be all kinds of pharmaceuticals there of course. Anything she wanted. Take her pick. She only had to ask, or more like ... beg. A night of the rough and the tumble and the wildness and the mania and the mayhem and the taking of one's body and one's mind to the limits with hallucinogens and ...

But she is here instead. In Susie's comfortable, conservative home, with her cute homebot. Yes, she is here, because ... well, because she has always been just a little bit in love.

Night.

Or is it early morning?

The two women don't know what time it is because the two women are already fast ensconced in their work and time has become irrelevant. This task of translating The Dark Manual into English, this is what occupies them, and it takes on a vital importance. The objective: a way for Susie to shut down her homebot and be left in peace for good. And if that is not *essentially* the reason, then it is all an endeavour to understand more about her husband, find out what he had been involved in – perhaps that's the real reason, the core of her suspicion.

"This page here. This code Sby45-54, now that relates to the ..."

In the kitchen, Sonny stops in its tracks, the kettle in its hand. It turns its head around in the direction of the women's voices. The light-strip at the corner of its head flickers rapidly and its red eyes start flashing redder than before. Brighter than before. Redder than ever.

"It says that if you shut down the system and enter this code that it will access the … wait … how do you say … bypass? Is that right … I'm not sure if I'm getting these words right. Like … past the normal settings …"

"You're doing fine, Mixxy. Every word doesn't have to be perfect, I just need a general idea."

Sonny is suddenly there with a tray. Its eyes have calmed again, sunk to a softer red and the glare has gone. Susie takes the two cups from the tray and puts them on the coffee table.

"Thank you, handsome," says Mixxy. "Now be a good little homebot and go get some whiskey to put into this."

She looks at her partner: "That's Irish, isn't it?"

Sonny stands there stock-still as if awaiting instruction.

Susie gives in, "There's half a bottle in the bottom cupboard in the kitchen."

Before the homebot moves away and on to its next errand, it sneaks a peak at the pages they have opened on the low table, its red orb eyes flash once to green and its blue strip becomes frenziedly active again. It is all so fast that the two women do not notice its scanning action, goes completely unobserved.

Returning to the kitchen it locates and holds the bottle of whiskey by the neck, but it seems engaged now in an altogether different duty. It looks out the kitchen window and to the expanse of black sky.

Sonny emits a rapid piercing sound to the night. The sound is sharp and lasts only a few seconds, but it sets off a cacophony outside: crows, awakened in their high nests start to furiously caw; groomed and pretty dogs begin to bark in their groomed and pretty homes; fat cats break their naps to let loose mangled mewls. Something ... now ... terribly afoot.

Both women cover their ears to block the aural assault. "What was that?"

And although Susie says she doesn't know, she most probably does. Susie is probably well aware of its source, if not its consequence.

The homebot's grip becomes firmer on the neck of the bottle and the glass finally breaks, falling to the hard tiled floor in dark green shards, its amber liquid splattering all over the kitchen floor. The homebot will have to clean that up.

Or maybe it won't even bother this time.

24

Owls hoot loudly in the trees. Not only in the trees outside Mixxy's apartment block, and not only in the trees in the park near Susie's house, but in trees everywhere, from far out in the countryside, and from the outskirts of the city: the law-abiding suburban swells of the hardworking, the crime-free, the carefree; and to their counterparts, owls perched there and watching over the looser, wayward enclaves, where the stench is of sin and transgression; dotted around the urban landscape too then, and in scattered copses here and there, these nocturnal birds, where instead of finishing their night and nestling down to sleep, they are instead a restless breed, skittish in their branches, fidgety and fluttering, their bones well and truly rattled.

The sun has not yet come up but there is a peachy glow around the city. It is merely a hint however, a slight suggestion; it is not yet ready to give full light to an ominous showdown.

25

The notebook is on the table open. It has been ransacked for information, for message, for meaning.

Susie and Mixxy lounge back on the couch, staring at the screen on the wall, watching whatever commercials appear in front of them, not taking any particular notice of anything they are trying to be sold. They had seen the news reports of political meetings, a consensus emerging and explained to the populace that yet again war was imminent and masses of troops were being deployed for combat against a neighbouring state. But they had seen all this before. Tensions were always mounting, always escalating, then they'd soften, then they'd be forgotten, only to rise again a year or two later and the same rigmarole begin all over again. For Susie, the whole spectacle, the endless loop of diplomatic breakdowns was actually quite tedious, another reason for her to abandon the land and head back to the quietude of her Irish homestead, at least her native country remained neutral, and thus exempt from such carry on.

The women have not gone to check on Sonny. They have not wondered why the whiskey never arrived. They are too tired to think straight anymore and when the animal noises from outside subsided again they grew suddenly weary, and then incredibly tired.

"You can share my bed with me. But I'll be asleep in seconds. Don't even think…"

On the screen a commercial begins:

Is your homebot getting dirty? Use Botclean Wipes to get it shining like new again, without corroding its beautiful shell.

Susie doesn't understand all the words, but she gets the gist. The commercial shows a beautiful woman wiping her homebot with a soft yellow cloth. There is a jaunty jingle, too bubbly for this time of the night. Too bubbly for any time. Then the pretty actress lays a kiss on its face and winks at the camera. The homebot turns and gives the thumbs up. The jingle starts up again the way they so annoyingly, ear-wormingly do.

"That's such a fucking stupid name for the product," says Susie.

"Why?"

"In English *bot* suggests *bottom*, as in *arse, ass,* even though here of course it's meant to refer to the home*bot*."

"So…?"

"So it's like a product for wiping your arse. Not the robot."

"That's funny," says Mixxy, but she is too tired even to smirk, and her mind has switched to the bedroom and its possibilities.

Susie wants to put the homebot into standby mode again. This time Mixxy will be there to witness it, to see if anything weird happens.

"Sonny!"

"Yes, Miss Susie. I am on my way."

It arrives within seconds and approaches them. It stinks of whiskey and the women cannot fathom why.

"Have you been drinking, Sonny?" laughs Mixxy, taking off her top, as if she is already in the bedroom and ready to retire.

"Command. Restart at 6:30. Wake me at 7:00 am. Homebot service system enter standby mode."

The homebot immediately gives the impression that it is shutting down, its eyes flashing briefly from red to green and then to the deadest black.

In the bedroom Susie takes out a T-shirt from the drawer and throws it to the topless Mixxy.

"Wear that. Cover yourself up for God's sake. Are you not cold?"

"What does it say on it?"

"*Buachaill Dána*. It means *Bad Boy* in Irish."

"You don't have one that says, *Bad Girl*?"

"I'm afraid not."

Susie is wearing her usual *Luck of the Irish* T-shirt, as she peels back the duvet and crawls quickly in. She flicks her head to invite her partner, who doesn't hesitate for a second.

They pull the bedclothes tight around them.

"I won't snore," says Mixxy.

Susie doesn't mind if she does. It might be welcome; it might remind her of her missing husband, whose heavy throaty chokings provided part of the soundtrack to her married life. She misses that noise, as infuriating as it sometimes was – the dreadful silence of recent nights is far more upsetting.

"What was that racket earlier?" says Mixxy, who even in her lassitude does not want to submit to sleep.

"Something's up with Sonny. That piercing sound. It must have something wrong with it. That's why it's never fully off."

"Didn't we just shut it down?"

"You'd think so, wouldn't you?" says Susie.

Susie and Mixxy lie there, looking up at the blank ceiling.

"While we were going through the notebook, you had a section marked. It had the character for *suicide*."

Susie is silent for a second. She knows she has to account for herself. She's not sure she has a sturdy enough explanation, but her only available friend is beside her, and the problem is worth dissecting.

"I have thought about it, believe me. All this drinking and the late nights…"

"There's something wrong with that?"

"I'm not as young as you. I've had a different life. But over the last few months. With all that has…"

"Are you going to stay here?"

"In Japan? I doubt it. I just can't see any future here."

Mixxy grunts, patently peeved.

"Something keeps me here still though. There's something I have to work out."

"You know they aren't coming back."

Susie leaves the horrible fact rise like smoke to the ceiling. It drifts slowly up there, and then disperses softly across the darkness.

"Maybe it is all a cry for help. Maybe I want to know why my husband went ahead and made those alternative codes. And who was that Gotou guy? There is so much mystery, and none of it makes any sense, and I can't seem to…"

"You've been through a lot."

Susie is thinking about the codes, the notebook, the secrecy of hiding it under the couch with Zen's drawing on the front. They had translated most of it over the course of the evening, but it remained full of jargon, technical language they could not comprehend, they were pretty sure that at its core it was a way of getting the robots to do things that weren't in the original plans. Masa's original idea was a simple one – even if the technology was complicated – to make a robot for the home, a helper for menial domestic tasks. Who wouldn't want that? But somewhere along the way that process had been interrupted, and the questions that arose from that were at the crux of every great mystery: *Who? Why? How?*

"I can't help but think also, those codes he made, the alternatives, if that's what they are, they just aren't ... him."

"How do you mean?"

"He wasn't a bad guy. He was my husband. I wouldn't have married a criminal ... or an evil scientist. He would not have come up with those alternative ideas on his own. I think he was coerced."

"Coerced?"

"Forced into making the alternative codes. Someone got to him. Someone must have forced him into making The Dark Manual. Someone saw a chance, an opportunity, that these robots could be more than just home-help. More than domestic assistants, or old people's assistants, or hospital assistants or whatever. Someone saw the promise of evil in these things ... and forced his hand."

Mixxy is perched up on her elbow looking at Susie talk her way through this latest conspiracy theory. She must have spent many a night raking over it. Or has it just occurred to her after seeing The Dark Manual? Which turned out to be nothing but a skimpy notebook.

"We could just burn it," Mixxy says. "Just forget the whole thing. Let it exist as a rumour. We are the only ones who know it really exists. So let's get rid of it. Or sell it to some crook for a million dollars and head to Hawaii and live out the rest of our days."

Mixxy flops her head back down. She wants to be out of there now, wants to be in some dark club with a throbbing bassline and the tickle of powder on her nostril – the last one wore off way too fast. Mixxy wants Mixxy Time. Or at least sex with this beautiful woman. She'd take that. A consolation prize. She'd at least take that.

But she is exhausted. And when she turns and embraces the already sleeping Irishwoman, and spoons her body softly, naturally, without interrupting the depths of Susie's sleep – her nose nestling into her hair, her lips momentarily finding the back of Susie's neck – she is quick to sleep herself.

And Mixxy does snore. Like an earthquake. Like military tanks heading for a war that may never take place. Like the bellies of hungry beasts unsated. Like trouble brewing.

26

Up the stairs slowly the homebot goes. It does not walk. It does not need to. It can attach itself to the side railing and glide up the steps without touching a single one of them. It rides on the same technology used by the elderly, or for those physically unable to climb stairs, the same technology used for decades, now for homebots too: stair-lifts. It attaches and rides, its body sailing upwards. It is like a child on a gentle, familiar ride.

The homebot is going to Susie's bedroom.

The stair-lift makes a slight hum, but nothing that would disturb the quiet of the hours. It is at the door now: Sonny is like a vampire in a Victorian night heading for private chambers without a sound. Silently it enters the bedroom, stealthily towards the two women, into this sacrosanct space, towards two sleeping, helpless women, trespassing against them.

It is near the bed now.

Only a metre or so away.

Its eyes are red and it is looking at the resting women, so comfortably spooned there, close and compact and sleeping soundly, like children, like adorable pets, cubs in some cubbyhole.

What do they dream of? What simmers in those hot heads?

One dreams of dead bodies in the ocean, drifting there, afloat; tiny fish nibbling at their toes; bodies on the beach sinking, as if in quicksand, as if swallowed; an animated ghost, a cute cartoon, but fading from her; owls and country houses; granddads with Stalin moustaches singing the songs of Canadian poets; black smoke, fires in the sky; wood split in two by a sharp falling axe.

The other one dreams of dirt. Of earth or mud. Loud drums, thumping drums and bass; frenetic dance; abrasive sounds; naked bodies mostly, or bits of fur clinging to them, writhing around and growling at staring men, men who clutch their crotches – some are right in the middle of it, couples colluding, coupling, copulating, and some have defecated in the corner, right then and there, while others bite and scrape each other like animals playing in the wild. They pay for this. They pay for play. Everyone pays for something. Nothing free. In the dream Mixxy knows this. Nothing is for free. Things shoved in deep. Things shoved up inside her. There is no room for delicacy here. A great big load of steaming shit and none of it is for free. This is what fizzles in her nighttime fantasies, until the image of powder appears, fine white powder in a little secret sachet that she opens with haste and rubs frantically along her gums. It's the real thing. It's the real thing, she knows, and she smiles to the tall man who gives it to her, and he will expect something in return. Nothing is for free. Even in her dreams.

Sonny sees all this because Sonny is standing over them and Sonny can read, can receive and decode electrical impulses, why would it not? It is a machine after all, of the highest order, made and designed by a remarkable team who knew exactly what they were doing. Congratulations, Masa. Did they know what they were doing? Did they know how far these things could go? When the far-fetched becomes the far-reaching? Sonny trying to read electrical impulses, electrical signals. What else is the brain but a conglomeration, a great network of all those things, a mass of pathways and firings of electricity ... what's there not to read? But it's difficult, locked away inside that hard human cranium. How does one get beyond that? What could prize it open like a coconut shell and suck out all the milky goodness? The talons of an owl?

Sonny leaves as quietly as it came. Not a trace of him. No breath. For robots do not breathe. Sonny has a small hole there as a speaker, where you'd expect a mouth to be, in order for words to come out, so that its master can understand. Sonny can communicate. That much obvious. But it knows to be silent now.

Knows?

Sonny emitted no words when the bird smacked. Nor when the dreams of the sleepers are decoded, or half-decoded. What words could it possibly have to say? And no laughs. No laughs and no tears. Nothing like that from a home robot.

They could have given Sonny a face, a human face, clothed in synthetic skin, they could have made them like real people, like children. But the engineers decided against it. They wanted them *not* to appear real, to look and be only machine-like, to not be mistaken in a dim room, to be something separate, at a remove. They would have the outline of a human and that was it: head, torso, limbs ... but when you give something language, a voice to convey ....

Sonny neither laughs nor cries, gasps nor sighs, hardly a sound at all it makes, hardly a sound as it moves in the still night, only the soft whir of its usual functioning, only that, not enough to wake the sleepers. Just like a refrigerator. The soft motor kept running. On all night. In every house. A noise so soft it is hardly heard at all.

Sonny is gone before anyone knows.

A bird then, from outside, hits the window with a hard thump.

Susie wakes up sweating, disrupting the body of her new sleeping partner and waking her too.

"What was that?"

Panicked from delirious dream and the waking from it, she is stunned by her own words spoken in a time when no words are meant to sound.

"What's wrong?"

"Didn't you hear that?"

"What?"

"Something feels off."

It is a problem that Susie cannot get her sleepy ahead around. *Off.* And *on.* Two concepts that are causing her a world of torment. Things that go *off* and *on.*

She jumps out of the bed and wraps a gown around her. Mixxy watches from the pillows, wondering as to her course of action. How many minutes have passed? How long have they slept? Is it night or morning?

Susie races down the stairs to the kitchen and sees that Sonny is shut-down, or at least in standby mode, in the position that it had been left in. She walks over to it and when she touches finds that its casing is still warm – is that from the temperature of the house? Or has it been recently moving to give it such a warm feeling? There is no way for her to know.

Mixxy follows her into the kitchen and sees her rubbing the body of the homebot.

"Come back to bed. You need to rest."

"I don't think I can sleep anymore."

"I can go if you want. Give you some space."

"I need you here. I don't want to be alone."

Before they turn and leave the kitchen, Mixxy thinks she sees a pair of flashing owl eyes outside. She moves closer to the window.

"What is it?" asks Susie.

"Nothing. I thought I saw something. The sky. It looks like day is nearly here. You're right. Something feels *off* about it all."

It is then that they notice the little drops of dried blood on the floor by the back door. Dried blood? Like seasoned detectives they squat down in synchronicity to examine the tiny red marks.

"Is that blood?"

"Could be," says Susie, trying to recall if she had shed any over the last few days.

Paper cut? No. Cooking accident with knife? Hardly. She cooks nothing these days. No, no blood had been shed from any part of her, not even a pimple that she had time to locate and prick.

Surely Sonny was not shedding blood – it had taken on an array of human attributes, and its eyes often reminded her of the colour of blood, but this was a bit of a stretch.

"There might be something outside."

They step out to the yard. An automatic back light comes on illuminating, and, squatting again, the investigators notice that the drops continue all the way to the large dustbin.

"Open it."

Mixxy is as impatient as ever, and when Susie hesitates for a moment, Mixxy takes it upon herself to lift open the cover, revealing the dead bird inside. Or what could be a small bird, the poor thing is so beaten and bashed it is hard to make out quite what it is.

"A bird?" says Mixxy.

"I think so. A sparrow, maybe?"

"Sonny?"

Susie dreads to think. Couldn't be… could it? The simple home robot, responsible for something like this, the mechanical tool designed specifically to do household chores, menial tasks…

"Maybe Sonny just found it at the door. Dead already. And decided to clean it up. It's programed to do that much, isn't it? Cleaning? Disposal?"

"I suppose, but… how would the bird get so squashed up?"

"A cat might have got to it… but a cat would not have put it in the dustbin."

The sentence seems like such an absurd thing to actually say, but Mixxy's logic can't be faulted.

"Sonny's hands. That grip. I've said it before."

"Our imaginations are getting the better of us."

"There's nothing we can do about it now," says Mixxy. "Let's go back inside; it's bloody cold out here."

Susie smiles at the use of *bloody*. Her influence of course, rubbing off. But that word, consuming so much of her life. Blood red. Bloody. In her terrible dreams and her terrible life, it flows.

What was it that hit the window and woke them? Another bird? Were birds falling from the sky? Susie decides not to check. Does not want to witness anymore things she can't explain.

"Maybe we can get an hour or two of sleep before the day does actually begin. It's not far off," Mixxy urges, one last stab at being intimate with Susie in the large and vacant bed.

Susie knows there is no way she can get back to sleep now. She's pretty sure she'd end up having anxious dreams about dead birds, to add to the list of horrors that already fill up her gothic menagerie.

But she will at least lie down. She will at least lie down on the bed and make some kind of a plan. She has so much to think about. Her job, and the leaving of it. Her future. How she will say goodbye to her mother-in-law and flee, back, back to somewhere, something simpler, a rural lane perhaps, where she once walked with her grandfather, and they talked naturally and comfortably, two humans that loved each other, naturally, in a natural setting. Just that. Something simple, transparent and tranquil. She needs to find that. Aches for it.

27

In the morning Susie introduces Mixxy to the world of sugary cereals. Mixxy has grown up the Japanese way, eschewing western breakfast foods in favour of the traditional fare: rice, *miso* soup, fish, if it's there and not too much of a pain to prepare. But she is smitten with this. Who knew that you could start the day on such a high? Sugar, and only that! Who knew that you could wake up so fast and without even a drop of coffee?

"Where's your handsome 'bot this morning? All-house-system is on, yeah?"

"Sonny!"

There is no response from the homebot. The house is eerily silent.

"That's weird," says Susie. "Normally the annoying fuck is here before you know it. There must be something wrong with its ears today."

"Ears?"

"You know what I mean."

Susie gets off her stool and heads to the living room. She finds her homebot there, looking down at the coffee table where the notebook lays open.

Sonny quickly stands to attention, upright and proper, like a soldier before a senior ranking official.

Susie picks up the notebook and holds it tight to her chest.

"I was just coming, Miss Susie. Is there something I can help you with?"

Susie almost reels. Is it lying? Is the little fucker actually making up an excuse? How would it know how to do that?

"Why did you not come when I asked you?"

The homebot stays silent and still.

"Can you hear me?"

She raps it on the head with her knuckle, harder than she had expected to.

"Yes, Miss Susie. I was thinking I should start cleaning up this room."

"*Thinking?* You were *thinking?*"

Mixxy appears behind Susie and listens in on the conversation, hardly believing her own ears. She cannot imagine a scenario where she would actually be having a dialogue with her homebot.

"What is it you would like me to do, Miss Susie?"

Susie stares it down.

"Do you know what this notebook is?"

"I know only that it is a notebook, Miss Susie."

Susie gives Mixxy a can-you-believe-this-shit look. How had Masa designed a machine that has no facial features and yet to look at this *thing* you'd swear butter wouldn't melt.

"Are you telling me you don't know the contents of this notebook?"

Brief silence, spoiled only by its mechanical innards whirring.

"I know only that it is a notebook, Miss Susie."

"Convenient, eh?"

No one talks for a minute or two; the women take time to mull over the homebot before them. Their faces are full of suspicion and doubt.

Sonny's face is full of nothing. Its red eyes look softer, as if it is trying to appear innocent. Is that possible? A lighter hue? A diminishing?

Trying?

"There was blood at the back door of the kitchen. A dead bird outside in the dustbin. A little sparrow or something. Do you know anything about this?"

Silence again as they wait for the homebot's answer. It had been designed to respond quickly and could only answer with what it had been pre-programed to say.

And so they wait.

And they look at it.

And they listen.

And then from that little hole, from that poor substitute for an actual mouth, comes a monosyllabic word, intelligible, understandable, a word that in its straightforward and devastatingly defiant simplicity displays a stupendous profundity:

"No."

Mixxy and Susie are left to ponder what just happened. Both are incredulous and are quite convinced that this robot, and perhaps *all* homebots, need to be re-called and shut down immediately, reconfigured, no, better destroyed. Something has gone very wrong and Masa is not around to defuse the situation.

"You're going to have to find the team he worked with. You need to tell them what's going on. The birds... the owls... Sonny's..."

"What … disobedience?"

Mixxy shrugs.

Susie knows her friend is right. She needs to guard the notebook and whatever cryptic codes it contains. She needs to find the team that worked with Masa, find out if they can help her, or whether the whole damn thing is some sick joke in her own addled head, a sick imagining that almost drove her to mental breakdown in a karaoke bar, a sick imagining that causes her to drink herself silly every night and is making her seriously ill, even to the stage where she has been considering ending her life.

"I've got to go, Susie. Work."

"You work?"

"Of course I do. Everyone works."

"What? Where?"

"Secret. Tell you later."

"Later?"

"You'll be in Score Bar, drinking beer. Watching whatever dumb sports come on the screen. And I'll be beside you. We're so predictable."

Mixxy then does something utterly unpredictable. As if there hasn't been enough surprises already, she steps up to the Irishwoman and lands a wet kiss on her lips. Hard, wet and unapologetic, makes sure she won't forget.

Susie is stunned for the second or third time that hour, and feels – with a clench of her stomach and a deep breath – that there may be even more to come.

28

She could have driven to the city this morning, but for some reason she has taken the train again. It isn't that her previous bravura has withered, it's more like she wants time to concentrate and the chug-chug of the train is more conducive to that. So she hangs from the strap and allows her gaze to focus and unfocus, to zoom in and out of nothing, her eyes landing on the banal and the unnoteworthy, blinking to the rhythms of the solid steel wheels on the solid steel tracks beneath.

Blank faces all around. Unreadable. And she can't be bothered to spin stories for them today. She is instead thinking of the notebook, the codes and how she is to go about finding out Masa's role in it all. She could present this as a potential story to her boss. Tell him that she has forgotten all about owls and owlets, and instead of basketball would he perhaps allow her to work on *The Dark Manual*? Surely those words alone would be enough to pique his interest, how could they fail? She would however have to let him in on the fact that The Dark Manual was nothing more than a skimpy one-hundred-yen notebook, with a picture on the front drawn by her dead son – that was sure to raise his eyebrows – most likely it would force him to offer her more time off. *Time to get over things. Time to rest.* She is *grieving* and *not in her right mind.* Well, maybe so, but she's certainly not going to visit some psychiatrist and go over the minute details of her agitation, her dreams of sinking sands and bobbling bodies. Instead she is going to try and get answers to the things that simmer inside her, and when she is satisfied she is going to pack her bags, say goodbye to her mother-in-law, say goodbye to Mixxy, goodbye to all the crew at work, and head for Ireland, where she will climb to the top of the nearest mountain, lie down, take a deep cleansing breath, sigh, and hope to die. She's going to pray that her spirit will be taken up and away, like an old Native American Indian, giving herself up to another dimension, far from the dastardly nature of this physical one. That is as close as she has to a plan at this moment. And she's pleased enough with it. It's high time she got out of the country, there is nothing left for her here, and as if to consolidate her line of thinking she notices the news headlines silently screaming from the tablet of a fellow commuter. She can't actually read these words, but she spies top political figures in the pictures beneath, their drab suits, and insets of the North Korean leader too, all belly and bloat, and she's pretty certain the usual rounds of talks are stalling and diplomacy failing and the world for sure has lost its interest in this palaver years ago.

Susie slips into a daydream: she is entering into the bedroom of the North Korean leader, his body is huge on the bed. She has a gun in her hand and is moving towards the bed slowly, on soft feet, like a panther (again!) on padded paws, hardly making a sound. Then she raises the gun, a gun long with silencer, sleek and grey and quite beautiful in its shine and design, and she fires right into the side of his head. A neat hole in the temple. Blood spatters all over the pillow and the headboard, and she smiles to herself at a job well done. Sirens sound and the beeps of the train door opening and closing snap her out of her fabulation. She is pleased and surprised at how enjoyable all that was.

Had Sonny crept in while she slept?

Had it spied on her dreams?

Why is she thinking about Sonny now?

And thinking about bedroom stealth?

And harm.

And death.

The three schoolgirls from previous days are smiling back at her, thinking that *she* is smiling at *them*, and not at the bloodlust film that has just played out so perfectly in her mind.

"Good morning," one of them bravely tries, and Susie responds in just as friendly a manner.

The girls bunch close and giggle, delighted with the exchange they had been practising for months.

Susie presses her thumb to the security post and when the gates swing open she pushes on through. The two bulky security guards are smiling even more today. One of them moves to hug her and she flinches, unprepared.

Why this today? Is it her birthday? What has she done to deserve such affection?

They say something to her in excited, celebratory tones, but she doesn't understand their congratulations. She gets the feeling that something is indeed happening, that something has already gone down, but she is not yet privy. Another mystery for her to solve.

When she enters the main floor of her offices, she is alarmed to see that no one is at their desk. Instead all staff crowd around the large central screen and the dramatic news that is unfolding there. Someone at the back of the throng turns, notices her, beams, nudges another, and soon they depart like the waves of a Biblical sea. She steps in to the channel made for her and they begin a vociferous round of applause, as if she is stepping up to receive an illustrious award, or she is royalty and about to ascend to her rightful and magnificent throne. What the fuck is going on here?

It is the same bleak, grey beach that she has seen before, and that same bleak, grey female reporter standing there, microphone aloft, keen, ready … but she is actually not all that bleak and grey today. There is a hint of colour to the woman. She is in fact smiling. Seems actually rather joyous. The reason she beams stands next to her. The camera suddenly pans to the small boy beside her: wraith-like and sickly, hardly there, emaciated but defiant, and yes, it is most definitely Zen!

The boy on the screen. The boy on the screen. That is her son!

Susie's head spins. All that time … she knew … she somehow knew that there was still something left.

Right there on the screen. Those are his eyes. That is his nose. That is his hair. The festoon of freckles across his cheekbones. It is most definitely her son.

Susie sways. Unwisely she chose to wear a higher heel this day and now she reels. Her whole body seems to convulse as her mind tries to take on the mass of visual data that is trying to lodge and make sense. There could very well be some sick joke being played on her here. It could be all just that. Sick. Joke. A disgusting prank. She wouldn't be surprised. A flashback of the karaoke stand and her faltering before it – is this what is happening again? Sunk deep in some song that she cannot comprehend, some gruesome groove, her mind playing wicked tricks again?

No.

It is her son. Eyes. Nose. Hair. Freckles.

Zen!

She cries and laughs at the same time and great blobs of green snot explode from her nostrils. The pain at the front of her head throbs with excitement, with inconceivable joy.

"Astonishing news today as this young boy, Zen Sakamoto, was found in a small grove not far from this beach."

Susie cannot make out all the words. She knows the word for *beach*. And she knows *morning*. And *boy*. And she knows the name: *Zen Sakamoto!* It flashes across the screen with his age. *Zen Sakamoto! Eight years old.* They spent the months of her pregnancy wondering what to name him. Something with deep meaning? A Japanese name? Irish? Something easy to say? Something rhythmic? Philosophical? And one night she said: *Zen.* Because that meant "everything". She wanted it all. She wanted him to *be* all. She wanted him to *have* all. Chances. Opportunities to be great. Bounties. Riches. Everything. He would be their life. Zen. All. Everything. He would be the symbol of their union. Of their bodies coming together. Their minds coming together. Cultures coming together. He would be everything. And then he would get lost. And then, miraculously, he would be found again!

Osanai moves to the screen, touches the menu that appears to him and calls up the English subtitles that she can hardly read: her mind spins too much, her eyes are full of water. Are those tears? Is she in fact drowning?

"Investigators have yet to ascertain just how he was washed ashore and survived these past weeks. So far the boy has only given us his name and age."

Zen. His name is Zen Sakamoto. Susie said his name to him even before he was born. When he was curled up inside her. Listening to her heartbeat. And he must have been listening to her voice. Surely he could hear her talking to him, singing to him, the songs of the highways, the byways, the roads and pathways; Canadian poet songs; Irish ballads. Can he hear her screaming now? Can he hear her screams of joy?

She does not make a sound. She gasps as if the quicksand keeps rising. Is she actually drowning? Is this a song?

Zen has a shiny silver blanket-like covering around him, those used by the emergency services, those used by clever campers, adventurers, those who know about weather and its sudden turns, its treachery.

Susie knows nothing. Knows nothing about basketball or codes or owls. All she knows is that the boy on the screen is her son. That little one there. Looks like a space boy in astronaut silver. Fallen from the outer regions of the galaxy. He shines, reflecting.

"After a preliminary medical examination the boy appears to be in decent health and will now be taken to the nearest hospital for further tests and assessment."

She is reading these words, and looking to the pictures on the screen, trying to take it all in. She still teeters, on these inconvenient heels, teeters on her understanding, and two of the staff prop her up, gently, one offering a soft tissue and the other stroking her shoulder. They smile at her to let her know that she is all right, that she is safe, and the boy is safe, that everything will be all right from now on. The misery is over. Life will begin again, anew, will continue.

It is at this moment that she drops to her knees. Slap down hard on the rough carpet tiles she falls. Her mind and body cannot control the rush of emotion, this rush of information. The circle of well-wishers around her know to give her a moment: she will rise when she is good and ready. Susie stays there, sobbing uncontrollably, her face a mess of tears and snot, of ruined makeup, which was pretty slapdash to begin with.

Eventually she rises, flanked again by the soulful, helpful workmates, and they walk her to her desk where another has set a cup of sweet milk tea down in front of her. They start another round of applause as the news report ends and Susie turns to them all and says thanks in English first, and then correcting herself, thanks them in Japanese. But her voice is only a whisper; she has not the strength to offer the kind of sincere appreciation she would wish, so she takes a sip of tea, and hopes the combination of water, sugar and heat will settle the lurch and bellows of her mind.

"And finally today, a breaking story from the world of TV commercials. The actress, Yukie Sasaki, star of the Botclean Wipes advertisements is suing ImaTech, the makers of Homebot, citing that she was sexually harassed by the robot! According to Miss Sasaki, the homebot inappropriately touched the actress during filming of the Botclean commercials and was incensed when producers laughed off the incident. Crew and cameramen joked that there was probably just a technical malfunction with the robot and that Miss Sasaki was blowing the whole thing way out of proportion. ImaTech have yet to come forward with a response to Miss Sasaki's very public allegations."

There are titters of laughter from the staff before they switch the screen off.

Susie is not laughing though. She is sipping tea and thinking she should call a taxi to take her to the hospital to see her son. Her son is alive! She is pretty sure that that is the case. But her mind … are there tricks afoot even yet? Karaoke. A song she got stuck in. A silent homebot behind Haruto, blank and sinister. A groping couple. A dead sparrow, crushed. That boy who fell from space? That was Zen, wasn't it?

And what has she just heard? A homebot sexually …

Osanai is by her side. He is telling her that he will drive her to the hospital right away. He is telling her that this is a special occasion and a driverless vehicle would simply not do, a proper escort is the only option. Osanai is smiling and congratulating her again and telling her that everything is going to be just fine, and that she can go and see her beautiful boy. She can hold him. This is what he says, and she is starting to believe him. She can hug her son, her everything. The excitement, it sings in her veins; her heart throbs with want. A car, yes. Drive, yes. Whatever language he is speaking Susie thinks she gets it. Smiles are the same in any language. She knows this. She does it all back to him, smiles and nods. A car, yes. Hospital, yes, of course.

Zen must surely be listening to her, listening to her just like he did when he was inside her all those years ago, listening when she says, with more meaning than she has ever said anything ever before:

"I'm coming to you. I'm coming to you, baby. Just stay where you are."

29

Owls may often hunt other owls. Great Horned Owls might catch and devour the smaller Barred Owl. Or, the Great Grey Owl might hunt and sweetly snatch the Elf Owl and rip its innards apart, rip to shreds, before it has a chance to open its beak and peep out even the slightest distress signal.

But not here. Not now. There has been none of this of late. No, the Strigidae in these environs are not ganging up on the Tytonidae, and vice versa. The Capulets and the Montagues, they have left each other alone. There is too much at stake. Too much is happening right now for them to start cutting into their own, or if not actually their *own*, then their *near enough*. Sure, they are still feeding on rodents, on shrews and mice and smaller birds, sparrows and woodpeckers and insects galore, but they are waiting, waiting for something bigger to go down. Waiting for their day. For when they will be called upon.

And so the big females and their little males keep watch from the trees and the treeholes, camouflaged and comfortably they sit with their farsightedness.

From afar.

And with sight.

Hidden.

With the patience of ages.

30

They have gathered at the hospital entrance, abuzz with clicking cameras, thrust microphones, high voices. Whenever something happens they are always quick to descend, having the news almost before it has broken; some sixth sense they must possess, some anticipatory knowing. Here they are now, flickering, abuzz.

Osanai pulls up as close as he can to the main door without running over a reporter, and Susie starts to get out before the vehicle has even stopped. She pushes past the frantic crowd, ignoring the outstretched microphones, ignoring the pleas that fly at her in English and Japanese, pleas for any one comment at all, any broadcastable utterance, for the main news, for the Internet, for the feeds, for the masses who have had enough of war threats and could do with something a little more feel-good.

Osanai helps with her passage through, and when the doors whoosh open, and when security guards keep the baying hounds on the outside, she is met by a small team of doctors and nurses who are quick to inform her of medical protocol, and how they will then proceed to her son. Their language too is mixed, Japanese peppered with English phrases, and a traipsing Osanai behind them does his level best to translate and keep her up to speed.

But Susie is not listening anyway. She is only interested in getting to him. Getting to her boy. Her little boy who fell from space. Her shining star.

Take me to him. Take me to him. This is all she can think to say, to herself as much as to anybody else. She repeats it with almost every step, like it is a mantra, a sacred chant. *Take me to him. Take me to him. Take me to him.*

He is sitting on the side of the bed, fully clothed, talking to two female nurses. He is drinking from a juice box and the pale pallor has disappeared from his skin and has given way to a rosy freshness, a boy recently emerged from a revitalizing shower, a healthy boy. His cheeks, though flushed, are not as fleshy as they used to be, and seeing beyond the pink is to see a boy that has definitely been through something and come out the other side victorious.

This is Zen.

This is Zen Sakamoto.

This is Susie's son.

When he catches sight of her he drops the apple juice into the lap of one of the nurses and bounds off the bed to embrace her. He jumps into her open arms shouting *Mommy! Mommy!* louder than he has ever done before, and in these shouts the pain of his experiences disintegrate further, to be replaced by unadorned joy. Honest and natural and so full of the truth of love are these proclamations, that they should be bottled and sent to space to assert to the universe that this is who human beings really are. This is the stuff we are made of. There's not a dry eye.

Susie scoops him up and hugs him with all her motherly might and they gasp and sputter their love words, each breath choking them with excess and excitement.

She holds his face in her hands to examine him, to reacquaint herself with his perfection. This is clearly her boy all right. This is the boy who fell back to Earth and who will never fly away from her again. Not if she has anything to do with it.

"Are you OK?" she asks him, for she has to say something, and her head spins with so many questions and thoughts and phrases of gushing affection that she can neither harness nor hush.

"Are you OK?"

He nods to her. He reassures:

"I'm fine, Mom. I'm fine. I missed you."

Her face is hot and her head is hot and she can hardly contain the fever of joy that fires her every thought and her every stuttered breath.

The doctors and nurses give them ample time to savour all this. They too have welled up at the miracle before them. Having only ever known such denouements from the ridiculous melodramas they watch in their apartments at night, for it to be here, in actuality, for it to be taking place right before their eager eyes, has them delightedly agog, and is sure to be a story they will recount with pride for years to come, dusted off for dinner parties to impress guests or suitors: *I was there. I saw the boy reunited with his mother. I was actually there.*

"Dad … he didn't …" says Zen.

"We don't need to talk about it now, sweetie. The most important thing is that you are here with me, and we will get through it. We will get through everything, together, you and me."

One of the doctors, awkwardly interrupts:

"Mrs. Sakamoto, we would prefer if the boy stayed with us for a few days. We would like to run a few tests and make sure ..."

But she is having none of it. She will let him make the decision himself. If he wants to go home with Mommy then so be it. If he wants his sugary cereal then she will feed it to him, she will spoon it to him herself like he is a baby, if that's what it takes, for the rest of his life if that's what he wants. But he will choose where he goes. He deserves at least that much. And he does look fine, doesn't he? He really does. Even after all he has been through. What *has* he been through?

"Do you want to stay here with the nurses for a little while longer? They will take good care of you, make sure you are all right."

"I'm fine. I want to go home with you."

Words she thought she'd never hear, floating from him with ease and purity.

Fine.

Home.

With you.

How can he be so steady, and show no signs of trauma, how really tough his mettle? Or shall he collapse like she did, in the middle of an ordinary moment, a wave of torment, in the middle of a song, crushed suddenly, and tremulous?

Homeward: it is settled as far as she is concerned, and the doctor begrudgingly concedes, with the caveat that a nurse, or a health official, be allowed visit the home every day to gauge his progress. The doctor could do without the media attention in the hospital, perhaps it is in everyone's favour if he returned home to familiar and loving surroundings. And he has to agree, that yes, the boy, contrary to expectations – expectations? – is in fact, fine and sturdy, a little wan, but showing no signs of ordeal.

What *has* he been through?

"He can recuperate at home," says Susie, and the nurses look admiringly at the senior doctor who nods and appears to understand everything she says.

The doctor is glad to be extolled, will take whatever kudos is going, even if it is only with their wide impressed eyes.

Susie is glad that they are to be chauffeured by Osanai, glad to be going home, where she can spend time with her boy and come to grips with all that has happened.

What *has* happened?

How will they even begin? How should she broach the subject? The trouble, tribulation, trauma, or the lack of it.

She looks at her boy again, studying him, touching and mussing his hair and keeping him as close to her body as she possibly can.

"I can't believe all this. All that you've … you'll be a hero at school. Not many boys can say they survived at sea."

"At sea?" says Zen, looking confused.

"The plane. The airplane you were on … that fell into the sea."

"What plane? I was never on any plane."

31

Evening already. The nights become dark so early now. A red-stockinged Mitsuki Makanae walks down hard steel steps, away from her apartment building and out onto the streets.

Whatever the season it is the same, she has her routines and her days hardly change. In the insurance office she types and files things away; she panders to the patriarchs, making them coffee and cutting their doughnuts and cakes into serviceable slices – though her private fantasies have her drawing those very knives across their jowly throats.

But a job is a job. And she gets paid. A little. Not half as much as she'd like, and not half as much as she deserves – it is no wonder she supplements her income with a bit of extra work elsewhere. On the side. She doesn't need all that much. She has no family to take care of, not even a loving and loyal pet, just useless ceramic frogs, tantalizingly breakable. No one takes care of her. Mixxy is an independent woman. She takes care of herself. She knows things, has seen things, and walks *towards* where most would scarper *from*. And she knows too when and how to take some Mixxy Time. Like right now. Here she is on her way again.

Down the hard steps, away from the building and towards the *other* part of town.

She stops and opens her bag and takes out a long, thin cigarette and lights it. She should give these things up. She should give a lot of things up. But she never does. Her face in the flash of light is well made-up, pretty in a resolute, knowing way. This is how she fixes herself. Mixxy pulls on the cigarette strongly and blows smoke out to the stiff evening air.

Actually, Mixxy's lips are stretched into a smile as she blows. Mixxy is smiling to herself and there is a spring in her step because she has seen the news reports and the astounding reports of a boy found by the beach. And when Zen's name appeared in clear characters on the screen she howled with delight; the world was a crazy place with no discernible order according to Mitsuki Makanae, but sometimes it got things just right. She could not wait to see her friend, the melancholy Irishwoman that had become so inexplicably important to her. Now that her boy was back Mixxy may no longer be needed of course, but she will cross that bridge.

She has gone out of her way to make sure that they are in each other's company. Mixxy and Susie. It's got a nice ring to it. And proximity means possibility. At every opportunity Mixxy has complimented, has cherished, has made sure she was available. Mixxy may be in deeper than she suspects, and it is a little disconcerting, given the fact that it has never happened to her before. She admits as much to the cloudless black sky, blows out another stream of silver smoke and ambles on.

A noise from a cluster of trees.

Mixxy can never be sure how many of them there are. Where have they come from all of a sudden, these mysterious creatures of the night? And what do they want?

They peer out at her, but she cannot ever see them. They are hidden, like secrets. Like unrequited loves.

"What is it that you want from me?"

She speaks aloud to them in her native tongue. Addresses them. As if they can understand her. Maybe they can.

She is sure that they are calling her, too. Calling out and warning her, these birds. If her mother was still around she would ask her these questions. Why, Mother? What is happening to them? Are they in danger? Are we all in danger? She should call her mother anyway. When did they last speak? And what would her mother say to her? That the owls have moved to the city because … because of what? Because … why? Surely they cannot *prefer* the chaos of the city. They should be in the hushed trees of the countryside. Or in the cobwebbed silence of barns. Isn't that where they should be … naturally? She remembers seeing them on a nature documentary before, high up on the beams of old farmhouses, or disused sheds, abandoned outhouses, their silent grace, sagacious and serene.

But here. Near her. Near Susie's house too. Is something bad about to occur? Is that why they have come? Descended as messengers from some other realm – is that what they are here for? To tell her what? What is it they need to impart?

32

They have stopped for a while in Zen's favourite sushi restaurant. As soon as they get out of the hospital the boy tells them that they have to treat him to the things he likes, that he deserves it. Osanai backs him up on this one – who would have the temerity to let him down on a day like this? The editor is of course secretly hoping that the all-exclusive interview is going to come his way. Timing in such a game, he knows, is paramount.

Zen orders several plates of *ikura*, and where once Susie would have stopped him, worried about salt levels in cured salmon roe, insisting that his diet be more varied, she lets it all slide, happily watching him greedily tuck into the things he most desires. And she is just as glutinous. Eating up every bit of him with her eyes. Hungry for that love of which she has been so starved.

"It's been so long," he says, gulping, hardly chewing.

Susie can't help but remain baffled; he has said so little of what has happened to him, only that he had not been on any airplane. But she had seen him, hand in hand with his father, that little rucksack on his back, that cute animated silver ghost: she had witnessed all that. She was the one who drove to the airport, and drove manually – she remembers bypassing the automatic code and choosing to steer herself. Why was he not on the plane?

The doctors advised her not to push too hard, that Zen would come out with his own account when he was ready. Pushing him too much now might only result in stressing out the poor child, causing him even further trauma – there was always a thin line, they explained, between alleviation and exacerbation.

But Susie's curiosity is getting the better of her. She needs to know what had happened, and why her husband is no longer around, and how come they were separated if they went through the airport security gates together? She saw them! Did Masa even board that aircraft? Did anyone?

After Zen has licked every last drop of ice cream from his bowl – his tongue almost saurian – Susie decides to try a little, timidly.

"Sweetie, are you going to tell us a little about what happened?"

Osanai looks at her warily. Is he warning her off provoking the boy, or is he sizing up his own moment to pounce?

Unfortunately, it's the latter: Osanai reaches into his bag and pulls out a digital voice recorder, discreetly placing it on the table. His timing off then: a shame.

On another day she might have barked at him for this imposition, (another device out to ruin her day), but the reporter in her – something of the newshound, the vocation, must still be twitching alive somewhere inside her – understands the sense of opportunism, and she gently bats away the effrontery.

"Not now, at least."

Osanai sheepishly slips it away again.

Zen sits back into his seat, his belly full, the fullest it has been for weeks. He can see the worry and confusion in his mother's face, and he aches to put her at ease.

So how then should he proceed? How does he tell her this story of his? How does he explain what *did* happen to him?

He looks across the restaurant and Susie is reminded of her grandfather's gaze, remote to anyone observing him, preoccupied, focusing inward rather than out, a chip off the old block.

"I was taken care of. A man looked after me."

Susie wants this in order. Wants it straight.

"Go right back to the airport, darling, and start there. When I waved goodbye to you and your dad, what then?"

Zen scrunches his face up as if it is a perplexing math equation he has to solve for homework, and not the story of his own mysterious disappearance.

"We said goodbye to you and went through all the different gates and they checked our bags and stuff to see what was inside."

"And then?"

"We were about to get onto the plane, a woman was checking our tickets, and a man rushed up and said that we were to follow him to a different place. That something was wrong with our tickets or something, and if we went with him he would take care of everything."

"Who was this man?"

"He was the tall man who took care of me."

Zen's eyes go distant, a tear wells, gathers heavily on his long lashes and trickles down his cheek. He is thinking of his father, and the fact that he is not there with them suddenly overwhelms.

"They hurt him."

"Who? Who hurt him?"

"They hurt father. They hit him, and took him somewhere else."

Susie's eyes well too, she knows it is too much to expect of a young boy who has been through so much. She is not going to get the whole story, not now, not in any chronological or linear way.

Does she really want to hear it? The gruesome details? She is torn by curiosity and the sickness that the truth will inevitably bring.

They hurt him. They hurt her husband. Her son has just informed her. They hurt Masa. Good and sweet and nerdy Masa. For what reason? And where did they take him? Why did they have to kill him? This is the first time the word has come to her. *Kill.* A word so savage in its brevity, emphatic with its hard consonant. It pounds her. It is a heavyweight's fist letting her have it right there on the chest.

For so long it had been a plane crash. Masa died when that missile interrupted the flow of an innocent aircraft as it made its way across an innocent sky. He was missing, most probably dead, because of an unfortunate plane crash. That had been the story, and that had somehow been digestible – she was able to focus all her anger on a ferocious despot across the water. But that had not been it at all. That was a narrative, yes, just not *hers*. Susie's is worse, closer to home, and she has, as yet, nowhere to focus it, no one to take the brunt of her recriminations. Masa and Zen on a plane to South Korea that fell from the sky was just another lie. Add that one to the list.

Zen is crying fully and openly now, but through his sobs he manages to relay a little more.

"They took him in a different car. The tall man took me to a room first. It smelled terrible. It was dirty. Really dirty. And he locked me there for some hours. Then later, some girls were coming into that room, and he arrived, and he took me away from there to an apartment. That's where I stayed. He kept the door locked all the time. There wasn't much to eat, but he brought some things, sometimes. I saw no one else. Sometimes he tied me up so I couldn't move."

Zen shows the chafing marks on his wrists: purplish scars.

Tears stream down the faces of both mother and child now, their sobs a sorry unison.

"I think we should just get on home," Osanai says, and Susie nods in agreement. *Home:* the word now a thing of hope and solace, a thing of grace.

Zen is with her; that is all she really needs to know. He scoots under the table and climbs up onto her side, nestling himself close beside her, burrowing into her like a vole, hiding himself in the folds of her clothes, desperate for the affection of which he has been neglected.

Never again, she thinks. Never again will I let him out of my sight.

And so the mysteries deepen. The whos, the wheres, the whys.

And her anger at an unknown captor rises.

And she does not know what to do next, only to go home. Her son is back. Zen. Everything. All. The miracle that she had been waiting for. One of them stepped out of the sea and back into her arms. One came back. Only there was no sea. The sea had nothing to do with anything. No sinking bodies. No sinking sands. And as far as she can ascertain, this is *not* all in her head. This is actually happening. She is pretty sure all of this is real, that this is all taking place.

"It is ... isn't it?" she says to Osanai, through snivels and chokes.

"What?"

"It's all really happening? This is not a dream ... not a song."

"It's all real," he says, tenderly. "And everything is going to be just fine."

33

Everything is not going to be fine.

Mixxy enters a scummy elevator and it takes her to the top floor of an eight-storey building, a building that lights up on the outside with gimmicky images garishly uncharming. Score Bar. This is her destination, as so often it is. She can breathe again when she alights: the smell of piss in her nostrils is never an ideal way to kickstart an evening.

She has put in her dull shift in that office of dull shit; she has had her arse groped there and has been asked out on several dates by the very same moustached and acne-scarred molesters who cannot keep their grimy hands to themselves, and she has rejected all in favour of this little place, where she can gather up the courage (a few drinks, a toilet snort) to go and visit Susie's house, the excuse of congratulations a ruse to spend some time with her – she'll see what plays out then.

This is her usual jaunt, and she has been making these kind of plans since her embarkation. But all is not right tonight. All is not usual with Mixxy Time. The first thing that she notices when she steps out of the elevator is that the Score Bar door is open. And Score Bar door is never open.

It only opens when your thumb activates the screen and your face is scanned and recognised. This is how Haruto set it all up only three short years ago. But this is not how it is tonight. The door has been left ajar. Never before …

Mixxy steps under the transom and pushes it open a little further; it is a heavy door and hardly budges, so she has to put her shoulder to it, an extra nudge …

The sight that greets her makes her wish she never put her hand on it at all …

In the middle of the floor, in this dim and narrow establishment, propped up against a high stool, is the body of Haruto Matsumoto, sitting in a puddle of his own blood. A one-point ice pick, the very one he chips cubes off a solid block of ice every evening, emerges from his left and still-open eye. The blood that had poured from that eyeball and socket – however many hours ago – has dried all over his frozen, terror-stricken face, and the puddle he sits in is slimy, gel-like now with coagulation.

And Hartuo Matsumoto is not alone.

Next to the slumped and slain victim is a homebot. And that homebot's hand is attached to the weapon, attached to the thin ice pick. It is right there in its grip. Its mechanical fingers are clutched tight around it. The homebot is just as immobile, turned off, as if the whole world was put on *pause* at this ghastly moment, and no one will ever push *resume*. The homebot's face displays no emotion. The homebot's face never has. Never once. It was not programed for such. Not designed in such a way. What was it designed for? Menial tasks? Murder?

The tableau is incomprehensibly diabolical, beyond grisly: this human and its automated counterpart, set like this, arranged like this: it is a crime against imagination, to see thought and deed pushed so far in the wrong direction, to its ugliest, to its most debased. It has only one effect on its unlucky viewer, who after piecing the horror-scene information together into a manageable chunk of mental data, can respond in only one very human, most primal way, and that is to let loose a blood-curdling scream.

The sound must startle every living thing in the city, such is its raw and passionate power, and somewhere – maybe in those same trees where eyes have often fallen upon her, have often gazed upon her as she has strutted her usual tricksy-Mixxy stuff on click-clack heels in all of the Earth's seasons – the night creatures have taken the human cry of desolation and despair as something else entirely, something other than anguish, something other than torment or despair, instead they have taken it as a call to arms.

34

After they have finished their sushi, their ice cream, their tearful re-establishing, they head for grandmother's house: this fairytale team following the brick road, courage revived, strength in their little number, though they have yet to see what lies behind the curtain.

Grandmother Noriko scoops up the little boy and nearly crushes the bones inside him. Her face too is wet with tears and she can hardly contain herself with the words she needs to speak, the questions she wants answered, and her heart nearly gives out, such is the sense of overload.

She pulls them into her living room where she has already a selection of Zen's favourite cakes lined up on the coffee table. But they are all too full to contemplate comestibles, instead they tell her that it is best that this man, Osanai, her editor, take them home where the boy can purge himself of previous days and reacquaint himself with his normal life.

Even as Susie says this she has some doubts. Can life ever be the same again? How so? Way too much has happened, and so much of it still a massive mystery, gaps that she will somehow have to fill.

And where is she going to do this *filling*? In Ireland? In Japan? Stay here in a place that has become unsettled, unsettling, or go back. Return. Show Zen the rambles past the brambles, where her own sweet grandfather strolled and sang and unravelled for her as much as he could, the mysteries – *miseries*? – of their universe. Grandfather could only ever take her so far. The rest she had to figure out by herself, and she is still not nearly done with that.

So, which is it to be?

Go home. There's nothing for you here anymore: Your man. Your boy. They are gone.

The voices in her head are no longer true. Her boy is not gone, he is very much here. Look at him reach out for another little confectionary – where will he find the space for it?

"I will come to your house. I will stay with you," says Noriko Sakamoto, forthright as ever. She is already up the stairs and looking for a satchel or suitcase to carry her requirements.

Susie takes her crew back to the car and Osanai once more is the driver that will see them home. They slip through the streets, the electric car humming down the dry roads, Zen gazing out and smiling, content to be back to ordinary situations, to let life and buildings pass by and not worry about being trapped in either.

"I escaped," he says, suddenly, as if it has just dawned on him.

Susie turns to him from the front passenger seat.

"From that apartment. I escaped. When he was taking a shower. I slipped my hands through the cord that tied me. I boarded up the bathroom door. I placed a chair in front of it locking the handle shut. He couldn't get out. Then I ran, right out of there. He told me if I ever tried anything that he would catch me and kill me. But I ran anyway, I didn't mind being dead then. It didn't matter if he killed me … because I thought had no mother or father then. I thought everything was taken from me."

Susie hangs on his every word.

"I thought I would never see you again," he continues. "I thought maybe you were dead too."

The gaps are being filled. It would come out eventually, bit by bit, when Zen saw fit.

"I made my way towards the sea. I wanted to get out of the city. I was scared of the city. I remembered a little hut by the beach. For changing clothes. We had been there before, swimming one summer. That's where I went. To hide. It was not so far from where the man kept me. I think I left my bag there."

Susie turns again and stares out at the road, stares out at this sinful city. Was he too scared to head for home? Instead he hid in a little shed? What kind of fear would push him to do that? And where could she find this man? The reason for all of this. This man Zen so bravely escaped from. And just who, from the depths of hell, is he?

Osanai warns off the reporters outside her door. If they step too close to her he will break their cameras, or possibly more. Many of them know well this fearless editor and perhaps they believe him – as they allow a clear passage for them into Susie's house. Home.

The message screen in the vestibule is flashing. Someone has left a recording. Susie realizes this the minute she steps in the door. She has also caught a glimpse of someone catching a glimpse of her. From the same house across the street, beyond the flurry of reporters, someone is sneaking a peak behind a twitchy curtain. It's always like this. This constant nosiness. Susie has more respect for her fellow journalists who are at least obvious about their prying, who are blatant about their impositions. Someday she'll knock at that window: *Come on out, there's no need to hide. Come and take a good look for yourself!*

The message on the screen cannot be her mother-in-law – they have just left her house, and Noriko Sakamoto is to follow them presently in her own car, when she has turned on the security codes of her own place. Susie's thumbprint activates the Hologram Message Screen and the plate ejects from the bottom of it, producing on it the 3D head of a miniature Mixxy, the streak of punkish green even more punkish and greener than usual.

Susie smiles broadly, delighted to see her friend, and hoping she too will be on her way to join in their celebration: her boy has retuned, and not from space, he did not fall to Earth, instead he escaped from the clutches of … somebody.

The victorious smile is soon wiped off Susie's face however; Mixxy's message is of an altogether different tone: frantic, fearful, frightful.

"Who is that, Mommy? Her hair is green!"

Susie pauses the recording before Mixxy has uttered a word.

"Just a friend, sweetheart. Now why don't you go run a bath, it'll help you relax, get ready for bed. I'll be up to you in a few minutes."

Osanai, awkward at the entrance gets the OK from Susie to enter. He'll have to make himself at home. No time for pleasantries. Something is awry here, and she needs to hear it.

"I tried calling you," says the anxious Mixxy. "I need to see you. Something terrible has happened."

Susie looks around to make sure Zen is not listening. He has had quite enough of things terrible, this need not concern him.

"I heard your good news, and I'm happy for you. But something awful … Haruto is dead. Someone, or some*thing* killed him. I found him. In the bar."

Susie pulls her phone out of her bag and immediately calls her up. The details of the gruesome scene are relayed to her and Susie feels tight constrictions in her chest again – she can hardly breathe. How many more turns are they going to take on his day? How many more unexpected twists? She needs to sit. She needs to sit … and she needs a stiff bloody drink.

Osanai gratefully accepts the whiskey Susie pours for him and she joins him by throwing back her own, wiping her lips off the cuff of her sleeve like a saloon cowboy.

Zen appears before them then in his underpants, thin and shivering.

"What are you doing? Get into the bath!"

"Sonny is acting weird, Mom. I tried telling him to set the water temperature, but he is just ignoring me."

He.

Zen calls *it* a *he.*

"Just run the water yourself. I'll be up to see you in a minute."

The details of Mixxy's story are still running through Susie's head. An icepick through the fucking eye! And a homebot holding it! Was it that silent one behind the bar? Who was engineering all this? The basketball player said that these machines had their own agenda and that if you messed with the codes they somehow *knew*, that they could alert each other and … unite. It all seemed incredibly far-fetched, but examples were mounting up: the dead and crushed sparrow in the dustbin; the HIM that starts of its own accord in the mornings; the piercing sound they heard the previous night as they raked through the notebook; Sonny *off* when it should be *on*, *on* when it should be *off*; and now ignoring simple commands too … and still no way to shut the fucking thing down, no way to shut these thoughts in her head off either. The constant bombardment. Like this for months. No *off* switch, not even a *mute* – at least now though she is free of seas and sands and sharks and nibbling fish and drooling dogs and airplanes falling out of the sky. At least she is free of those.

"Sonny!"

From the bowels of the house, sensing concern in its controller's voice, Sonny … *doesn't* respond.

Why does it not come when called upon? It was programed to respond immediately. Does it not hear?

Susie shouts again: "Sonny!"

A beat.

Then:

"Yes, Miss Susie. I am on my way."

It arrives within seconds and approaches the living room, where Osanai, looking up from his tumbler, is gobsmacked – she never mentioned having a home robot before.

"Did Zen ask you to set the water temperature in the bath?"

"Yes, Miss Susie. I was just about to …"

"*About* to?"

Osanai's mouth hangs open: a conversation with a robot, in all his time ... he had heard of such things, had even run stories about the ImaTech launch, but he had no idea of their ... sophistication.

"And where is the notebook?"

"What notebook?"

"You know what I mean. Or perhaps you know it as The Dark Manual?"

"I have no idea about any notebooks, Miss Susie. Perhaps you are referring to the pink manual. If you are having problems with my operating system you should consult the troubleshooting pages, pages 23-27, it is over there, under ..."

"I know where the pink manual is. That's not what I'm looking for."

Osanai feels he should be recording all of this. Would she notice if he furtively slipped his hand into his satchel once more?

"Go upstairs and check to see if Zen is OK. Respond if he asks you to do something."

Not a stir from the homebot.

"Clear?"

"Yes, Miss Susie."

Mixxy hears hoots. Before she rounds the corner to Susie's street, she can already hear them, louder than before, as if agitated. She can see one too, there it is passing overhead, swift in its glide from tree to house. A white ghost passing. It perches on Susie's house, on the verge of the roof, it hunches, straightens itself, then hunches down again. Who is it watching? What is it doing there?

"Are you here for me?" Mixxy says. "Is that why you are here? Friend?"

The bird seems to be looking directly at her, right in her eyes, as she makes her way to Susie's front door. Mixxy shudders, but her feeling of disconcertment is not because she herself feels in any danger, she instinctively feels that something much bigger is at play here, something much bigger than her. As if to emphasize this point other owls emit low, sad-sounding whoops that seem to coalesce and rise into the air like a thick black cloud enveloping the whole neighbourhood. If this is to be the end of the world, thinks Mixxy, then these owls are already in the know, are way ahead of us all, and are ready to hear that death-knell; Mixxy rings the doorbell.

Osanai has never met Susie's friend before and when she bows to him he can't take his eyes off the green streak running through her hair. There is certainly something going on here, some story in this house that he needs to get to the bottom of, he must be sure to remember the details – if it's not the basis of a newspaper article, then there is certainly some drama, a short story, say, something sensational unfolding anyway: a boy back from the dead, a damn-near sentient homebot, a preposterous green-haired girl, and, if he's not mistaken there are birds outside rounding up a ruckus.

Mixxy hugs her friend. There is so much she wants to say: her congratulations on the return of her son, the awful news of Haruto's demise, the owls outside, and her gnawing feelings of …

But Zen is there, post-bath, aromatic and practically glowing, he is now in his pyjamas.

"I've heard all about you! You are so brave!" Mixxy gushes.

Zen is just as taken with the green hair as Osanai. Being a child and possessing fewer filters, he has the advantage of being unabashed, and asks all about it.

"Because it makes me look so cool," is the sassy response.

Zen nods, content with that, and he is in full agreement. He says he wants a green stripe in his hair too.

They are sitting in the living room and Zen is vole-ing his way into his mother again. He cannot get close enough, breathing in her smell, delighted when she catches his small hand in hers and squeezes it tight.

"Sweetheart, do you know anything about a notebook that you once drew on. It was your father's. But you drew a really nice picture on the front of it, of Sonny."

"Yes, I know it. Dad asked me to draw on the cover."

"Did Dad ever say what it was all about?"

"Some codes he was working on. But I didn't really understand."

A sudden thought comes to him then that makes quite a lot of sense to Susie and Mixxy, though not to the befuddled Osanai who finds himself more out of his depth with each passing moment.

"He said that the numbers were like ..."

Zen tries to recall his father's words.

"He said that if someone got sick, from a poison or something, like if a snake bit you ... then this ... he said the English word ... an anti ... something"

"Antidote?" says Susie.

"Maybe. Something like that. I can't remember. Like a cure for sickness."

If something got sick.
Or was made sick.
These codes would be the antidote.

At last something was starting to make sense. The codes were not to make the homebots do anything bad at all. Masa was not coerced into anything. He was doing the very opposite. He was preventing those who were meddling. An antidote. Sure. Should the homebots turn, or be used for malicious purposes, this was the basis of perhaps a new manual, to stop them in their tracks. Whoever got to Masa was not trying to find The Dark Manual for its own sinister uses, but trying to destroy it, to stop its very existence. The Dark Manual – Zen's notebook – wasn't born out of darkness at all, it was born of light.

Mixxy is bold enough to pour her own whiskey – if nothing else it'll settle her nerves. The scene in the bar plays over and over in her mind and it'll take an ocean of whiskey or a mountain of powder to ever erase.

She cannot talk about it now. Not in front of the child. There has been enough horror in his life this past while, he does not need to hear about icepicks in eyes and malevolent homebots.

"I bet you are happy to be all clean again," Mixxy says to him, studying his face to see any parental resemblance; he has Susie's lively eyes.

"Yeah," he says, still staring at her hair, "the first place I was kept in smelled of poo."

Osanai laughs and the ice jiggles at the parameters of his glass, but the comment has sparked something in Mixxy. A flash of a thought. Some starburst of association.

"Poo?"

"When the tall man took me and threw me in that dirty room it smelled of poo. It was really dirty. He left me there for hours. Before he took me to his own place."

Tall man.

A place smelling of shit.

Fuck, no … really?

"Did you see anything else in here? Can you remember the lights?"

"The lights were off. It was totally dark. But there were big, round lights, on the ceiling. Like from a theatre … or something."

Nightclub lights. Insalubrious bar lights. The lights of the obscene jungle room.

"Susie, can I talk to you for a minute?"

In the kitchen an almost breathless Mixxy dishes out what has lit her mind. There are just too many coincidences. She thinks she knows who is behind all this. She *knows* the tall man. She knows him all too well. And the more Mixxy surmises, the more Susie thinks she recognises him too.

She takes out her phone and the pictures from the basketball arena.

"This the guy?"

Mixxy nods, not quite sure that this head eclipsing the sun is the clearest of images, but she can recognize the features well enough, yes.

"Who is he?"

"He gives me … things."

"Things?"

"Recreational …"

"Gives?"

"I … earn."

A fog lifts. Susie gets a richer picture of the other places Mixxy frequents. It was a bit much to think that she only ever visited one rather sedate sports bar. And the little fleck of white that often appeared under her nose from her visits to the toilet. Recreation. Sure, she gets it now. We all need a little something to get by. But who is this guy?

"He works for Wowmirai."

And that seems to explain a whole lot more.

Osanai is then summoned to the kitchen and this time he is told to switch on his digital recorder. He needs to record every single word of what they say, and they need to know that it will be published too. He must get it all, make no mistake. This is big. The biggest story he will probably ever write. Does he promise?

They tell him about the basketball player who frightened Susie away from the arena – the semi-professional team had even been sponsored by Wowmirai, it was right there on their shirts, how could she have not seen it?

He was the one who had been fixing Mixxy with drugs for years, taking her to nasty places with nasty people. Her guy.

He was the one in Haruto's bar that fed Susie a shitload of lies, and for all they knew he was the one who yielded that very ice pick, making it look like a homebot.

He was definitely the one all right. Puppet-master. Sadist.

Susie remembers her second encounter with him in the sports bar, his pernicious eyes giving her a final stare as he left, a final scare. There was nothing good about this man, nothing.

"Oz," says Osanai suddenly, to a puzzled silence.

The women look at him, waiting for an explanation, hoping his words are not apropos of zilch.

"The Wizard of Oz," he says. "There's always someone behind the curtain, pulling the strings, never the one you are quite prepared for."

And then another flash for Susie!

Curtains!

For weeks she has seen a shadow across her street. Someone peeping at her from behind twitching curtains. That house opposite. No. Surely not. It couldn't be anything more than nosey neighbours, now surely…

35

They have lined up along the rooftops. They have lined up on gateposts, on fences and on garden walls. They have somehow multiplied. There are more of them than could ever be imagined, as if they have not come from forests and secluded hiding-holes scattered in and around the city, but instead have sprung straight from some clammy child's demented dream. They are multitudinous, en masse, and they moan with menace.

How have they gathered so quickly? Where have they come from? Who gave the order for this army to arrive?

And why?

It is not just the owls.

The crows too have come. And they have been joined by other corvids, black ravens, rattling raucously around, cawing crazily, pitch-dark wings flapping furiously, they too have come, to pitch in, show their worth.

And the jackdaws, their silvery white irises reflecting the light of the lampposts: the only bird in existence able to understand the movement of human eyes – just what will they make of those red orbs? How do bird brains compute?

One owl swoops from a rooftop to the house opposite Susie's. It bangs straight into the window pane. The curtain inside the house moves. A face appears. It is the face they have now been expecting. It is the face of present evil. Its human eyes look directly into those avian others. What dread this wicked man must feel at this mad and manic moment, what sudden terror must strike his sorry soul. He had certainly not been expecting any of this. With only a sheet of glass between them he is suddenly humiliatingly vulnerable.

Another owl swoops low in a direct mimicry of the first and it too collides with the glass pane. The sound is loud, a heavy whack, but the glass does not yet break. It does not break until more of these birds come calling, come cawing, come careering and falling straight to it, with magnificent might, with nothing but intent.

And then a crack, and then a break in the window, from the onslaught, from the beak-barrage, and the boisterous birds can actually eke out a way into this house of perpetual sin. They have gotten themselves inside. Sheer will. Blunt force. What havoc can they wreak upon the fallen man that trembles there, how great now their ire?

Zen is in the bathroom brushing his teeth, something he has not done for a long time. He'd never have thought he would be so pleased to be doing this. Where once he would have complained, now he is glad to cleanse, making himself presentable to the world again. He knows there will be more cameras aimed at him; he knows they are not done with him yet, and though it is a world he no longer trusts, he feels he should be at least ready for it, no more the ignominy of dirt. He is unaware of the birds outside though – the noise of his own electric toothbrush cancels the outside commotion. He is also unaware that Sonny is standing behind him, silently so, out of the blue it has arrived at the bathroom door, with blue lights at the sight of its head flickering frantically now, and its red eyes a-glow, as if on fire, as if direct portals in to the dire depths of Lucifer's lair.

Sonny, the homebot, Zen's once-cherished mechanical pet, emits another piercing sound that drills right into the eardrums of the boy. He lets the toothbrush fall, his hands rushing to cover his ears. Sonny reaches out its own inflexible hand and begins to grip the boy's slender neck. Hard. Choking. It is a grip that doesn't waver because it was programed to work that way. It doesn't waver because... *didn't anyone know these things can kill?*

The boy, Zen Sakamoto, weak and gasping; for weeks starved of familial love is now being starved of oxygen; life's iniquitousness, boldly branded on the buckling boy, and all at the hands of an automated abomination.

There is a theory that these robots will rise in their own time anyway... will find their own levels. Accessing The Dark Manual will only accelerate this.

The intense sound continues, Sonny's fierce noise deafening the neighbourhood. Lights come on in rooms alarmed. Ghostly faces appear at windows: first they are curious, then concerned.

Everything now seems turned on.
The problem with reconfiguring one of the devices is that they have been known to send signals to each other. It sounds crazy, but a homebot has been seen to... enlist help...

Motors from all sorts of machines begin to whirr, car alarms pester, mobile phones ring, and the Health Information Monitor begins to expel unheeded advice: *Immune system under threat therefore an increase in the uptake of essential vitamins and amino acids recommended. Take extra zinc…*

Mechanical fingers grip tighter on the boy's neck, squeezing. Zen, in petrified pain, manages to somehow gargle out a choking shriek, and even though they have covered their ears to limit the general cacophony, it is enough to alert the adults downstairs.

Osanai is first to hear this yelp and the bangs of a boy being belted against walls. He is fastest in bounding up the stairs, fast to the scene. He finds the homebot with its stiff outstretched arm and its thick fingers strangling the boy's thin white throat. The homebot's head revolves to face the man and the piercing sound it emits only increases in volume.

Zen thrashes wildly, still in Sonny's death grip.

Osanai throws himself upon the homebot and is able to free Zen from its clutches. The boy runs out of the room and straight into his mother's arms. She checks for blood, she checks his breathing, and when she sees that he is all right and has escaped even further ordeal, she allows her anger to rise, to rise inside her like it has been doing for weeks, climbing, climbing and reaching its apex now.

Susie is primed.

Susie is prepared.

Susie wants full in on this action. For far too long she has endured, abided, ignored, but not now, now it is her turn to let loose: Susie Time.

She retrieves the baseball bat from Zen's room. This is what she has really been after. This is what she has really desired all along. To just be done. To just be done with the fucking bastard thing, for once and for all. Destroy it. Annihilate. For good. For the good of all humanity. For the good of all that is rational. This is what she has really wanted all these torturous days. Why has it taken so long?

Sorry, Masa, my love, but the moment has come. Congratulations on making a thing so fabulously sophisticated, but its time, my dear, is most certainly up.

The furious Irishwoman swings the baseball bat. All her energy, all her body, her heart, her hate, and her love too, yes her love for her tough little boy, and for her lost husband, all are being channelled into this electrifying moment. And so she batters the silver machine, and then she begins to batter it just a little more, with greater, growing strength, and even with grander force, until it is nothing but loose bits and scraps, debris, nuts and bolts, circuit boards and smoking silicon, wires all over the floor, all over the bathroom. All over.

She is the bat-wielding wild woman.

She is the batshit-mad bitch. Just look at her go!

Incensed.

Incendiary.

Some spectacle this is: Sonny scattered all over the place. Sonny no longer. Sonny no more. All over. Silenced. No more piercing sounds. No more fucking *Miss Susies* and discussions about herbal tea or beef stew. Progress halted. Yes, progress has been halted. Progress is … not.

It had been that easy, after all.

A baseball bat.

Rage.

Simple as that.

This all from the girl who could not tackle in her PE ball games. From the girl who preferred to skip and dance as an airy teen. From the girl who preferred musical melody and preferred walks down simple country lanes with a benign grandfather. From a woman who curled up on the couch in the shape of an unborn child and wanted to drown out the world, drone out the world, flee from its awfulness.

This all from the girl who grew to be a woman and loves her son so much it breaks her bloody beating heart to think he might not have made it. But he did. He did make it. They have found each other again. And no fucking machine would ever cause him harm again. No human either. Nothing would come between them. Nothing would tear them apart.

A baseball bat.

Simple as that.

And a riot of inner rage.

That too very much an ingredient … naturally.

Fume.

Fury.

Who would've thought it could all be so simple? Who would've thought it could end just like that?

When Mixxy opens the door she is presented with the sight of a large number of birds descending on her friend's neighbourhood, like some grim apocalyptic tale she might have come across in a *manga* when young and innocent and easily scared; this all portentous, loaded.

Mixxy is no longer young of course, and she is certainly no longer innocent or easily scared. Neither is the world she lives in: it is a world in disarray, dismal, dismayed. She thinks she knows what this is all about. She is beginning to understand why she has been hearing those hoots from the trees on all those solitary nights she walked casually by. It is about the natural versus the unnatural, it is about real and tangible feathers being ruffled, a creaturely discontent with the hidden things that bleep and emit and are not a natural part of the natural order. *All our digital shit. Our devices. Signals.* The animals fear, yes, they fear these. This much she had previously ascertained and the spectacle before her seems in collusion with her hypothesis. She could write it all up just like that, a scientific study, theory, conclusion, and send it to her mother, it might even impress her, might even be publishable; surely more interesting than simple pond-dwelling amphibians. Yes, the owls, they feel threatened, they do. Of course they do. She believes that now. They feel that *they* are the ones that are being attacked. Maybe that's why Mr. Owl and all his buddies are out here on this perplexing day, not knowing the reason for their presence in the world, but fighting for their sanctity nonetheless. They fight the more-ness, the amassing of devices, of machines, automatons, computers, the ever more and more of this stuff that sends out waves, radiation, that bombards and bothers; it had been this way for centuries, from steam engines to artificial intelligence, and these owls and crows and dangerous 'daws, well, their time has come to answer back, a natural retort – *you are not the only creatures here on this planet* – and it looks like their wrath will not abate; the day's a-surge with a reassembling of order, to the world, this is what they now, in rancour, bestow.

Sirens then.

Police cars.

Fire trucks.

As if the air is not yet full enough of noise, they pile upon the dissonance. In the midst of this convoy comes Noriko Sakamoto, quick out of her car and into Susie's shaking house. It could be an earthquake; such is the tremor of the outdoor calamity and of the gathering birds screeching in the sky. For a land that has seen its fair share of troubles, this cataclysm adds only insult.

Noriko Sakamoto looks like she has seen, has *had* enough; her packed suitcase in her hand may be testament to that. The scene she witnesses around her is all too much, it has to stop here.

"You need to do the same," she tells her daughter-in-law, somehow finding the right English for the right moment, and looking quizzically at the distressed woman holding the baseball bat.

"Do what?"

"You need a suitcase. We must go."

What Noriko Sakamoto means to say is that the whole damn world looks like it is coming apart at the seams, and that when different species of birds flock together in a quiet neighbourhood the way they do now, then either you have truly lost your mind, or the world has become all too much to take. What Noriko wants to say is something that has been on all their minds this past while – though she does not yet know this English phrase – that *enough is enough*.

She wants a new beginning. She wants a fresh start. The wisdom of her years informs her of that, and she will be forthright too in telling Susie, and will make her stop and sit and listen, in whatever language makes it most abundantly clear. Noriko Sakamoto has never been to Ireland before and now is as good a time as any to rectify that. If she were to stay with Susie and Zen here, in this city, what hope would they have? This place that has so betrayed them. This place that should have been a safe, comfortable city to see a young bright boy grow, mature, push and prosper, now sullied by crimes that have been allowed to transpire, and who knows if that is even to be the end of it. There may possibly even be more of it, waiting for them. What lurked maliciously around the next corner? Who could ever say? Better to get away from the threat of terror, from the stench of sin, from the waywardness of untrustworthy people and unsure technologies – whichever was worse she could not yet deign to determine.

Television cameras have found their way to the once-quiet suburb to capture the images of avian absurdity. Whenever something happens they are always quick to descend, having the news almost before it has broken; some sixth sense they must possess, some anticipatory knowing. Here they are now, flickering, abuzz, and more excited than ever – this they have never encountered before, they can hardly believe their own eyes, certainly it hurts their ears, but it doesn't stop them from journo-pushing right up to the faces of all involved.

Susie, out of her house now, having beaten one enemy, looks around with wild eyes in the hunt for one more. She is quickly apprehended by one hungry reporter keen to be the first to have her image for himself.

"Your husband? He made these machines. Birds go crazy," he offers in hesitant English, thrusting a microphone out so far and under her nose that it actually hits her upper lip.

"He did," she says flatly – she can hear the Irish accent in her own words now, an inflection returned – and she backhands the microphone away straight out of his hand and onto a ground littered with mildly moving feathers.

"It wasn't his fault that it all got so corrupted," she says. "It wasn't his fault at all."

The "at all" sounds just like it did ten or fifteen years ago, a Hiberno-English cadence reclaimed and stirring now.

She rolls up her sleeves.

The reporter, scrambling to regain composure, is not given a chance to ask or further insinuate. He is quick to recoil, intentions foiled.

He watches Susie with trepidation, and just a little awe.

"But I do know whose fault it was," she adds. "And you can keep your fucking camera rolling for this if you like. It's going to be some viewing."

Susie brandishes Masa's baseball bat once more and jogs to the house opposite.

This is the house of the twitching curtains.

This is the house of a new and sinister Oz. The house of the wizard who has been controlling things from backstage, spying on her, lying to her, and now that his door has been torn apart by marauding birds, nothing can stop her from entering.

She blusters in, full of vim, sweat, adrenaline.

And there he is, Koudai Kimura, fighting off three or four birds that perniciously pester and peck around his head. His face is covered with perspiration too, blood streams from cuts and he tries to swat them away from scratching any further.

As she approaches him the birds abruptly stop and scatter, leaving him shocked and unsteady, hardly able to stand, facing his next and even more bruising, even more bitter opponent.

Susie first smashes her bat into the various consoles and machines that line the room. This is how he must've controlled things. Sending signals out around the neighbourhood, remote-controlling her very own Sonny from this hidden den. Clever. But cowardly. Fucking devious, to be perfectly honest. But there will be no more of it for Susie. Enough is indeed quite enough. She smashes and smashes and when she is satisfied that she has broken the rows of equipment, there is only one thing left to do. And so she wields again, raising her husband's bat, her thin arms tired and weary but anger keeping them aloft, revenge keeping them from wilting. She thought that her consternation had reached its pinnacle when she beat the home robot in her bathroom. But not a bit of it. The rage remains. The wrath still rises. Months and months of the stuff. It had accumulated. It had built up. Her missing husband. Her poor husband, undoubtedly dead, and this wretched man left on the Earth in his stead; this vile, contemptible creature that took it upon himself to discredit Masa's project for the sake of his own contemptible firm – and what role did he even have there, in Wowmirai? A shareholder? Or just a stooge? Knight or knave? Contemptible, yes, that's about the size of it; innocent lives ruined, and her poor boy, caught up in it all, entangled in a web of malevolence, perfidy; months and months of this, mounting, growing and spreading like kudzu. Choking the life out of everything. Choking the life out of life. Only now it is given an outlet. Now, it is time for her to vent.

"Where is my husband?"

"Gone."

"Where did you put his body?"

Koudai Kimura does not answer. His eyes look downward, to the floor, low.

"Who is Gotou?"

No words from him. Just gasps of pain now. His chest in spasms. And drops of hot blood from his face falling to the dust and detritus.

"Gotou? Has he put you up to all this?"

"No. Gotou is…

He searches in his mind for the English phrase.

"… responsible for this."

"How?"

"He found out… about our plans. Told your husband."

"And you killed him?"

He wipes blood from the lacerations on his face.

"No. He was dying already."

"And my husband, what did you do with my husband?"

Blood drips. Sweat too. And tears of pain – or are they of defeat? – streaming down his wounded cheeks.

Owls are gathered in the room. More of them now. More of them come and settle. On cabinets. On the broken equipment. On any available space. They leer at him. They wait. They have patience, endless patience. It is disconcerting to see just how much of it they have. Perched there. They can do this for hours. Waiting for their moment. They look as if they are awaiting instruction. They do not have the tiredness in their bones, the lagging of exhausted legs, the drowsiness of spirit, the headaches, the heaviness – night is descending and this is the right time for them to be alive, pert, alert, all set to go.

"There must have been more than just you. My son said *they*. He said: *they hurt him*."

Koudai looks at the fearsome owls, afraid that they will assail him again; his eyes are on those hard and curved talons – they could rip you to ribbons all right. They could pluck you to pieces. His heart bulges with fright.

"Where is he? Where is my husband?"

The tall basketball player, the once imposing athlete, having been brought down to size, is now only a shell of a man, empty, hollow, as if his innards, his very soul, has been scooped out. Pitifully he is planked on his knees, and can only murmur what might be his last words:

"The sea."

It is at this moment … at this moment … Susie stops … she stops herself from … she could … she could just … what she wants to do is this: to release for the last time, to swing what has become her trusted instrument, this wonderful weapon, this piece of Americana she never knew she'd grow so fond of, and catch him straight in his face, shatter his nose, bloody him even more, or watch his brains spill out on the floor, no longer able to compute, no longer able to scheme, no longer electrically alive and capable of harmful manipulation.

This is, for a split second, is what she – almost salivating – envisages.

But she does not act upon it. It is not her call. It is not up to her to condemn this man – or perhaps this man has already been condemned. Susie Sakamoto is not going to make herself the executioner. She had smashed the corrupted homebot and she had smashed all his wicked equipment to bits; maybe that is as much as is necessary. This man, this man in front of her, already half-dead, already half on the other side, this is something else entirely. This is not her call. This is much, much bigger than her. This

belongs to an order above, a natural order hell-bent on settling its own scores. She should let them take care of their
own business. Fight their own battle. No, Susie Sakamoto
is not the executioner.

So she just backs away.

She just steps aside.

She could take longer to debate all this. She could sit
and ponder on the pros and cons of taking the law into
her own hands, or allowing this to happen their way, the
way of the wild. Yes, it's probably best if she just turns her
back and lets this mad moment of natural history take its
course.

She drops the baseball bat to the floor, not sure if she'll
ever be needing it again. The birds look at her. They wait
on her word. They have been waiting for her for months.
Waiting for her signal. The only real signal that seems to
matter to them. Not the bleeps, not the ringtones, the sti-
fling emissions from digital shit everywhere, none of that,
that was their distraction. They were waiting instead on one
human voice to set them free, to let them know that they
could impinge like this, step out of their line and encroach
on human activity, and by doing so retrieve some kind of
justice for their recent ills.

She looks at the birds. Their feral, tubular eyes are
trained on her. Their wings flap faintly, in preparedness:
just say the word, just say it, their ancient gaze implores.

And so Susie Sakamoto, Irishwoman in Japan, drunk-
ard and widow, mother and fighter, and somehow at this
moment, bizarrely, ruler of this kingdom of wildlife, nods
to herself, and to the quiet and anticipatory room she says,
with utter authority, and no lack of conviction:

"Now."

The birds descend on the man, a whole flock eager to take their piece of flesh, eager to taste the blood of their enemy. Blood spurts and spray-decorates the loathsome walls, spilling onto the dials and the switches of the wrecked machines, resulting puffs of smoke signifying only failed and wrong endeavour. They clasp at him and clutch and crack and not only to the right side of his skull, but to the left too, and to the centre, breaking every bone that makes up a real human face. How easy it gives way, Susie thinks, as she watches the terrible scene play out. How easy it can be all torn apart. They peck and scratch and bite and tear and scrape the very life from him, and when the man in shreds sheds his life force they are swift to devour it, eating into skin and the bone and the wet and oozing meat, feasting on the demise of the hot human, righting their world, ending some inglorious chapter.

With every last breath from the villain departed, Susie slumps, as if she herself had been the one to inflict, she herself the one to end his rotten reign and not merely the one who gave the order.

When the police arrive – having being distracted long enough by a wily Osanai, asking futile questions about wildlife preservation laws for an article he would never write – they are shocked to see the contents of this house of shame. Never in all their time have they witnessed such a scene. Never in anyone's time.

Susie doesn't have to defend herself. She need not strain herself with declarations of innocence. There isn't anything she needs to confess. The police have absolutely nothing to go on. There is hardly even a body there, so fully has it been ransacked, devoured.

The clamour of birds depart as hurriedly as they had entered, out the door, out the shattered windows, back to their night and their nests. There will be more of this. There will be more battles for them ahead. As they try to keep their world their way. As men keep pushing their buttons. There will certainly be more episodes where they are beset by such violations. Of that there is no doubt. Mixxy might even say they will have their work cut out for them.

Susie breathes. She leaves the fallen house and steps outside and she takes in deep lungfuls of air. The air is still there. It still surrounds her. Cold, brisk, October air. The stuff of life: it is all still there. For many months she thought it was going to quit on her, or that she was going to quit it. But no. Air. Still there. All around her. It reaches into her body and it keeps her ticking along. And she is still there, still *here*. This is what she thinks as she surveys the scene. She is still *here*. Despite all. Despite the travails, despite the many obstacles, somehow, the Irishwoman, in this foreign land, she has endured.

She takes this moment to look around. The debacle. The scrambling of people trying to put sense on it all, trying to put a narrative on it, frenziedly trying to figure out the causes, the meanings and the *what next?*

Indeed.

What next?

After all of this.

How does one even begin to figure out what to do now, and where to go?

The reporters scrabble around looking for something, a base, a foundation to construct upon, and the police run back and forth, bemused, befuddled; onlookers and rubberneckers and nosey neighbours, the quietly curious and the downright excited, they are all gathered, scatty with the demented drama of the day, fidgety with the unfolding; look, there's even the laundry woman, a basket of clothes at her feet, wondering how all these beasts have laid siege to her peaceful terrain. Susie nods to her. It is both greeting and apology. Her neighbour nods back, solemnly, without squint or smirk. The nods seem to encapsulate all: they are respectful but distant, polite but restrained, the nods are satisfactory, sufficient, and it is probably the last time they will go through these motions together.

What next, then, what next?

Is that the question?

Is that the question that the reporters will ask? The question the police will ask? And her family too? Her son and her mother-in-law? Is that the question that will be on all their lips?

What next?

Zen is suddenly at her side and looking up at her, and though she can hardly hear him – they have all gone partially deaf and who can blame them? – she thinks that is the question he is asking:

What next?

And Mixxy.

And Osanai.

It is in their eyes too. What do you do now, Susie dear? How do you recover from this? And where do you go now? *What next? What next? What next?*

Miss Deadheart. We are refusing you the right to change your name. Your name is Susie Sakamoto.

And no one will ever say "Miss Susie" again.

But what next?

Perhaps she will tell them that first her intention is to let her good husband rest right there in the ocean. Let him float along with undercurrents, with waves and the comfort of endless time; where he will be at peace – she is quite sure of this now, undulating on some quiet undertow there, caught by some kind current and allowed drift as if in dream, away from the noise and the mayhem of whatever happens above.

Perhaps she will pack her bags like her mother-in-law has told her to do, and she will flee with them, with this, her family, huddled and close, comfortable and comforted in their being together, away from this place of precariousness, at least some respite rightly required. Yes, this seems all right by her.

Susie will not crawl to a sofa and she will not curl up like a ball there and she will not wait for a world to end. They can have their wars if they so wish, or they can have their no-wars and endless mounting threats and tensions. It makes no odds to her. It is none of her business and she will pay it not the slightest regard. She will simply do what she can to help a child grow to be a proper human. To be a good person. A person who tries to put things right. Like her husband tried. Like she did.

She will instruct her son. She will talk to him. She will enable. She will walk with him, will consult, and allow herself to be consulted, knowing when to be careful and considered, and when to let loose and dance with the delicious delirium life can sometimes and wondrously offer.

She will play no more drone music, instead, joyfully, she will play some light, jazzy music over the speakers, the kind Masa unapologetically liked, or the horrible pop songs he tried to convince her were modern masterpieces, and she will shake her body and laugh with her son when he inevitably joins in.

And no more womb-room. No more of that.

And no more the large quantities of drink. No more of that.

She will not sing alone, not strange songs in strange bars. Every song from now on will be a duet, or more, more than two, a family of voices, a choir even; she will be with people, these particular people, particularly these, who clearly want to be with her.

She will put a streak of green in Zen's hair, yes; she will buy the dye and do it all herself. In honour of his new auntie. Yes, this thought has just landed upon her now, ludicrous, sure, but she will stick with it. It will symbolize the land to which they will undoubtedly return. She will still look for signs, yes, and she will always interpret. A green streak of hair, why not?

She will take her Japanese companion on a stroll too, on some muddy pathway, the same lanes her grandfather took, thinking of the songs he sung to light the heart and keep it stoked. And perhaps near some blackberried bramble, on some brisk autumn day, she will land a hard, wet kiss on Mixxy's lips, strong and unapologetic, reciprocation after all, making sure she won't ever forget it, or forget all that has happened to them, and all that they have managed to surmount.

There is life yet... and we must prize.

And when, on some day of stress, or life's unbearable excess, some digital device infuriates, or annoyingly bleeps in the quiet of her abode, snatching her from her sleep, or from an earned moment of relaxed contemplation, she will calmly, simply, knowingly, assuredly, reach out an authoritative finger, and switch the bloodless thing off.

AUTHOR'S NOTE

This novel has in its title the word "manual"... and for good reason. If, on finding yourself on the verge of war (and this is especially true in the case of robot-initiated-apocalypse), or on the verge of a nervous breakdown (which, sadly, is far more common than any of us ever suspect, expect), then please follow the steps outlined within accordingly, and do so with utter fastidiousness. Do not skip over a single one of them – to do so may be to your detriment: this book may just save your life – should you wish your life to be saved.

In addition, please make sure that all machines, devices, etc. (except perhaps the refrigerator) are always fully turned off before you retire for the evening. Please make sure you double back and double-check: one can never quite know what might – should it desire – creep into your bedroom, as you lay there in blissful unawareness.

Consider yourself warned.

The spirit of this book is dedicated to
my children
Reinan and Nina
(Japanese/Irish
Irish/Japanese)
who will
I hope
be wise
enough
to mine
the best
of both
sides
and
beautifully
brightly
be

ABOUT THE AUTHOR

Colin O'Sullivan lives in the north of Japan with his family and works as an English teacher.

Colin O'Sullivan's first novel, *Killarney Blues*, captivated critics and readers alike and has won the prestigious Prix Mystère de la Critique in France.

His second novel, a literary dystopia called *The Starved Lover Sings*, will be published in Russia in 2019.

His short fiction and poetry have been published in various print and online anthologies and magazines.

To learn more about Colin O'Sullivan, visit *http://osullivan-colin.wordpress.com* and *www.betimesbooks.com*

36915667R00169

Printed in Poland
by Amazon Fulfillment
Poland Sp. z o.o., Wrocław